HE HAD BEEN HUNTED, HOUNDED, FOR SO VERY LONG.

A tapping on the car window drew Jackson's attention. He swiveled his head and stared at the visored face of the policeman. He wished the polychromatic helmet didn't cover the rest of the man's head. Somehow the short antenna sticking from the helmet, coupled with the silver sliver of the mouthpiece, gave the man an insectoid look. Cold and distant and artificial.

Jackson read the man's lips.

Roll the window down.

Reluctantly, Jackson rolled the window down, leaving his finger in place.

The police officer touched the pressure-sensitive switch that released the static energy charge holding the visor in place. The dark crescent slid back up into the helmet. Revealing crystal eyes. Over an unmerciful grin.

"Time Police!"

Volume 3

STRANDED

By

Warren Norwood and Mel Odom

A Byron Preiss Book

LYNX OMEIGA BOOKS

New York

Special thanks to Richard Curtis, Michael Fine, Lou Wolfe, Judith Stern and David Harris.

TIME POLICE
Volume 3: Stranded
ISBN: 1-55602-008-X
First Printing/March 1989

Printed in the United States of America

0 9 8 7 6 5 4 3 2 1

Cover painting by Paul and Steve Youll
Cover Design by Dean Motter
Edited by Mary Higgins

CHAPTER ONE

    Praetor Centurion Lieutenant Colonel Friz Brelmer stared at the face of the Time Policeman sitting behind him with acute interest, watching as the man's features expanded and contracted in some unknown rhythm with the undercurrent powering the time machine.

    Around them, seemingly pulsing through the crystal windows of the time machine, colors glowed nuclear-bright, chasing themselves through unending spectrums. Dot-to-dot pictures collapsed into impossible zodiacs then spiralled away into a monstrously cloaked Death that ruled whatever domain they traveled through when the time machine rattled between years.

    "Sir!"

Brelmer forced his eyes open again, not realizing until then that they had closed. He focused on the Time Policeman and sorted through his memories for the man's name. So much had happened. "Yes, Sgt. Jameson?" The Time Policeman's head swelled up like a balloon at the top, stretching till it looked like the crash helmet had become a thimble sitting on it. Traveling through time had many different side effects and the medtechs working on the problems had only accounted for a few of them. The vision problems were one of the least important. Usually, if you were alone or if you kept your attention on the images that constantly swam by outside the crystal windows, you weren't even aware of them.

Sgt. Jameson's forehead shrunk, working like the sounds of an hourglass, exploding the mouth and chin into ponderous dimensions. The teeth seemed to work independently as the man talked. "Sir, your daughter has stopped breathing."

Without warning the time machine seemed to hang suspended for a moment, then just as suddenly, it fell off of whatever shelf of "present" it had been lodged on.

The interior of the time machine whirled around Brelmer in insane fury. He tore the sickness bag from the clips of the helmet as he twisted in the seat to look at Suzanne.

His daughter appeared two-dimensional in the rear seat, chalk-white. Her blonde hair covered most of her face, but he could see the slackness of her jaw, the spittle that trickled down one cheek. The time machine hit another unseen dip, found invisible tracking, and slid weightlessly through another corridor of time. Twirling end over end, it refused to compromise whatever path it had locked onto.

A black cloud seemed to drift up from Suzanne's pores.

Brelmer watched, unable to break the fascination it held for him. What was it? Could it be touched? Tasted? Smelled? His analytical mind locked onto the problem, forgetting where he was as it recorded the experience for later research with the theorists who still pondered the variables of traveling through time.

Then the scientist in him subsided as the father consciousness pushed it roughly to one side, demanding to help his daughter. His hands ripped clumsily at the restraining belts. The crash helmet bounced off one of the crystal windows. He squirmed through the narrow opening between the two front seats to reach Suzanne.

Brelmer's hand wrapped around Suzanne's narrow wrist as he felt for a pulse. Nothing. He turned back an eyelid, finding only bloodshot whiteness. Panic seized him and cold talons seemed to squeeze threateningly around his heart.

Did pulses beat during time travel? Why didn't he know that? Everyone was so preoccupied with the other intricacies of the voyage, with the distances that could be traveled, with the possible changes that could be wrought with each journey. Why didn't he know if

pulses beat? Shiva, he was breathing, wasn't he? And
Suzanne wasn't. Pulse or no pulse, his daughter was not
breathing. She was dying.

"Get up front," Brelmer ordered.

Sgt. Jameson hastened to comply, oozing across the
top of the time machine as it developed an outwardly
directed centrifugal force.

Brelmer rolled off his daughter's lower body and into
the vacated seat. He wished there were more room to
operate in. But the basic geometrical design that was
necessary to explode the time machine across the time
barrier limited the machines to a cramped capacity of
four people. If it had not been for the self-replicating
factor that had been discovered to be inherent in the
system, traveling through time would have been cur-
tailed to observatory journeys only.

Perhaps, that would have been better, Brelmer had
often thought.

And perhaps Voxner would have still demanded the
impossible.

Silently, Brelmer cursed the Senator as he took off
the hooded poncho he had worn on the last jump back to
Mexico 2074. None of the hidden-tech wired into it
would do him any good in the present situation. It was
combat gear, constructed solely for battle. He peeled
the chest holster and mini-Matthews off after disengag-
ing the static electricity charge that held it in place,
dropping the gun to the floor.

Visions of the carnage his team had left in Mexico

City of 2074 fluttered through his memory as he worked to loosen the tee shirt from around Suzanne's neck. He remembered the way the Chavez building had collapsed into ruin after being mortared with the missles he had ordered, remembered hoping Jackson Elgin Dubchek had perished inside, remembered how he had hit Suzanne to knock her out so he could get her out of the building, remembered the maroon uniforms of the Time Rebels. How many people had died in that assassination attempt? How many at his order?

Was Suzanne going to be a delayed fatality of it?

Feverishly, he freed her from the restraining belts and removed the crash helmet. Shiva, she was so beautiful, so soft. She couldn't die. He wouldn't permit it.

Reaching behind her, he fought to bring her to a sitting position, fighting against the angle he was forced to lift against the crazy way the time machine skipped and burned its way across the surface of whatever centuries lay between it and its destination.

"Jameson!" Brelmer bellowed.

"Sir?"

"Get me the emergency oxygen system. Direct it through one mask."

"Alabama, Colonel."

How long did it take to make a time jump? Brelmer didn't know. Chrons didn't work once the jump was underway. You could figure on getting any kind of reading from a chrono at the other end of the jump. A minute. An hour. A day. Some of them moved backwards. Some didn't move at all.

Brelmer gripped Suzanne from behind, placing his hands just below her sternum. Maybe the time travel sickness had taken her early and something had lodged in her throat. He squeezed firmly, trying to force loose whatever might be there.

He heard her breath whistle easily from her lungs.

But there was no drawn breath following.

Squelching the panic he felt rising inside him, Brelmer rolled Suzanne back over. He cupped the back of her neck, forcing her head back and her mouth open. Taking a deep breath, he expelled into her lungs, willing her to live. He counted between breaths, finding a rhythm that left him light-headed and gasping.

What had happened to her?

He had hit her hard in the Chavez building, true, but not hard enough to cause any lasting injury. Or had it been something else? She hadn't seemed quite herself somehow when he had tried to convince her to not pursue Dubchek into the building. Something about the brightness of her eyes, the loss of motor-reflex motion. He could recall that now, but he hadn't realized it then. There had been too much happening around them.

"Oxygen, Colonel," Jameson said as he held the plastin mask between the front seats.

Brelmer nodded. Come on, Suzanne, breathe. He tried to resuscitate her again, feeling a weakness in his own lungs as black spots wavered in front of his eyes. The familiar sickness associated with time travel spun like kneaded taffy into the pit of his stomach. He tried to put the frailty of his flesh to one side, tried to force his body to become the machine it was designed to be.

The odor of freshly squeezed oranges and coffee grounds and ammonia filled his nose. This was the only indication that the time jump was almost over: the sickness and the unforgettable odor. But even once those came into being the arrival time was indeterminate. There was still enough time for Suzanne to die in his arms while Brelmer's body was wracked with pain and nausea.

He came up for breath again, his senses swimming around him, fighting back the taste of bile. From up front he could hear Jameson and the time machine pilot giving in to the sickness with wretching sobs. He grabbed the oxygen mask from Jameson before the man lost it and the mask reeled back into the hidden recess where it was stored.

He could feel his heart hammering inside his chest. Tears came to his eyes as he gazed at his daughter's inert form. She could not die. He would not allow it to happen. He remembered the last few times they had been together. Anger had been an unseen conflagration between them and both parties sensed the heat. True, Suzanne favored her mother in her looks, but the soul and mind inside came from her father. She was curious, headstrong, self-willed, analytical, tactful only when it suited her purpose to be so.

She was his daughter.

He came up for air again, knowing the sickness no longer would be kept waiting. He felt it reach into his stomach with knotty fingers, multi-jointed for the extraction of excrutiating pain.

Suzanne shivered against him, then gasped as her breath rushed into her lungs on its own again. She fought against his hold, rolling over to vomit on the floor.

After making sure her throat was clear, Brelmer clamped the oxygen mask across her nose, leaving her mouth free while the sickness ran its course.

Then he gave in to the retching himself as his guts strained into complicated Moebius strips of life, connecting him to nothingness. Everything seemed to come apart in his mind as he became disassociated with himself. In the eternal blackness that was often showered with impossible colors and images, Brelmer's mind searched. Somewhere in the void he found something, a piece of string/bread crumbs/spoor. A something he could not identify but could follow back to its source.

He searched for Suzanne, closing his artificial crystal eyes, blotting out the impossibilities on the other side of the crystal windows. A pegasus had just flown by, riding an invisible wind on its four wings, glaring with eyes made of comets that trailed twin greenish fires in their wake.

Trickles of sound whispered down the tunnels of his hearing. Sounds of sickness, of retching, of knowing death was so near. His voice was mixed somewhere in the center of it all.

Then he felt the warmth of Suzanne's back against his palm for a moment. The sensation flickered away before Brelmer could grasp it. Panic welled in him, throbbing incessantly. He groped with mental fingers, tracing the path back along convoluted lines. Was Suzanne still breathing? Wind from a thousand shutting doors whipped into whatever face he wore as he hunted.

Where was Suzanne?

The time machine skated in a downward spiral, suddenly braked as it tripped over something, falling over, then up. Impossibly up and impossibly high, caught on some wave of centuries that seemed as if it would surely dash them on some stone shore of past/present/future/will be/won't be.

Suzanne. Brelmer would not be denied. Somewhere/somewhen. He felt his fingers move, drag across texture(time?) till they reached his daughter. Breathing. Relaxed, he let the sickness pound at him again, driving nails into his flesh that would leave no scars. He maintained the tenuous link between his corporeal body and that of his daughter even as his mind was liberated into the prison that time jealously kept between its moments. He focused on his palm, feeling the pained rise and fall of his daughter's back as her lungs continued to suck in oxygen between bouts of retching.

How often had he spent his nights just so? Brelmer could remember many times that Suzanne had shared his bed, sleeping between himself and his wife. At first when she was small, when they both feared something would happen to her in the darkness of the night. He had slept as he was now, with one hand on baby Suzanne's back, thinking if something happened to her, it would wake him. And later, when she was plagued with the nightmares that troubled every child as they came to realize how big their world really was and how little control they actually exercised over it.

What were Suzanne's nightmares like now? Brelmer wondered. Time travel had opened whole new worlds, hinged like Chinese puzzles, that hung from this corner or that. Worlds that held dangers for them as they explored. Other worlds that poured dangers into their world in the form of Time Rebels from the future as well as events triggered in the past that could sweep away their "real" present.

A heaviness forced him deeper into the reinforced seat of the time machine, trapping him once again in the body that was struggling against the sickness.

Brelmer blinked his eyes open again, looked past the strangely distorted shapes of the Time Policemen in the front seat, through the crystal window. Evidently they had been sucked into the gravity field of some as-yet-undiscovered asteroid lost in Time. He watched it spin above them as the time machine slid from side to side in an effort to break free.

He couldn't control the impulse to reach forward and seize the controls, knowing it would do no good because they were locked into the destination already programmed in.

Abruptly, the time machine shifted directions, plowing through a glowing red energy field as it headed directly for the bleak and barren asteroid. If time occupied space, Brelmer wondered as he found himself unable to look away, didn't it also make sense that the space should be filled with something?

Present theories argued in favor of the subconscious mind being responsible for the visions that swam across the black sea of Time. If not for the ability to dream and visualize, the theories espostulated that all travelers through time would have breakdowns before they reached their destinations, reduced to gibbering idiots and madmen.

Life was based on sensory input.

What existed in nothingness? In the time that held no time?

The asteroid swelled enormously before the time machine, filling the crystal window.

Brelmer regretted not having the restraining belts on. The coming impact would be impossible to survive. He wanted to shut his eyes, to outlaw the incongruous ending that seemed so imminent.

Yet, it wasn't unknown for time machines to get lost somewhere between then and now. True, the percentage figures were down now on government trips, but it was still far from being an exact science. Time travel was only a little over a year old, having been invented in

2249. Only ten months had passed in Brelmer's current year of 2250, but he had seen more days than that go by when he counted the trips into the past he had made. Surely he could add at least another biological year onto the chronological age he was filed at in Temporal Projects' records.

He had often wondered how old he would really be five years from his current present. Much of it depended on how many trips back Voxner insisted he take, and how long he had to spend each time.

And that was only assuming he lived that long.

Time travel was a Pandora's box of mayhem that Brelmer was sure Voxner did not understand. As Secretary of History and head of Project Clio, Voxner was aware of the multitudinous paradoxes involved at TP, yet the Senator chose to disregard them, insisting they were Brelmer's problem. Voxner had his own course to chart and it did not matter who he washed over in the attempt.

For a moment, Brelmer considered the good that would come when the time machine fragmented against the black, crater-pocked asteroid that raced toward them. He would not have to deal with the impossibilities anymore, not have to argue with the blindness Voxner exhibited about the paradoxes. But not now. Not when Suzanne was with him.

Not when there were so many unanswered questions he was sure would follow him into the next turn of the Wheel.

•

Shiva, he couldn't be taken away now. Not until he knew some of the answers.

The time machine fluttered briefly as the broken surface of the asteroid split in front of them, metamorphasizing into a gigantic, splinter-toothed mouth that swallowed them into darkness.

Nova-white lights shot into Brelmer's crystal eyes and he felt them respond immediately as they were created to, shutting out the brightness to a more manageable level. Then he was aware that his proper weight and balance had returned to him. He looked outside the crystal windows at the familiar surroundings of Temporal Projects.

Techs stood by their monitoring machines, waiting for the away team to open the doors.

Glancing at Suzanne, Brelmer found her gasping weakly for her breath. The pallor had continued to the point it seemed possible to see through her skin and count the blood veins beneath.

"Get out," Brelmer ordered.

The two men in front staggered out at once, falling to their knees as the last vestiges of the time sickness still held them.

Gathering Suzanne in his arms, Brelmer removed the oxygen mask and muscled her out of the time machine. He forced himself to walk when he could barely stand, carrying his daughter close to his chest.

"Gurney," Brelmer ordered, looking at one of the medtechs.

"Alabama, Colonel," the man responded as he sprinted for the door.

"Alert the medvault we're on our way," Brelmer bellowed at another man.

"Alabama, Colonel."

What would he do if Suzanne died? He pushed the question away, denying any attempts at rationalization. He swayed uncertainly, checking a nearby Time Policeman's move toward him with a glare that locked the big man into immobility. Brelmer was already aware that Voxner did not trust Suzanne, just as he was aware the Senator would have no qualms about ordering someone to kill his daughter. He would not trust anyone present with her safety. Except the precious handful he had culled from Voxner's ranks.

And if it meant he had to carry her himself to the lower floor medvault at TP, then he would do it.

CHAPTER TWO

Perspiration covered Jackson Dubchek as he labored under the hot Mexican sun. Sandy loam stuck to his fingers as he carefully slipped the watermelons from the leafy vines and laid them in the center of the row he was working. The melons weren't huge. Maybe weighing thirty to thirty-five pounds for the most part. But how many had he slipped since this morning?

He stifled a groan as he reached for another, wrapping dirt-encrusted fingers around the melon as he muscled it toward him. His right shoulder still ached, not yet recovered from the bullet wound he had received during his impromptu attack on the future rebel assassins in the Chavez building four weeks ago.

Only occasionally would a Buddha-blessed breeze sweep gently across the flat land of the field and bring momentary bliss with it.

The thin cotton shirt and white pants he wore were drenched and stuck stubbornly to his back and thighs. Sweat beaded in his eyebrows and stung his eyes. Removing a handkerchief from his back pocket, Jackson dried the area just around his eyes, leaving the rest of his face alone. Already his body had expended a lot of energy and resources to spread the protective moisture over his body. He put the handkerchief away and adjusted the other one he had tied around his head, hoping to stem sweat flow. He pulled his wide-brimmed straw hat lower, trying to cut out the blinding rays of the setting sun.

He back ached with the prolonged agony of toiling in the same position. But he had learned in the last week and a half that it was better to endure than try to change it. There was nothing around him but the almost silent sounds of the other migrant field hands as they worked the melon rows.

Hefting another melon to juggle it into position, Jackson felt his sandy fingers slide from their precarious hold. The watermelon started a downward spiral that left a sick feeling in his stomach. Without thinking, he bent lower, throwing both arms under the melon as if it were a falling child. He cradled it, stopping it only scant inches from the hard-baked surface of the row.

Jackson gave silent thanks to Buddha as he rolled it into the center of the row.

Every one he broke he had to pay for and with the slowness at which he worked, even one would deeply affect the pittance he was given at the end of the day.

Memories of the air-conditioned hallways of New Ninevah Library haunted him constantly as he worked. The almostness of the once-was tortured him. Despite the inclement heat, the dull repetitiveness of the job, and the fatigue that ate at him with dulled fangs, Jackson could not turn off his mind.

A year ago, in his native time of 2250, he had been a useful part of a useful society. His work as translator at New Ninevah had held no ground-breaking discoveries, but it had been something that worked his mind as surely as slipping the melons worked his body. It had been something he had been trained for basically since the Birth Stat recorded his delivery.

It was hard to imagine that the same elation which had once filled him after completing a successful translation of a difficult Sargasso scroll would flame inside him as it had when he kept the melon from smashing against the ground.

But then, it was hard to imagine that the small translation Temporal Projects had asked him to do in 2183 would change his life as dramatically as it had.

Yet, the change had come.

In 2249, he had been driven from his job at New Ninevah by Friz Brelmer and the Time Police. He had spent a year in Branson, Missouri after agreeing to never cross paths with anyone connected with Temporal Projects again. And it had proved to be an almost comfortable existence, living as a pick-up dulcimer player around Silver Bullion City.

But a year later he had wound up again tangled in whatever vicious web the Time Police wove across the centuries. Brelmer had left him stranded here. In Mexico City of 2074. Without the knowledge of whether he had managed to insure his sister-in-law's existence.

Jackson often thought of his older brother, Martin, in the dark and quiet hours of the night. It seemed strange to think that his brother didn't miss him. Over four weeks had passed for Jackson. Yet, if he was able to find a time machine and return to 2250, he knew that at the most only 9.6 hours would have passed for Martin. That was one of the strange guidelines of whatever physical laws governed time traveling. No matter where you traveled or how long, there was always that 9.6 window that allowed you access back to your present.

A shrill whistle screamed into Jackson's ears, signalling the end of the work day.

Sighing, Jackson continued working to the end of the row, knowing the farmers who had hired the picking crew would watch to see who stopped halfway down a row. Then he turned around and helped the white-bearded old man who had been working behind him carry the melons to the small fleet of ancient pickup trucks at the edge of the field.

The old man gave him a small smile, looking slumped under the weight of the melon he carried on his shoulder. The cotton shirt was grayed with sweat and age and had a handful of holes scattered across the chest. A dead cigar was clamped firmly between the old man's yellowed teeth.

Jackson had feared the man for the last three days. He was twenty-seven and knew the old man had to be at least twice that age. Yet the old man never seemed to bend under the heat of the sun, never seemed to wilt against the constant dry breezes. To Jackson he had seemed as knobbly and wear-resistant as the pads of cactus that flowered in the arid ground. He had felt threatened as he worked the melon rows because the old man seemed to constantly dog his heels, making Jackson even more aware of the slowness he worked at. As well as exposing that slowness to the owners of the farm.

"Eh, muchacho," the old man said as he placed his melon on the pickup truck beside Jackson, "you are getting much better with the hands, si?"

"Gracias," Jackson said.

The old man slapped him on the shoulder. "You do not work so bad for a Yankee," he said as they returned to gather the last two melons. "With just a few more weeks of practice, I think you will be ver' good at slipping the melons."

Trying not to wince at the sudden pain in his injured shoulder, or the thought of continued work in the field, Jackson only nodded. One thing he had learned from his experiences with the Time Police and from being around the farm laborers was to keep his mouth shut.

"At first," the old man said as they shouldered the last two melons, "I think you were ver' much trouble. I think that something or someone ver' bad must be following you from the States for you to come here to work."

Anxiety trickled through Jackson as he and the old man walked back toward the waiting trucks. The other laborers were finishing up as well and none of them seemed interested in him. The drivers had already gotten behind the steering columns of the pickups and were waiting impatiently for the rest of the load to be put on.

"See," the old man went on as they stood in line behind a handful of men and women stacking their melons, "I think to myself a lot. I wonder about things and try to find meanings in things for myself. Whether they are right or not. So, I tell myself, Santiago, I say, this Yankee boy does not belong here. Not in this land and not in this way of life. Yet, he is here. Why? So I tell myself it must be because you are in ver' much trouble and bad men must be following you. I guess this because of the way you always look over your shoulder when we work and because of the way you guard your back during noon meal periods."

Jackson felt chagrined. He had thought he'd kept

those paranoid feelings to himself and had been less noticeable.

"But I watch you, Yankee, and I see how you treat your job. Like you care for it. Like you are helping build yourself over again with everything you do. It takes you time to learn things, si, but once you learn them, this knowledge is yours and you use it. Not like some of these young vatos who come to the farm to buy new compact disc players so they can listen to Yankee rock'n'roll. I think you are a man of good heart. And if evil follows you, as I think it must, it is not of your doing."

Jackson studied the muddy depths of the old man's eyes, wondering if the man knew the whole story, if he would be amazed at how closely his guess hit the last few events of Jackson's life.

Gently, the old man laid his burden on the over-filled pickup. "I know you are living with the Franco family now, and I know they are good people and will take care of you. Just as I know you will let no harm befall them. I just want to tell you, Yankee, that as long as we work these fields together, I will be another pair of eyes in the back of your head."

"I think my trouble is long gone, senor," Jackson said, "but I thank you just the same." He extended his hand and felt the leathery roughness of Santiago's palm against the tenderness of his own.

"Maybe, Yankee," the old man said. "But if you haven't solved your troubles, I know from experience that they have a ver' bad habit of popping up again and again."

"I know," Jackson said. But his trouble lay 176 years in the future. If Brelmer had left anyone behind to search the survivors for him, he had not seen the person or persons. True, he had kept a low profile, staying at the motel where he had had his wound tended till the money he had received from Paress Linnet ran out. Then, at the suggestion of the night manager at the motel, he had introduced himself to the Franco family and had been accepted as a border.

He had been so watchful at the beginning of the last month. He never went anywhere outside the Franco house unless it was to run an errand for Carmita Franco. Even then, when moving among the suburbs of Mexico City, he had carefully scanned everyone for the telltales of the Time Police: the crystal eyes, the long and pointed ears, the broad nose, and the brightshades that was an unofficial symbol of office. Now that watchfulness was an ingrained survival habit. Before, in 2183, the Time Police had been satisfied with simply losing him in time. Displacement, they termed it. A slow death wrapped in suicide and insanity. Now they were willing to kill him.

Brelmer had proved that.

The Praetor had fired at him even as Jackson saved Brelmer's and Suzanne's lives.

Suzanne.

Memory of the woman still brought pain to Jackson.

Suzanne Brelmer was at one the most alluring and most dangerous women Jackson Dubchek had met in his life. Three times now he had walked away from her, swearing never to become involved with her again. But her memory haunted him with an unfamiliar bittersweetness. Often he had laid awake, listening to the soft sounds of little Mateo Franco's snoring, remembering the warmth of Suzanne's breath on his cheek when they had made love.

Regretfully, he pried the shadow of memory away, folding it carefully into the corner of his mind so he wouldn't crease it and mar what he was able to remember.

"I will see you manyana, eh, Yankee?" Santiago said.

Pulling himself back into his current present, Jackson said, "Yes. Thanks again."

The old man nodded and reached into his pants, pulling out an ancient Zippo lighter he used to fire up the cigar stub between his teeth. Someone called his name and Santiago turned away with a final wave to Jackson.

Removing the handkerchief from his pants pocket, Jackson doffed his straw hat and wiped perspiration from the back of his neck. He fell in with the flow of field workers lining up in front of the water tanks to slake their thirst and get their day's wages from the farm owners. It would still be a long walk back to the Franco house because Pepe Franco was in Mexico City getting a part for the house water pump.

Jackson stood in line, gratefully erect, and felt the tiredness coat on him layer by layer, hermetically sealed into place by the hot sun. He closed his eyes and felt himself sway to some internal rhythm. For a moment he felt dizzy, lost, like he was experiencing time travel flashback. So many memories to choose from. Which one could he use to escape the screeching ache that throbbed up and down his back and shoulders?

"Jackson! Jackson!" a shrill young voice called.

Turning, Jackson saw grimy-faced Mateo Franco running through the mass of people waiting patiently in line for their chance at the water and the money man from the farm. The eleven-year-old boy's continued exuberance despite the full day he had just put in always amazed Jackson.

The boy lunged at Jackson in a flying tackle. Jackson squatted and barely managed to catch Mateo, feeling the boy's weight thump solidly into his ribcage. Even braced as he was, the boy's charge nearly toppled them both into the dirt.

Regaining his feet, Mateo clapped the palms of both hands on Jackson's shoulders, a gamin's grin spread almost from ear-to-ear. "Eh, vato, how are you today?"

"Tired," Jackson said as he kept his hunkered down position to talk eye-to-eye with the boy. At first he had been surprised by the feelings of attachment he had for the boy and at the fact that Mateo easily returned them. He had been an outsider to their family, an added burden when his injured shoulder kept him from doing much more than helping with the housework. Yet, not even Pepe and Carmita, Mateo's mother and father, treated him as such. At first Jackson had assumed it was because the hotel manager had been a member of their family and they extended courtesy to him out of those familial obligations. Then he realized how open they were with him and how much they appreciated the time he spent with their children.

"Too tired to tell stories tonight?" Mateo asked. A concerned look filled his face.

Jackson smiled, remembering the way the boy and his two-year old sister, Theresa, listened to him as he told them stories he cannibalized from his readings at New Ninevah. Little Theresa always listened intently as he spoke, but she was always the first to nod off to sleep. Unless he was playing the harmonica he had purchased with the first money he had earned. It had been the only thing he had bought for himself. It wasn't Odar'a, his dulcimer, but it permitted him to play the music that seemed to be locked inside himself. The rest of the money he had given to Carmita, who had protested and said it was too much. But he had insisted. Money would do him no good where he was presently stranded, and Jackson knew it. Until he figured out what his next move would be, he wanted to help the family out.

In a way it was strange. Jackson was a fugitive, hiding from the elite corps of the Time Police, dodging the reach of Temporal Projects and Brelmer, yet he was trapped in a culture that had not yet joined the Second Republic. A country that would have benefitted from the vast reforms that were available under the provisions of the Second Republic. Mateo's schooling was infrequent and lacking in its view of the world, but the basics of homelife, of being a positive influence in the family, those were the strong points. Jackson had felt fortunate in his own time period to have a brother like Martin, one who stayed close and didn't drift apart like many of the other families did. The Second Republic kept busy with caring for its citizens and promotions often flew thick and fast. Sometimes it was hard to keep up with your family when you were transferred from post to post.

Jackson had many good remembrances of the Second Republic, of the way it cared for the people within its reach, but could never shake the thought that the same government housed a dark heart like Temporal Projects. No matter what else the Second Republic did, everything TP touched gradually filtered into everything else. He pushed the thoughts of future rebels and the Brelmers from his mind as he tousled Mateo's hair.

All those problems were literally in tomorrow. And, if he didn't find some way to break the chains of Time that held him hostage here, Jackson knew he would never live to see tomorrow. Again.

"No," Jackson said. "I'm not too tired." "Bueno. But can we skip the music? That is so boring."

"To you, maybe, but I think it's the only part Theresa cares about."

"Si, I know. But she is only a girl. And a baby as well. When you tell stories, I can see them. Like when Odysseus was tied to the mast of his ship and the pretty women called to him."

"The Sirens."

"Si. The Sirens." An inner fire lit the boy's eyes. "I can see these things, Jackson. Mamacita says you have a gift for story-telling, that you are a ver' smart man."

"Gracias," Jackson said. He hugged the boy briefly, wondering if big brother Martin had ever experienced the feelings for him that he had for Mateo. If it had not been for the memories and the feeling of displacement that constantly plagued him, Jackson was sure he could have been happy where he was. He could have put even those aside eventually, he often thought, if it wasn't for the constant fear of the Time Police. How long would Brelmer allow him to be simply stranded in time before assigning someone to make sure he would never be a problem again? And why had Suzanne been so content to let him vanish? For a few moments, while locked in a post-coital embrace in the hotel on their first trip to 2074, it seemed like Suzanne cared for him. Or did she believe him to be dead?

Jackson moved through the line with Mateo holding his hand.

Another problem that gnawed at him was that if he did stay in this time period, sooner or later there would be a record of his existence. A red flag in the flow of Time that would alert the records-searchers at TP. Was he living a life that ended a week from now? Two weeks? A month? He couldn't live his life in a vacuum no matter how hard he tried.

Then there were the questions that would not leave him alone. Was Martin alright? Was he able to save Ana's history enough to reestablish her existence? How would TP call a halt to the interference in history from the time rebels? And were the adjustments the Time Police were making really necessary? Irene of the Mnemosyne didn't think so. She and her followers had mapped out history through oral memory and there seemed to be many contradictions between what they could remember and what the Second Republic offered as general information. Why?

The questions were pointless because Jackson knew he wouldn't be able to answer them. He'd tried before. The only thing that came as a result of the endless sessions of examining the little he knew were blinding headaches that ignited a dark anger within himself.

When he reached the water container, he sipped sparingly from the dipper, knowing too much at one time would make him sick. That had happened to him the first two days he had worked in the field. He had been afraid he'd contracted some disease the Second Republic had eradicated until Mateo corrected his water consumption.

Jackson was handing the dipper to the old woman

behind him when he heard Mateo's voice cry out his name. The pain evident in the boy's yelp snapped Jackson's head around.

A large man wearing an angry frown held Mateo at the end of one beefy arm, shaking the boy unmercifully.

CHAPTER THREE

Jackson pushed his way through the gathering crowd, apologizing in English as well as Spanish. When had Mateo left his side? He had released the boy's hand when he picked up the water dipper, but that had been only seconds ago. What had happened?

Mateo screamed in pain and fright.

The big man held both of the boy's arms in one large hand. He shook the boy again when Mateo kicked him in the shins and tried to push away.

Jackson paused on the inner edge of the crowd, already drawing curious stares from the other field laborers. He addressed the big man in Spanish, holding his hands well away from his body so the man could see he held no weapon. "Put the boy down," Jackson said as he approached the man.

"Who the hell are you?" the big man demanded, turning so his bulk interposed itself between Jackson and the boy.

"I am with the boy," Jackson said. He caught and held Mateo's gaze for just a moment, seeing hope in the boy's eyes. Tears made dirty streaks down Mateo's face.

"You are his father, then?"

"No. A friend of his family's."

The man stood a half head taller than Jackson and nearly doubled him in weight. The constant running from the Time Police across the centuries, the bullet wound, and the harsh, demanding labor slipping the watermelons had all contributed to stripping the extra flesh from Jackson's already lean frame. Moving easily, offering no real threat, Jackson pushed the insistent thought of trying to take the boy from the man away, trying to use reason instead. He was no stranger to violence or to killing, but that was not his chosen path. Rather, it was an alley he had been forced into on different occasions. A dark and lonely alley filled with dead who refused to stay that way. How many nightmares had disturbed his sleep since he had crossed the paths of the Time Police? Laszlo Slye, Lance Paulson, the future rebs in the Chavez building, they were all still there, waiting for him every time he closed his eyes.

"This boy is a thief," the big man said. His beard was short and thick, wisps of it crawling down his neck to disappear inside the sleeveless denim work shirt he wore. The black eyes were only hard glints over his sunburned cheeks.

"He is no thief," Jackson said. The undercurrent of voices behind and around him whirled with sickening dizziness that echoed his own thoughts. Reason. The man had to listen to reason. Think placidity. Zen. Step outside the violence, radiate only calmness.

Mateo cried out again as he renewed his struggle to free himself.

Jackson felt his resolve weaken. He didn't want the boy hurt. And if a confrontation between himself and the big man took place he was sure it might happen despite his best intentions.

"He is a thief!" the big man roared. "I felt him stumble into me only a moment ago and, when I checked, my wallet was gone."

"Maybe you lost it somewhere else," Jackson said.

"Maybe this boy stole it, too, eh?" The big man shook Mateo again, eliciting another howl of pain. "Maybe you and this orphan are working together, eh?"

Unable to hold himself back any longer and recognizing that the man could possibly break Mateo's arms without being aware of it, Jackson stepped forward, looking upwards into the man's face. He kept his own face expressionless as he spread his hands further outward from his body. "You are hurting the boy. Release him, por favor. He has done nothing to you."

An evil grin gleamed through the wiry beard as the man started to shake his head and say something further.

Jackson lifted a leg and kicked the man in the crotch without saying another word.

The man released his grip on Mateo as he doubled up and fell to the ground.

"Come on," Jackson said as he stooped to help the boy to his feet. Mateo came into his arms eagerly, crying silently, his sobs thudding softly into Jackson's chest. For a moment Jackson held him, talking soothing words no one else could hear. He backed away from the big man, watching as the man tried to unroll himself from the fetal position. The crowd parted behind him, unwilling to take sides in the battle.

The big man got to his feet before Jackson cleared the outer fringe of the crowd.

Jackson let the boy's body slide to the ground, staring at the big man who was running toward him. "Run," he told Mateo, "run and don't stop till you reach your mother's house."

"But . . . "

"Vamoose!" Jackson pushed the boy in one direction then back-pedaled in another. He saw Mateo turn and sprint for all he was worth just before the big man's bulk rolled over him like an avalanche. An immense fist, seemingly loaded with some kind of explosive, drilled into his left cheekbone and he felt skin split. A kaleidoscope of colored lights, as many and as varied as any of those generated by the time machine, clouded his vision. A talon of blunt fingers bit into his injured shoulder, flooding into a sensory overload that almost took him away from his body.

"Pig!" the big man yelled into his ear. "Lying, thieving, gringo pig!"

Jackson struggled to get away, grabbing a fistful of the man's shirt with his left hand in an effort to lever himself out from under the man. His right shoulder felt incapacitated but he forced it up anyway, doubling his fingers into a fist, not aiming for any particular target. His fist landed ineffectually against a sweat-slick shoulder.

The harsh sand cut into Jackson's bare back as he tried to slither away from the heavier man. The man gave up hitting him for a moment as he shifted for a new grip. Foul sweetness blew into Jackson's face as the big man breathed on him.

As the man tried to circle him in both arms and cover his body at the same time, Jackson levered his uninjured arm under the man's chin. He pushed, straining every muscle in his body that helped provide the proper leverage. His breath came in sobbing gasps. He locked into position, feeling his arms shake with the effort. The sick craziness of displacement swirled inside him, building from distant eddies to full-fledged hurricane force. Lester Wu had died before he was born. So had

Slye and Paulson. And others. With no one to mourn them. Was that how it would be for him? He remembered how the bloody shadow had seemed to rip from Lester Wu's body. But had it really been his friend that died? The creature Jackson had gone back to save had been infected with whatever madness seized traffic left behind by the Time Police.

Jackson struggled, flipping through his erratic memories as he tried to focus on Chrys Calvino and the classes in Tae Kwon Do she had gotten him to attend with her. Chrys had been his sex partner before the business with Temporal Projects, and for a while afterwards. Till Jackson was edged into a search for the truth behind the disappearances at TP. But the only thing that came to mind from the classes was the thought of pain from overtaxed muscles and the discovery of yet another sport Chrys could defeat him at.

Something bright flicked under Jackson's wrist holding the big man's head back. Knife, he realized with keen interest, but where the hell had the big man found another arm to hold it with? The original two were still pounding away at him.

Then he saw the edge bite warningly into the big man's neck just under the Adam's apple. He felt the big man stiffen in response.

"Get up, Luis," a man's voice said threateningly.

"Si, si," the big man said. Slowly, he gathered his feet under him, rising off of Jackson.

"Are you all right?" Santiago asked Jackson. The old

man held the switchblade to the big man's throat, making the skin white around the blade.

"Yeah," Jackson said hoarsely as he forced himself to his feet. He tasted blood in his mouth and realized the big man had busted the inside of his cheek when he knocked him to the ground. He moved gingerly, checking to see if anything had been broken.

"This is Luis," Santiago said. "He believes himself to be one bad vato. Big man. Strong man.

"The big man spit into the dust, still glaring at Jackson. "You got no business in this old man. This Yankee and that boy stole my wallet. They're thieves together."

"The boy didn't take your wallet," Jackson said.

Santiago lowered the knife but didn't put it away. "That boy is the son of Pepe Franco, Luis. What do you think Pepe is going to do to you when he finds out you were trying to hurt his son?"

Luis tried not to show it but Jackson could tell the big man felt uncomfortable with the idea. He could understand why if the man had met Pepe Franco. Mateo's father wasn't as big as Luis, but his shoulders were easily broader, his chest deeper, cut into a large vee draped with heavy muscle. Mateo had once shown Jackson a coin his father had bent in his bare hand for a keepsake. Jackson had seen the man easily manhandle engine parts on the family truck, lifting assemblies Jackson knew he himself would never have been able to shift without some kind of pulley system.

"Hey, Luis," someone in the crowd yelled.

A wallet dropped into the dust at the big man's feet.

Luis bent to reach it and Jackson felt himself tense up painfully in response. Santiago's knife wasn't there any more to keep the man at bay.

"Is it yours?" Jackson asked as the man opened the wallet.

Luis nodded.

"Is everything there?"

"Si." The big man didn't look happy as he put the wallet away.

"The boy did not steal it," Jackson said in a low voice.

The big man didn't say anything. His baleful glare told Jackson the matter was anything but settled.

"If I were you," Santiago said conversationally, "I would not show back up here, Luis. I think Pepe Franco would consider it an insult if his son had to work with someone such as yourself."

Without another word, the big man turned and walked away, striding forcefully through the thinning crowd.

"Gracias," Jackson said to the old man. He touched his fingers softly to the swelling below his left eye. Already the eyelid had almost closed. "I don't know what would have happened if you hadn't stopped him. I'm not much of a fighter. In fact, I'm probably better at slipping melons."

Santiago clapped him on the back and laughed out-loud.

Jackson couldn't remember seeing the man put the switchblade away but noticed it had somehow vanished.

"Not a fighter," Santiago repeated. "Yet you were willing to risk fighting Luis than let harm come to young Mateo."

"It happened before I realized what I was doing. I could have caused him to hurt Mateo even more than he did."

Santiago shook his head as he took Jackson by the elbow and guided him to the water tank. "I was watching. You were faster than me, but you did what you did because there was no choice."

"Maybe I could have gone about it a little more intelligently. I don't like fighting."

"Yet you are no stranger to it."

"No." Images whirled inside Jackson's mind as Santiago had him sit at the base of a small scrub oak by the water tank. He watched the old man wet a handkerchief with a dipperful of water. Laszlo Slye's head exploded again in his memory as the gun bucked in his fist. Lance Paulson died again back at the German concentration camp. Thoughts of the way the Chavez building had shivered and shook under his feet as he fled for his life made chill bumps race down his arms.

The handkerchief felt cool against his face as the old man washed the blood away. Jackson closed his good eye, focusing on the pleasant feeling of being cared for.

"You do not have to be a warrior to fight in a war,"

Santiago said gently. The timbre of his voice told Jackson the man spoke from experience. "If this were true, there would be no wars, no revolutions. When you fight someone, you don't just fight from the training in your body and the knowledge in your brain. You reach into your heart if you wish to defend those that you love. Just as your love for young Mateo drove you into the confrontation with Luis."

And just as his love for Martin and Ana had driven him into the conflict with the Time Police again. As much as he hated the thought of being stranded in this time zone, Jackson knew he would have done everything over again if he had to. "Maybe, you're right."

"Of course I'm right, Yankee. A man doesn't get to my age without learning much along the way." Santiago helped Jackson to his feet. "How are you feeling now?"

"Better. At least now the shaking has gone away."

"You will be sore tomorrow."

Jackson grinned. "It can't be any worse than from slipping the melons."

Santiago cackled and clapped him on the back.

"Do you think there will be any further trouble with Luis?"

"No. Pepe will see to that. But you will want to watch yourself when you are alone. Luis is not a man to let his revenge cool quickly. He is mucho hot-blooded. You've seen that for yourself."

Jackson dusted himself off, grimacing at the blood staining the fabric of his shirt. He thanked the old man again and turned to go.

"Hey, Yankee," Santiago said.

Jackson looked over his shoulder.

Santiago rubbed his fingers together in a gesture Jackson recognized as belonging in most of the cultures he had pscyho-studied in the Republic schools. "You are forgetting your wages. You worked hard for them."

Jackson nodded and followed the old man to the farmer.

Cupping his palm over the harmonica, Jackson played as he walked back toward the Franco house. He followed the weather-beaten dirt road that wound through the dry land, knowing the sun would be down by the time he got back. Had little Mateo made it back safely? He felt bad about sending the boy back alone, but there had been no guarantee that Luis would not have attacked Mateo after finishing with Jackson. And the boy had made the trip by himself several times before, hadn't he? Carmita and Pepe had both told him that.

Long shadows from the chaparral on either side of the road streaked across the baked yellow hardness of the road.

Follow the yellow brick road, Jackson thought, remembering the book by Frank L. Baum and the holotape starring Judy Garland. Only Dorothy's quest took her back home at the end of it. True, there was the menace of the flying monkeys and the Wicked Witch of the West, but Jackson thought he would have gladly traded them for the deadliness of the crystal-eyed Time Police. The yellow brick road didn't leave you with your guts twisting through themselves like the time machine did. It also went in only one direction, with no unexpected side jaunts to Wheeling, West Virginia.

And Dorothy had companions on her journey, as well as a home to return to.

Jackson had no one, and no home.

The only people who seemed the least bit inclined to care about his welfare were also wanting to use him every chance they got. Irene and the Mnemosyne wanted him to do their research in the past, to confirm whatever inconsistancies they believed were evidences of Temporal Projects' tampering. Brother Martin didn't know the whole story, and telling him would only have involved him too deeply and made him a liability to the Time Police. And Suzanne Brelmer.

Who knew for sure where Suzanne's true loyalties lay?

He played deftly, wrapping himself in the music as he walked. The harmonica was a poor substitute for Odar'a. He missed the way he could involve his whole body in the playing of the dulcimer. Missed the way he could feel it resonate against his body. Yet the harmonica allowed him to sort through the chinked and cracked pieces of himself and keep himself in some sort of order.

Music was timeless. Jackson was grateful for that. No matter what time line or reality he found himself in, there would always be music and an instrument for him to play. He knew that dulcimers were in existence in this NOW. It was just a matter of time before he found one.

People on the same road watched him as he walked, smiling at the gay noises he warbled from the harmonica. He warmed to the exercise, pushing his problems away as he reached for the completeness he knew as Jackson Elgin Dubchek. The threat of Luis faded into the darkness of nonthought as he assembled the Ozark folk songs in his head and strung the melodies together for all the passersby to hear.

A little girl hardly older than Theresa Franco clapped her hands in obvious glee as she trailed behind her mother.

Jackson winked at her with his good eye.

She laughed at him and covered her gap-toothed mouth with both hands.

Giving himself over to the music, Jackson played on. New energy seemed to possess him as he slid into a plane of existence that held no worries or fears.

How many times had he wanted to be like Robinson Crusoe, Gullivar of Mars, Michael Valentine Smith, or Horatio McQuay? As a boy reading through those literary classics, he had felt at home with the idea of being stranded on a desert isle or a barbaric planet, of being a stranger in a strange land or being lost in the nether world of psychoses.

Now it was real.

He felt the chill of fear leaking iced water balloons down his back.

Traffic.

The word sounded so innocuous at first. Yet, now, so lethal. Permanent and grim.

For a moment the shadow of insanity possessed him. A madman cackled inside his head. Time travel, the madman croaked, nice time to visit but I wouldn't want to stay there.

His fingers felt stiff and cold on the harmonica. His lips seemed bloodless and rubbery. He missed a note, almost off-key. Nothing, he was sure, that anyone around him would notice, but something that sounded sharp and painful to him.

Something that sounded lost.

A rattling brown pickup coming down the road drew his attention. He kept playing while an animal part of his mind prepared to push him into flight. Then he recognized Mateo standing in the bed of the pickup so his head looked over the vehicle's top. He saw the boy point and wave, pounding on the cab of the pickup.

An unfamiliar lightness filled Jackson's heart as he put the harmonica away and began trotting toward the pickup.

Carmita Franco had a worried look on her face when the vehicle stopped for him. She was dressed as Jackson had always seen her, in a dark skirt and simple white blouse. Her black hair was still up in a bun to keep it out of her face while she cooked, though, and usually she refused to be seen out of the house unless it was let down. She worried an embroidered dishtowel in her hands. When she saw Jackson's closed eye she made a pained "O" with her mouth.

Sitting behind the steering wheel, Pepe Franco's face was unreadable. He easily dwarfed his wife in bulk, though none of it was fat. Carmita was almost as tall as Jackson, and boyishly slim. Pepe was a short giant with a thick mustache that trailed down to his chin on either side of his mouth.

Jackson smiled at little, dark-eyed Theresa standing on the seat beside her mother, knowing he probably looked strange to her with the swollen eye. She took her thumb from her mouth and smiled back shyly.

"I did not want to leave you, Jackson," Mateo said as he leaned over the wooden railing of the pickup, "but I knew papa could help you."

"You did well," Jackson said as he tousled the boy's hair.

"Where is Luis?" the boy wanted to know. "Did you kick the vato's ass?"

"Mateo!" Carmita's stern voice yelled.

The boy's face reddened as he apologized.

"No," Jackson said as he clambered into the pickup.

"Maybe next time, eh?" the boy asked.

"Let's hope there's not a next time."

"Are you all right, Jackson?" Carmita asked. She

still
had trouble pronouncing his name and it was often a
joke between them.

Theresa slid across the seat and sat in Jackson's lap,
cradling her head against his chest as she continued to
suck her thumb. "I am now," Jackson said.

"Luis?" Pepe asked.

"A problem for another day, perhaps. Santiago mentioned your name when he pulled Luis off of me."

Pepe nodded and ground the shift lever into gear.
"Santiago is a good man."

"He may have saved my life," Jackson agreed. "Was
Mateo alright? I didn't have time to check."

"Si," Carmita said as she braced herself against the
dashboard. The pickup bounced roughly across the
uneven road as Pepe swung it around. "A few bruises,
perhaps, but nothing requiring medical aid."

"I'm glad." Jackson caught Pepe's eye as the man
checked the windows for pedestrians. "Thanks for coming for me."

Pepe shrugged. "The Francos take care of their own,
Jackson. It is one thing my father taught me when I
was ver' young."

The words warmed Jackson, walling off some of the
chill displacement had filled him with. Stranded, he
may be, but not without somewhere to call home. At
least for awhile.

Little Theresa reached out with one small hand, tracing a fingertip across Jackson's swollen eye. "Ouch,"

she said in her tiny voice.

"Si," Jackson replied as he laughed at her. He hugged her tightly, feeling her short arms attempt to hug him back, becoming a small anchor that held him closer to the security he missed so much.

CHAPTER FOUR

Struggling through layers of sleep and tattered dreams with kernels of memory tucked into the center of each, Jackson forced himself awake.

The attic bedroom was silent around him, almost too warm from the wood burning stove in the kitchen below. Faint illumination from a downstairs lamp glowed softly on the unvarnished woodwork of the bedroom. He blinked his good eye in an attempt to clear the sleep from it, forgetting for a moment that his left eye was still swelled shut. Pain nipped at him with sharp teeth as he shifted on the hard bed. He sat up and pushed the sheets away.

Reaching under the frame of the bed, he gripped the

handle of the dagger the female Tysonyllyn had given him. He held the sheath in his left hand, wrapping the fingers of his other hand around the polished black handle.

Mateo was a small bundle on the other twin bed.

There wasn't enough room to stand in the make-shift bedroom and Jackson had to move crablike through the support struts of the roof. He pulled on his pants as he moved, securing the sheathed knife at his waistband.

What had wakened him?

He searched his fragmented memory for the answer but it was impossible to find the seam between whatever it was and the nightmare that had tried to swallow him while he slept.

He paused at the square-cut hole in the kitchen ceiling. The stovepipe running through the roof beside him radiated heat onto his face as he peered cautiously down the collapsible ladder.

Voices.

Jackson could hear them now but couldn't identify them. He glanced at the alarm chron Mateo had by his bed. It was 3:14 AM. Carmita Franco wouldn't even be up to prepare the family breakfast for almost another two hours.

Who could it be?

The ladder was out of the question for the moment. Jackson knew the squeaks it made would announce his presence at once. He rocked back on his heels, using his arms to redistribute his body weight as he stepped to the front of the house, staying on the 2 X 12s that framed the house. He felt something furry and sharp-clawed run across his foot and restrained a curse.

At the front of the house he pushed a shutter out of the way and looked down.

The Francos lived on a small dirt road in the middle of dozens of other houses coated with the same white-washed color. Scattered amber lights showed in a handful of the other dwellings.

The long, dark-colored Cadillac with its ruby-tinted brake lights and the clear white of the head beams was the only thing out of place.

Jackson felt panic seize him. He strained his eyes to penetrate the dark tint of the car's windows but couldn't see anything.

Time Police? But how had they found him? Sweet Buddha, had he, by agreeing to come to the Francos in the first place and by finding himself unwilling to move on, sealed their deaths as well as his? He knew from experience the Time Police liked to leave no loose ends.

He moved away from the shuttered window, duck-walking his way back to the rectangular opening and the ladder.

"Jackson?" Mateo's sleepy voice croaked.

Jackson whirled instantly, silencing the boy with a finger to his lips.

"What's wrong?" the boy asked.

Jackson shook his head, returning to his bed long enough to grab his work shoes and the clean shirt

Carmita had given him.

"Where are you going?"

"Nowhere," Jackson responded, remembering how he had resented the answer when big brother Martin had given it to him. But that had been before Martin married Ana, before their parents had died in the Great Plaza Fire.

Jackson's mind raced as he tried to figure out how to get out of the house. If the Time Police couldn't find him there, maybe they would leave the Francos alone and continue their search elsewhere. But what if the Time Police didn't leave the family alone? They wouldn't have revealed themselves if they weren't sure of themselves. Or would they? The Time Police Jackson had encountered hadn't been overly stocked in the intelligence department.

The sound of voices from below came to a sudden stop and Jackson found himself holding his breath. Footsteps, sliding with papery quietness across the polished wooden floor below, approached the rectangle.

"Jackson," Carmita Franco's voice called softly. "Jackson. Come down, por favor. There is a man here to see you. He and Pepe are waiting."

Returning to the attic opening, Jackson looked down at the woman.

Carmita had her long black hair tied back in a ponytail. She wore a flowing housecoat and kept her arms across her breasts.

"Who is it?" Jackson asked.

"Tyrell Czenlyn. He is a doctor."

"Do you know him?"

She shook her head. "No, but I have heard of him. He is a good man, Jackson, ver' learned in medicines. Many times he has helped sick people in the city who could not afford to go to the hospital or who the clinic doctors said they were unable to help."

"Is anyone with him?" Jackson placed a foot on the first rung of the ladder. Carmita steadied it for him as he clambered down.

"No. He has a chauffeur who waits in the car."

The wooden floor felt cold to Jackson's feet. He leaned against the small white refrigerator long enough to slip his work shoes on and shrug into his cotton shirt. He followed Carmita into the living room.

Soft light from a small lamp splashed against the dark curtain covering the room's only window. Pepe sat in a worn easy chair Jackson knew they had gotten second-hand from somewhere because it was covered with cigarette burns and none of the Francos smoked.

The other man sat in the center of the couch Carmita had told Jackson she had received from a grandmother when she and Pepe were first married. The man rose as Jackson entered the living room.

Dr. Tyrell Czenlyn was a big man. He was almost a meterpointfive tall, with broad features and shoulders an axe handle wouldn't have spanned. He was overweight, yes, but certainly not fat. Jackson could tell that from the way the man moved as he easily got to his feet. Czenlyn wore an expensive dark blue suit and held a hat in his hands.

Relief flooded through Jackson when he saw the big man's eyes were of flesh and blood and not the genetically altered ones of the Time Police. Then suspicions flared anew when he realized Brelmer might have sent someone like Czenlyn back. Someone who wasn't tainted with the stigma of Temporal Projects' elite corps.

The big man stepped forward and extended a hand. "I'm Dr. Czenlyn," he said in a deep voice that fit the cavernous chest. He also spoke English with a 23rd Century inflection.

Jackson glanced at Pepe Franco's face but saw only calmness there. He forced himself to relax and take the hand.

Czenlyn smiled. "I've been trying to find you for over a month, ever since I saw you during the address for the Second Plan de Iguala, but I still don't know your name."

"Jackson. Jackson Dubchek." A wandering thought settled into Jackson's mind as he answered, reminding him of the cultures he had studied in linguistic classes who had refused to give their real name to anyone for fear of being put into that person's power.

"Should I have heard of you?" Czenlyn asked.

Jackson smiled tightly. "Perhaps it's better if you haven't."

"Maybe you've heard of me, then?"

"Only what Carmita has just told me of you."

Czenlyn shook his head. "Not here, young man. From where you came."

"No." How much did the man know? That he had been seen at the plaza during the assassination attempt was no surprise. Jackson had been there twice. At the same handful of moments in time.

"Perhaps this will help explain," Czenlyn said as he pulled a pair of glasses from inside his jacket and put them on. He took a wallet from another inside pocket and opened it up, rummaging through the contents. A brief smile flickered across his lips as he handed an ident to Jackson.

Jackson looked at it, noticing the Temporal Projects emblem in the background of the tri-D ident. A much younger Tyrell Czenlyn presented both full-face and profile views on the ident. The man had worn a beard for the ident and the hair contained none of the gray that was now readily apparent. He read over the rest of the information. Eye color, weight, height, the rest of the physical description didn't matter. Some things had changed and some hadn't. He handed the ident back.

"I debated with myself about coming here," Czenlyn explained as he put the ident away. He removed the glasses and cleaned them unconsciously. "But I took a chance. Buddha, it has been so long since I have taken chances and I have been so afraid." He shrugged his shoulders against the invisible burden he felt. "But after seeing you, after seeing the carnage the Time Police left in the plaza a month ago, after watching some of those poor people die in the street as I tried to help them, I couldn't stay away any longer. Not as long as there was a chance I could help. Do you understand?"

Jackson was surprised to find he was no longer wary of the doctor and had even relaxed to an extent. Czenlyn's despair sounded real to him, familiar. He remembered the haunting voices of Rosito Alvarez and Lester Wu and how the experience of being displaced in time had ripped the fabric of their personal realities to shreds. There was something of that in Czenlyn's tone.

"You see," Czenlyn said as he focused on Jackson again, "I thought the assassination attempt was another of Temporal Projects's goals to correct their future. Until I heard the policia found bodies of men they could not identify with weapons that did not exist. I arranged through an officer to view the bodies myself and found enough evidence to lead me to the conclusion that these men were from an even farther future than my own. I pondered what that could mean for days, then realized I had to have more answers." He looked at Jackson expectantly.

Seeing the pain stirring in the depths of the doctor's light gray eyes, Jackson said, "I'll tell you what I know but it may not be much."

"Thank you."

Turning to Carmita, Jackson asked in Spanish, "May I borrow your kitchen to make a pot of coffee."

"Si, I will make it for you."

"Let me, por favor. It will give me something to do while I arrange my thoughts."

"Si."

"Jackson," Pepe asked from the easy chair, "is everything well?"

"Si, gracias. The doctor and I have much to discuss."

Pepe nodded. "Then I will be off to bed again if you do not need me. Listening to you two talk is making my head hurt and I have many things to get done tomorrow."

Jackson led the way into the small kitchen after saying goodnight. Czenlyn followed after him, walking tiredly himself. "What about your chauffeur?"

"Lorenz is monitoring the surveillance equipment in the Cadillac to make sure no one from Temporal Police discovers us."

"You can track them?"

"To a degree."

"I didn't know that was possible."

"To most people, it wouldn't be. I can. And it's only fitting I should be able to. I helped create the Time Police."

Jackson paused in prying the top off the gaily colored coffee cannister. "You helped create them?"

Czenlyn nodded.

Jackson didn't know how to feel. The Time Police had usurped control over his life, left him rootless and stranded. And now their existence even shadowed the small and hard life he had managed to put together here.

He had watched Carmita make the evening meals in this room, had shared thoughts with Pepe as they sat in front of the potbellied stove and fed small sticks to it. Little Theresa had smiled at him with chocolate covered lips while he and Mateo played card games at the same table Czenlyn was sitting at.

"I take it you have no love for Temporal Projects or the Time Police."

"No," Jackson said as he spooned coffee into the top section of the tin coffee pot. How much easier it had been in his apartment when all he had to do was tell the kitchen to prepare it. Carmita had laughed at him the first time he tried to make it by himself. He had seen her make it before but really hadn't paid attention until that night the nightmares wouldn't go away and he had finally given up and crawled from the warm bed in the attic. She had heard him in the kitchen and made the coffee, giggling at him the whole time. He put the pot on one of the stove's heating plates and took a seat opposite Czenlyn.

"When are you from, Jackson?"

"2250."

Czenlyn nodded. "Buddha, only two years," he seemed to say to himself, "and how much has gone wrong?"

"How did you get here?" Jackson asked.

"I came here of my own choice, initially, now I seem to be held prisoner from the future."

"What do you mean?"

"I've tried to return to my original time line but I can't. Both times I've made the attempt, my time machine seems to rebound from something and ends up somewhere else. Once I ended up at some place called Wheeling, West Virginia."

Jackson nodded. "I've been there. Twice."

"I came here from 2248, just two years in your past, but I took a very involved path leading here. Maybe that had something to do with it. I don't know. I'm practiced in surgeries and medicines, not in theories of quantum mechanics."

"I'm a linguist by training," Jackson said, "and a musician through passion. So I haven't had a lot of exposure to the possibilities and plausibilities of time travel. But you should still have access to your time line. What about the 9.6 hour window?"

"I don't know." Czenlyn sounded shaky and unsure of himself. "I've been gone from 2248 for over twenty years."

Jackson studied the man again. At first he had assumed the gray hair had turned prematurely and that the doctor was actually younger than he looked.

Czenlyn gave him a small smile. "Yes, Jackson, I'm actually almost sixty years old. Almost half of my life has been spent back in the past. Most of it here, just outside of Mexico City."

"But why? How did you get Temporal Projects to authorize you to do that?"

"I didn't give them a choice. See, I was very idealistic when I was a younger man. I was very talented also, which is how I came to be working for Temporal Projects initially. I had a project I had been trying to interest the Second Republic in for some time: chemically, genetically, and surgically altered men and women who would become a new force in the military. It was an expensive project, to be sure, but I felt strongly about it. However, the Senate was convinced the Second Republic had already fought its last war. I had shelved the idea and the team for three years before I was approached by Ronald Reul Voxner, the Assistant Secretary of History. He offered to house my project under the new Temporal Projects Research Fund he was helping initiate. I quit my job immediately and gathered what I could of my project team. We were given a floor at TP and a security clearance but we were not privy to what TP was actually all about."

The coffee pot perked and Jackson reached back to get it, pouring a cup for himself and Czenlyn.

"The Director of TP then was Dr. Otis Minor, a callow little man who jumped every time Voxner wiggled a finger. Still, he was able to run a tight ship as well as keep Voxner informed on all our activities. By that time, my team had progressed to our first human patients: men and women from various penal institutes around the Republic. Not my choice, you can be sure, but Dr. Minor insisted these people were expendable. Later, there were some good soldiers from the militia, but these were few and far between. I gathered that these men and women were to be the commanding officers of the others. My department turned into a full-scale production plant. As we added people to our staff, no longer were they fully versed in every operation or procedure involved, they each had a particular duty relating to the creation of the Time Policeman. There was another name for them back then, but I can't remember what is was."

Jackson sipped the coffee and found it too strong and too hot. Czenlyn didn't seem to notice. "How did you find out about the time travel?"

"By accident. One of the Time Policemen I had augmented had been in an accident. While I was operating on him in an effort to save his life, he kept talking, speaking of a pirate ship that had been sunk off the coast of Miami. Then there was the 'accident' itself. When I operated on the man, I found a flint arrowhead in the wound. Later, I pulled some of the Time Police into my chamber for periodic check-ups and hypnotized them. I got the story in bits and pieces, but I got it."

"Voxner never knew?"

"No. The department was in too much turmoil as it was. Senate investigators were already looking into the disappearance of Dr. Rosita Alvarez, the previous head of Temporal Projects. And Dr. Minor was ousted after losing favor with some of Voxner's peers."

"That's when Friz Brelmer was brought in?"

"Yes. His was an interesting choice. He was a military man by training, but a scientist at heart.

Apparently he had upgraded through the science department in the militia and had been discovered as possessing a certain flair for leadership. Voxner had no trouble whatsoever in getting Brelmer nominated to the post. During the relocation of Praetor Brelmer, I connived my way into my first experience with time travel. I told the techs that I wanted to see the nausea firsthand that the Time Police kept complaining of. It was a short jaunt, no more than one hundred years back. I visited the southern coast of California thirteen years before it dropped off into the ocean. It was so unreal, so breathtaking. I was born and raised in southern California, in Patterson, a small town on what is now the coast. To be able to walk on ground that no longer existed. Buddha, it was so incredible."

"It can be," Jackson agreed. "As long as you're only there to visit and no one is trying to kill you."

Some of the excitement left Czenlyn's eyes and he held his coffee in both hands as if to soak up some of the warmth it offered.

Opening the door on the potbellied stove, Jackson pushed in a few more sticks, stirring to build the flames. The room seemed colder now to him as well but he didn't know if it was actually a physical thing or a psychological one.

"Then, through the continued use of the hypno-questioning, I learned that the Time Police were not just there to observe and record, duties which most of them would have found almost impossible with their educations. They were also being used to terminate events as well as individuals who were a threat to the continued existence of the Second Republic."

"They were also triggering events that would move in their favor," Jackson said. "I'd heard that Texas became a separate country in 1836 and stayed that way."

"Who told you that?"

Jackson related the complete story of how he came to be involved with the Time Police and Temporal Projects, mentioning Friz and Suzanne Brelmer, as well as the female Tysonyllyn who had given him the veritas dagger and the Satan-faced Tysonyllyn he'd met in New York City in 2183.

"Traffic?" Czenlyn repeated.

Jackson nodded, then reached for the coffee pot to pour refills.

"A totally impersonal word," the doctor observed.

"For a totally impersonal function."

"The story about Texas interests me, though," Czenlyn said. "I don't listen much to current political affairs. Most of my time is spent studying the past, trying to find whatever trails of the Time Police back there that I can."

"It is a global effort now. You'll find Time Police guards everywhere in the past now."

"Are these men being trained for the time periods where they are posted?"

"I don't know," Jackson replied. Then, thinking of Laszlo Slye, he shook his head. "No. I'm almost sure they aren't."

"Doesn't Brelmer realize the paradoxes involved with all of this tampering?"

"I don't know, but from what I gathered from his daughter, Brelmer doesn't have much choice. Voxner is the actual power behind TP. And he's no longer Assistant Secretary of History any more. He's Secretary now. As far as the paradoxes go, everyone involved with TP in 2250 knows of them. You'll find Time Police who belong in our future back there now, as well as future rebels who are fighting everything the Time Police have ever done. Whichever Time Police you care to discuss."

"And this war between 2250 and the future is what caused all the killings in this version of the past?"

"Yes."

"This is madness. Brelmer uncovered what I was doing in 2248 and planned to displace me as he did with you. But I was able to get into the time machine lab and take off with a machine of my own. I bounced through several time periods, sometimes only waiting long enough for the POES to recharge the machine and sometimes spending days in the past. Ultimately, I jumped here, to a time twenty years ago, and figured I would be spending my life here."

"Why?" Jackson couldn't understand why the man would choose banishment to the past if he had a time machine. Buddha, it would mean a return to sanity, to a world he could understand.

"First of all, because I love this area. I spent time with my grandmother here when I was a boy. And the second reason you should have figured out for yourself."

Jackson waited patiently, trying to put together the things he had learned with the things he had only guessed at. Something gnawed at the edge of his conscious mind.

"The second reason is this, Jackson," Czenlyn said as he leaned forward. "Even though I have spent over twenty years of my life in the past, much of it here, when I return to the future, it will still be 2248 and Brelmer and his assassins will be waiting on me. Even if they had to wait the entire 9.6 hours of the return window. Even if they have to search every inch of the Second Republic. Your presence here, from two years into my future, tells me I never made it back. Or if I did, I was unable to escape the Time Police. You've spent a month back here, yet only 9.6 hours would elapse for you if you returned to your present. Brelmer would still be waiting on you as well."

Jackson slumped back into his chair as the enormity of his situation settled across his shoulders and stripped away the false sense of security the last month had given him. "But you said you tried to go back?"

"Twice during this last month," Czenlyn agreed. "I felt I needed more information after the assassination. But I couldn't break through whatever barrier seals me off from my present. I believe something in the past has changed enough to shut this past off from the future, or maybe only my access to it. Or there is the possibility that I've simply stayed out of my present too long and closed myself off from it."

Jackson shifted his gaze to the kitchen window, noting the pale pastels of the rising sun coloring the sky. A month he had spent in this time, trying to live half a life or less than that. How long was too long?

CHAPTER FIVE

The scan-screens and digital readouts around the medvault changed dramatically as the surgeon in charge called out orders to the computerized scrub-techs. A phalanx of micro-equipped laser arms hung from the hovering compnurse just over the surgeon's left shoulder. As the surgeon called out orders after ascertaining data from the scan-screens and readouts, different robot arms unlooped from the compnurse to complete whatever the desired action was. An adjustment was made to regulate the oxygen flow to the patient. Another arm swooped into place to tuck an IV needle into the patient's right forearm while still another hooked up the plasma bag.

To Brelmer, standing on the other side of the op table and wearing a sterile mask like the surgeon's, Suzanne seemed lost in the complexity of the OR. He tried to follow the logistics of the surgeon's search for the cause of his daughter's pulmonary failure but the scan-screens and readouts flickered through mode function too quickly. From what he was able to gather, the man was narrowing the field down to a variety of chemical substances foreign to the body.

The surgeon's facemask pushed in and out as he breathed and called out instructions to the scrub-techs. Without being called on, another arm unlooped from the compnurse and toweled the surgeon's forehead.

Glancing up to relieve the tension in the back of his neck, Brelmer noticed a crowd had gathered to watch the operation. He glared at the dozen or so faces staring down from the observation hatch at the tip of the domed room. "Privacy mode," Brelmer growled through the facemask. "Execute now."

Obediently, the OR shut itself off from the rest of the Temporal Projects building. Hatches closed over the observation posts and recorder dampers switched on.

The surgeon might run the compnurse and scrub-techs, but Brelmer was the heartbeat of Temporal Projects. Which was how he had been able to get TP's top surgeon out of bed and into the OR in less than fifteen minutes.

"Stomach pump," Hoban ordered as he continued to check the scan-screens.

Following the surgeon's gaze, Brelmer watched an iridescently glowing silhouette in the general shape of Suzanne's body on the scan-screen. Pink swirls of colors fed through the two-dimensional figure, gathering in what the Praetor judged to be the stomach and kidneys. He knew the audio implants behind Hoban's ears gave him access to even more information.

A thin, clear hose with a cybernetic acti-skel uncoiled from somewhere inside the compnurse and inserted itself down Suzanne's throat.

Brelmer could feel an empathetic scraping inside his throat. He wanted to reach out and touch his daughter but steeled himself against the impulse. It had been against Hoban's better judgement as a surgeon to even allow him in the OR. But corporate survival rated higher than better judgement. Shiva, Suzanne was so cold. So pale and still. It hadn't been possible for Brelmer to be there when his daughter had been born and thoughts that he might be present as she died burned nova-hot in his mind. He kept the tears from his eyes just as he refused to let his hands touch his daughter's face for even a brief moment.

"Sweet Buddha," Hoban said.

"What is it?" Brelmer asked.

"Her entire system has been poisoned," Hoban said. He ordered a new line of demographics to be displayed.

"Someone tried to kill her?" Brelmer asked. He strained to keep the rage from his voice. Dubchek? The lunatic was definitely a possibility. He wished he had not listened to Suzanne's impassioned plea to let the linguist live after the first time he involved himself in Temporal Projects' affairs. Dubchek had much to answer for already.

"I don't think it was intentional," Hoban said as he turned his attention to the stomach pump. "Suction."

The compnurse hummed in response. A brackish gruel filled the thin tube, making the silver cybernetic acti-skel stand out in sharp relief.

"Then how?"

Hoban flipped one of Suzanne's eyes open and shined a small flash into the pupil. "If I'm correct in my assumption, Colonel, I think your daughter ingested a dangerous amount of drugs that counteracted with the effects of time travel. As you know, during the process of the time jump, there is the constant danger that the humans aboard the time machine will be absorbed into the material of the machine. Fuse. It is the Knegel damper that keeps everything separate when the time machines reintegrate. The counter-effect is the acute nausea that accompanies the arrival. According to the mandates of the Knegel damper, everything is kept separate, which means things not identified as being part of the organic unit is reintegrated separately. Of course the alterations we do on the Time Police are all organically bonded and register as such. However, food preservative, red dye food coloring, MSG, all of these things which constitute a heavy majority of our meals now, as well as the obvious synth-food groups, are recognized as being something other than the human animal. During a time jump, these impurities in the foods are gathered in a person's stomach and are thrown violently from the body. This is what happened to your daughter. Everything would have been alright except that some of these drugs she ingested are very accessible to the human system. Bulked as they were in her stomach, they became a lethal overdose and caused the pulmonary and kidney failure."

"Have you identified the drugs?"

The stomach pump tube turned clear again.

"Retract," the surgeon said.

The tube withdrew cautiously, snaking inside its shell again where Brelmer knew it would be sterilized by radiation as well as chemical agents.

"Some of the drugs, maybe," Hoban said. "A hallucinogenic was introduced into her bloodstream through her lungs in the form of a smoke. Others entered through the stomach. Evidently there had been enough time between doses that the drugs would not have a cumulative effect."

"Until the jump."

"Exactly." Hoban leaned back, rubbing his lower back with both hands. "I'm fairly certain I was able to get most of the drugs out of her system, but she is going to be very tired for the next few days. I'd recommend lots of bed rest and plenty of fluids, especially those containing electrolytes. If I were you, sir, I'd keep her here. You won't find any better facilities in Kansas City and I'll personally keep an eye on her."

"I know, Dr. Hoban." The thing that niggled at the back of Brelmer's mind was that, in addition to having access to the finest hospital in the Second Republic, Suzanne would also be accessible to whatever action Voxner wanted to take against her. Suzanne had already earned the Senator's ire over the last episode with Jackson Elgin Dubchek. What would this present predicament do to augment that? Brelmer lived his life in the grim realities of the political power Voxner wielded. The Senator would use this new lever to his advantage. Brelmer was also sure of that. The man never missed an opportunity. Or a weakness. Voxner was a fat jackal and Brelmer had never thought of the Senator as anything less. But the man held power over what went on at TP and Brelmer didn't think he could free himself of the powerful love/hate relationship he had with the project.

Suzanne would be in danger and Brelmer didn't try to fool himself about it. Unless he was able to divert most of the pressure from his daughter to a more deserving subject. Someone like Dubchek. Even if that someone was dead, as he believed Dubchek to be.

Even Voxner would back off at some point if Brelmer drew a line. And there would be the added luxury of the lever the Senator would have over him. But Brelmer could survive that. He had chafed under restraints all of his life. He had always been one of the boldest and brightest in whatever group of individuals he had found himself surrounded by. Survival in politics was too often decided by the refusal to be simply worn away. And to know when to stop being aggressive. That was one thing he knew he had over Voxner: the ability to know when to hold himself in check.

"Very well, doctor," Brelmer said.

"We'll let her rest here for a few hours before we move
her to a private room," Hoban said. "I can put off the operations I have scheduled for this morning till later this evening."

"Thank you."

"Suzanne is breathing on her own, now, and kidney function has been restored. I could give her a stim if you want to talk to her but I don't really want to cloud her system with any more barbituates unless I have to. She can use the rest."

Brelmer shook his head. "No, let her sleep." Maybe by the time she woke, he would have a plan formulated for her protection. The difficulty lay in coming up with one that would suit her and appease Voxner at the same time. He stepped forward and closed his steri-gloved hand over Suzanne's fingers. What words would he have for her when she woke? Shiva, there had been so many arguments. And her demotion. He had engineered that only hours before she went with Dubchek. Had he been right in wanting to make sure she could not be considered the unknown leak at Temporal Projects? Yes. He still believed that. But Suzanne hadn't seen that it was a move designed for her protection as well. Voxner was all too ready to point the accusatory finger in her direction.

"Colonel?"

Brelmer looked up from his daughter's still face. Hoban stood at the entrance to the medvault unable to pass the security initiated by Brelmer's voice.

"Open," Brelmer said.

The activation lights across the top of the door flashed on as the sterilization field locked into place. The   door slid away.

"I'm going to put her on oxygen for a little while to finished flushing her system," Hoban said as he paused at the entrance. "Purely a precautionary measure."

"I understand, doctor."

"You'll be staying, sir?"

"For awhile."

"It's not necessary, Colonel, I've wrist-banded with the compnurse to alert me the minute any problem arises. If you want someone to stay with her, I'll be glad to get someone or stay myself. You look like you could use the rest, if you don't mind my saying so."

Brelmer permitted himself a small smile, sliding out of the role of project head for a moment. "Your opinion is duly noted, doctor, but there are some things a father has to do for himself. Thank you."

"Good night, sir." Hoban stepped through the entrance and the door slid closed behind him.

"Privacy mode and one-quarter illumination,"

Brelmer said softly. "Execute."

Quietness filled the medvault as any exterior build-ing noise was excised by the aud-dampers.

A click sounded from overhead as the compnurse hovered into a new position further away from Suzanne. An opening unsealed on the op table by her head and a translucent oxygen mask opened, trapped between the twin fingers of a cybernetic acti-skel arm. The flimsy mask filled with a hiss, covering the bottom half of Suzanne's face.

"Chair," Brelmer said. A seat hummed from under the edge of the table and he sat on it, adjusting the height vocally.

He continued to hold Suzanne's hand, marvelling at how large her fingers seemed in his. Surely it wasn't that long ago that his hands had dwarfed hers. Where had his little girl gone? Was little Suzanne trapped somewhere in the depths of the woman time and society had conspired to make of her?

Why was he thinking of the child? he wondered. Was it because the child was what he missed most, or was it because he felt safer dealing with the impression-able part of Suzanne rather than the woman? He remembered other times he had watched her sleep. How often had he stood at her crib and wished he had made it home in time to share part of her day with her? He remembered the innocent face of her, tucked tightly into the side of the teddy bear he had gotten for her even before she was born.

Unexpectedly, Brelmer felt Suzanne's fingers twitch in his hand. For a moment he thought something had happened, then he saw her eyelids flicker open, searching the darkness of the medvault.

He touched her face with the back of his free hand. "It's all right, Suzanne," he whispered.

Her head jerked back toward him, eyes glassy as they tried to adjust to the dim lighting.

Brelmer couldn't hear her, but using the infra-red function of his crystal eyes, he saw her lips mouth the word, "Daddy," as her breath fogged the oxygen mask.

Suzanne rolled over, moving weakly and slowly. Her other hand covered his, then her eyes closed again and her breathing became deeply regular.

Brelmer adjusted the IV line, knowing the compnurse would have done so had there been any danger of entanglement, but feeling the need to do so anyway. He called for a sheet and watched it unfold itself the length of Suzanne's body. He tucked it under her chin, remembering how she could not sleep well without some type of covering.

For a long time he sat in the darkness with her, trying to figure out when their relationship had become so complex and aggressive. Who was trying to prove what to who? Did he feel threatened by her in some way? Brelmer wasn't sure. He shoved the thoughts away, wanting to be nothing more than Suzanne's father again for a few moments longer before duty to Temporal Projects called him back again.

Clearing his voice, he ordered a com-link from the medvault.

"Which department, sir?" the tinny compvoice asked.

"Costuming," Brelmer answered. His chron told him it was only a little past midnight. Only four hours since Suzanne and Dubchek had made the jump into the past. Realizing that left 5.6 hours on Dubchek's window back into the present, Brelmer made a note to double the security around the time machine labs. In case a miscalculation threw the linguist back to his point of origin. Otherwise, Dubchek had access to the rest of the Second Republic with the self-replicating factor built into the time machines.

"Costuming," a woman's nasal voice answered.

"Colonel Brelmer."

"Yes, sir." The voice instantly sounded more crisp.

"Who is in charge of this shift?"

"Well, Paress, sir."

"What is she doing here? She just got off shift at five." Dark suspicion welled up inside Brelmer. Paress Linnet had been with TP longer than he had and her loyalty had never been challenged. Yet, she was a big influence on Suzanne. Or had been lately. Since Dubchek had become a problem with the project. He shelved the thoughts tumbling through his head for a later time of introspection.

"Senator Voxner called her in, sir. I thought you knew about it."

"No." Anger burned inside Brelmer as he realized

how deeply the Senator had insinuated his control into the nerve centers of TP.

"Yes, sir. Apparently Senator Voxner is planning on taking a trip back himself and wanted Paress to make sure the costumes were correct."

"To what time?"

"I'm not sure, sir, but it has something to do with the Dunkers. Paress could tell you more."

The Dunkers? Brelmer thought of the small religious faction and tried to fathom Voxner's reasons for pursuing them in the past.

"Sir?"

Turning his attention back to the person at the other end of the com-link, Brelmer said, "I'm still here."

"Should I get Paress, Colonel?"

"No. She is probably busy organizing the Senator's snipe hunt. This is a small matter." He told her what he wanted, waiting to hear the bafflement in her voice when she repeated the order.

As his office door closed behind him, Brelmer felt himself relax for the first time since he had attended Voxner's party earlier the previous evening. He had spent most of the last hour with Suzanne but she hadn't come to any more and had seemed to be sleeping peacefully.

Tiredness drifted over him like fog, chiseling away at his physical and emotional resolve with broken teeth.

The holo came on automatically when he entered the room, filling the empty space between his authentic mahogany desk and the door with brightly colored shapes and sound. Guthrie, his personal secretary, had left the prepackaged selections earlier in the day but Brelmer had not had the chance to view them. It began again, as it had before, with a news documentary about advanced techniques in micro laser surgery.

Seating himself in the old fashioned swivel chair behind the large desk, Brelmer watched the holo for a moment, hoping it would capture his attention and slow his racing mind. As always, he was amazed by the solidness of the tri-D holos, intrigued by the way they left no shadows on the carpeted floor. Intangible, yes. Yet, he couldn't see through the images even with his crystal eyes.

He left the lights off, comfortable in the darkness. Vocally, he flipped through the selection Guthrie had left, finding nothing that kept his mind from Voxner.

Since he had been project head of Temporal, he had known of no time that the Senator had journeyed back in a time machine himself. Voxner had left that for Brelmer and the Time Police to do. The Senator had seemed content to have his schemes carried out through proxy.

So what was so different now? Why the personal interest?

Brelmer shifted in the swivel chair as he sorted through possibilities. What interest did Voxner have in the Dunkers? They were a barely tolerated religious sect even in this age of liberal tolerances. Or perhaps the Dunkers would be better called an embarrassment that was only inches away from being extinct.

Feeling a headache coming on, Brelmer reached into the bottom drawer of his desk, back beyond the specially-bound editions of Carl Sagan's works and holos of his wife and daughter, to the brandy flask he kept there. He had never been much of a drinker but the brandy had become one of the best headache reliefs he had found over the years.

He poured a shot into the stainless steel cap that also doubled as a cup and drank it down. He followed it with another quick shot then put it away. He shut the holo off with a vocal command. The room fell into darkness. But it was a comfortable darkness to Brelmer. Everything, all the problems and questions plaguing him, seemed to be lost in the miniature chunk of space he had created in the office.

He summoned the office vid and watched a much smaller holo shimmer into being only inches above the mahogany desktop. "Messages," Brelmer said as he leaned back in the swivel chair.

The vid holo splashed a rainbow of colors through the palm-sized space of air, then resolved into a head and shoulders view of Brelmer's wife, June. She left a message for him to call back as soon as he could.

The second message was from Voxner, ordering him to report as soon as he came out of the medvault.

Ignoring the anger that suddenly lighted inside him, Brelmer shut the vid down and glanced at the wall of books opposite the desk, reading the titles from the spines even in the darkness. How much did the Senator know about Suzanne's condition? And how had he found out? How much did he know about what had happened in 2074? Both times?

The vid hummed musically, drawing Brelmer's attention from the books. He watched disinterestedly as the recorded holo flashed onto the vid. A small, tri-D copy of Brelmer's head floated disembodied over the surface of the desk. The smaller self seemed more at ease than he felt. The bald head and jutting beard were tinged with a greenish cast and Brelmer knew he would have to make a new copy for the recorder soon.

Just as the recording neared the end, a ruby beam shot through the closed blinds of the office's only window, lancing through the forehead of the holo Brelmer and leaving a scorched place on the desktop.

Brelmer threw himself to the floor, pushing up against the reinforced wall as he bellowed for the office security network to engage. A solid steel panel erupted from the bottom of the window and sealed it off.

There was no message for the recorder. Which didn't surprise Brelmer. Whoever had vid-linked with his machine had left the message they wanted to.

But who had it been? And why?

CHAPTER SIX

"Why do you have to go?" Mateo asked.

Jackson struggled to find the words as he packed the small duffel bag Carmita had found for him. Uneven dawn had snaked into the room from the shuttered window, leaving stripes across the bedroom. "It's something like a quest," he told the boy. For weeks he had worked out his own personal problems, often in the forms of stories he created for Mateo and Theresa in the evenings, forcing himself to focus on the realities of his situation and the options he was presented with. Sometimes Carmita and Pepe had listened as well, but usually they gave him the time to the children and took a few moments to themselves, usually spending it in the small garden behind the house.

"Like Odysseus trying to return home to his wife and children?"

Jackson thought the example suited the truth more closely than was comfortable. Like the Greek hero, he had found himself on the shores of a world very far from his own with no easy way back. "Yes."

"Where do you live, Jackson?" The boy shifted on the bed, talking in a quiet voice.

The aroma of baking bread and the spatterings of frying grease in a skillet from the kitchen below punctuated the feeling of early morning.

Almost, Jackson said, a long time from now, but caught himself at the last moment. "Very far away." He put the last of the three shirts Carmita Franco had purchased for him in the duffel bag, folded neatly on top of the other pair of white slacks and black market blue jeans. His bagged work shoes occupied the last remaining space and he tucked his shaving kit in beside it. He wore his tennis shoes, preferring them to the heavy clunkiness of the work shoes.

"Will you come back?" Mateo asked. His voice almost cracked from the emotion he was trying to contain.

Zipping the duffel bag, Jackson hung it over one shoulder and walked over to the boy. He knelt in front of Mateo and pulled the boy close, feeling the boy start sniffling into his chest and pulling fiercely at his shirt. Jackson's voice felt thick and heavy as he spoke. "As long as I am able," he promised. He hugged the boy, wondering at how quickly friendships and love took root when you lived in a world filled with the hardship and challenge of surviving from one day to the next. Living in the Second Republic promoted no such searches for another facet of the self beyond one's own life. But here, amid a way of living that seemed a travesty of the lifestyle he was accustomed to, he had found life to be more layered than he had known it could be. The courtship between Pepe and Carmita, the way they held hands and looked at each other, had made him realize much of what was missing in his relationship with Chrys Calvino in his own time. And had raised more than a few cases of introspection about his sporadic relationship with Suzanne Brelmer.

Gently breaking the embrace, Jackson led the way down the ladder to the kitchen, finding Carmita behind the stove cooking breakfast while Pepe and Czenlyn sat at the table drinking coffee. Theresa sat on the kitchen counter, clad in an ankle-length nightgown, and playing pat-a-cake with the floured tortillas her mother was using for breakfast.

Czenlyn emptied his coffee cup and stood. "Are you ready?"

Jackson nodded. "I wish I could stay for breakfast, Carmita," he said, "but . . . "

The woman turned from the stove and put her spatula to one side. "I know, Jackson, the doctor has explained. At least as much as he was able. You have much in front of you to do and it is time you returned to your work. Pepe and I are only glad we could help you." She came to Jackson and hugged him, then turned away quickly to wipe moisture from her eyes.

Jackson reached for Pepe's hand but the big man disregarded it and threw his arms around Jackson in a fierce bear hug. "Eh, muchacho," Pepe said in his deep voice, "you will remember you always have a home here, eh?"

"Si, Pepe, always." Jackson stepped between little Theresa's outstretched arms for a floured kiss and tickled her to make her laugh. Then he stepped back to follow Czenlyn out of the house that had become a home to him, moving once more toward an uncertain future that might no longer hold a place for him.

The back seat of Czenlyn's Cadillac was spacious and the air conditioning seemed to take Jackson light-years away from the existence he had known for the last month despite the chaparral at the edge of the road. According to Czenlyn, it would take more than an hour to reach his hacienda hidden away in the broken hills south of Mexico City. Tiredness soaked into Jackson, completing the job the luxury car started. He felt himself start to drowse, drifting away from his surroundings.

Until he saw the cherry glow of the flashing lights ahead of them.

He blinked back sleep as he straightened in the seat. Glancing over at the doctor, Jackson saw a concerned look on the man's round face.

"Sir?" the chauffeur said from the front seat.

"Drive on, Lorenz," Czenlyn said. "We will see what the men want."

Jackson found his gaze riveted on the police vehicle and the two men standing on either side of it. Trepidation filled him and the familiar ache of the weeks' old shoulder injury flared to ghostly life. There was nothing there, he told himself. Calm down.

"It is nothing," Czenlyn said. "Only a roadblock to make sure every driver has the proper credentials. You see this done occasionally."

Jackson only wished he felt as sure as the doctor sounded. The black-handled Veritas dagger was an uncomfortable weight hanging upside-down in the make-shift sheathe across his chest.

The chauffeur edged the Cadillac through the small line formed in front of the police car. Only two cars separated them from the policemen now.

Jackson's hands sweated and he rubbed them across his pants legs.

"Easy," Czenlyn said in a whisper. "It is nothing. A mere formality. You'll see."

What if they were searching for people who had been in the plaza the day of the assassination? Jackson recalled the self-impelled cameras that had been hovering around the stage area. It wasn't hard to imagine that stills had been made from the camera exposures.

And he had been there twice at the same time.

It would be hard to overlook him. The Cadillac slid to an easy stop in front of the police car.

"Could I see your papers, sir?" the first officer asked as he stepped to the driver's side of the car.

Jackson heard Lorenz give an affirmative answer and lean to reach into the glove compartment.

The other officer began a circle around the luxury vehicle, as if inspecting it for road-use violations. He tapped his leg with the stun baton he carried.

Forcing himself to keep from watching the circling policeman, Jackson turned his attention to Lorenz and the sheaf of papers he was showing the other man. An itch, moving as slow as a coiling rattlesnake, climbed up Jackson's spine, threatening to splinter into a sensory overload of panic. Buddha, he had been hunted, hounded, for so very long.

A tapping on the window beside him drew Jackson's attention. He swiveled his head and stared at the visored face of the policeman. He wished the polychromatic helmet didn't cover the rest of the man's head. Somehow the short antenna sticking up from the helmet, coupled with the shining silver sliver of a mouthpiece, gave the man an insectoid look. Cold and distant and artificial.

Jackson couldn't hear the man through the thickness of the polarized window but he read the man's lips.

Roll the window down.

Reluctantly, Jackson thumbed the window down, leaving his finger in place. He caught Lorenz's eyes in the rearview mirror and knew the chauffeur was paying attention to everything that was going on.

The police officer touched the pressure-sensitive switch that released the static energy charge holding the visor in place. The dark crescent slid back up into the helmet. Revealing crystal eyes. Over an unmerciful grin.

Reacting instantly, giving vent to the building anxiety that was flooding through him, Jackson thumbed the window back up, yelling, "Time Police!" He slammed a palm over the locking mechanism that sealed the door, praying it would hold against the Time Policeman's augmented strength. "Floor it!" he screamed at Lorenz.

Before the chauffeur could make a move to put the Cadillac into gear, a black-gloved claw seized his face and shoved him back into the seat.

Jackson released his seat belt and struggled to reach over the seat to help the chauffeur. A movement, caught in the corner of his eye, caused him to shield his face. Only a heartbeat later the stun baton crashed through the window, scattering polarized fragments all over the interior of the Cadillac.

The Time Policeman, spewing vulgar curses, reached for Jackson through the shattered window.

Knowing there was no room to maneuver in the car, Jackson unlocked the door and kicked it open, driving it into the Time Policeman's ribs. A painful "oomph" sounded as the man fell away from the car.

Slithering through the door, Jackson dove for the stun baton lying in the dust only a few feet from the downed Time Policeman. Desperation fed into his already adrenaline-charged system and he missed the weapon on his first grab.

"You goddamned little qwerk!" the Time Policeman howled behind him.

Jackson could hear the rasp of leather boots against the hard ground as the man got to his feet. His fingers curled around the vibrating haft of the stun baton and he rolled to his feet, holding it before him.

The Time Policeman rushed at him, crystal eyes glinting with the redness of the desert sand.

Gripping the baton with both hands, Jackson side-stepped the man, dropping the weapon below the outstretched arms to thud heavily into the Time Policeman's mid-section.

The Time Policeman whirled away from the baton charge like a leaf before a gale wind.

Without waiting to see what happened to his opponent, Jackson ran at the other Time Policeman, screaming at the top of his voice, praying the man hadn't killed the chauffeur.

The Time Policeman spun around at Jackson's approach, almost too quick to follow.

Already committed, Jackson couldn't break away from the all-out dive he had centered on the man. The Time Policeman's foot exploded against his chest. For a moment everything went black in Jackson's mind. Hold onto the baton, he yelled from the void to his fingers. There was a moment of freefall, then he collided with the baked earth of the desert. The air whooshed out of him and it seemed as if his lungs had locked up. Unwilling to give up and die, he forced himself to his knees, taking care with the injured shoulder, not knowing how much strain it could take before becoming crippled up again.

"Dubchek," the Time Policeman said in satisfaction as the glittering eyes assumed a studious look. "It is you, isn't it?"

Jackson didn't say anything, wondering if he had met the man before, or possibly if he would meet the man sometime in a future which lay somewhere in the Time Policeman's past.

A weak, coughing sound came from the front seat of the Cadillac and Jackson knew he could expect no help from Lorenz. The baton in his clenched fists seemed painfully inadequate to him when the Time Policeman reached for the long-barreled Matthews at his side.

"You mean a bonus to me, little man," the Time Policeman said, "and I mean to collect it. Brelmer said he didn't give a tuerc whether you were alive or dead, so it's your decision."

The laser sights of the Matthews seemed to heat up the patch of shirt it focused on over Jackson's chest. He had seen the terrifying carnage that was left behind by one of the weapons. The stiff shoulder was a constant mute reminder.

He felt his breath catch in the back of his throat as he prepared himself for the attempt to get to his feet. The glow in the Time Policeman's eyes told him that the man was not going to be surprised by the move. But giving himself over willingly would only prolong his life, not ensure it.

To make matters worse, he saw the other Time Policeman getting up, shaking off the rougher effects of the stun baton.

A bullfiddle roar of lower range octaves screamed from nowhere.

A pained expression covered the Time Policeman's face as he whirled to face the new menace.

Jackson was in motion at once, throwing himself forward. He caught a glimpse of Tyrell Czenlyn holding a weapon with both hands, steadying it on top of the luxury vehicle. Then the gun was jumping again as the doctor moved it to a new target.

Using the baton, Jackson touched the Time Policeman's back, bouncing the man to the ground unconscious.

The bullfiddle roar of Czenlyn's weapon was punctuated by three-round bursts from the other Time Policeman's Matthews.

Jackson felt something pluck at the loose folds of his pants leg, then he was airborne, diving for the heavy security of the Cadillac. He hit the hood of the luxury vehicle awkwardly and forced his continued slide across it till he was spilling over the side.

Metallic clangings that rang through the Cadillac's metal body told him the Time Policeman's reactions were only heartbeats behind.

Glancing over the hood, Jackson watched the Time Policeman drop into a semi-crouch and hold the Matthews in both hands, aiming at Czenlyn.

Czenlyn's weapon rumbled in the bullfiddle roar again. This time an uneven row of multi-colored fletchettes sprang into violent life up one of the Time Policeman's thighs, winding across his chest, then thinning out to three blue-veined triangles piercing the man's left cheek.

A burst from the Matthews blew the back glass out of the Cadillac only inches from the doctor. Then the automatic pistol clunked to the ground as the Time Policeman raged and stumbled.

Ignoring the frightened people still held up at the roadblock, Jackson opened the passengerside door and helped shift Lorenz to the back with Czenlyn after ascertaining the man was going to be all right. The chauffeur's breathing was hoarse and strained, but it was regular.

Jackson slid in behind the wheel and slipped the transmission into gear. He put his foot down hard and saw twin spumes of dust fly into the air in the rearview mirror. He also saw one of the Time Policemen struggle halfway to his feet only to fall again.

He returned his attention to the dangerous twists of

the road as he steered with both hands, alert to the possibilities the two Time Policemen hadn't been alone. After all, Jackson Dubchek was worth a bonus now, and Friz Brelmer was offering it. Dead or alive. Buddha, his hands were still shaking.

"Those guys were still moving," Jackson said to Czenlyn.

"I don't carry anything lethal," the doctor said. "The fletchette gun is loaded with neuro-toxins designed to incapacitate rather than destroy. I keep it with me out of habit. I've found it useful many times on my excursions into the past."

`"How long will it keep those Time Policemen down?"

"I don't know. Usually a handful of darts is enough to keep the average man down for three to four hours. But with the enhanced nervous systems those men have, it could be only a matter of minutes."

Jackson pressed his foot down harder on the accelerator. Thoughts of the com-link equipped helmets the Time Policemen had been wearing tumbled through his thoughts like the ball in a game of vid-tennis. Surely there were back-up units stationed around Mexico City. Would Brelmer be there? The question brought up the painful subject of Suzanne and he dodged it. It didn't matter. Brelmer didn't have to be there to guide the altered guardians of Temporal Projects and the unholy secrets there. They only needed to be unleashed once they had found the scent.

Glancing in the rearview mirror, Jackson saw Czenlyn administering a hypo to the chauffeur. "Is he going to be okay?"

"Yes. The larynx was severely bruised but there was no permanent damage. He was fortunate." Czenlyn thumbed down a window and threw the used hypo out.

The man still looked at least a dozen shades too pale to Jackson. The chauffeur leaned his head back against the seat, eyes closed as he seemed to use his whole body to draw in each breath. Feeling himself start to breathe in the same laboring fashion, Jackson returned his attention to the road. He checked the speedometer and saw the big car was loping down the highway at almost 140kph.

The speed was too fast for the road conditions, Jackson thought, and too slow to escape the Time Police. How had they found him so quickly? The question scraped the back of his mind with long-taloned paws as doubt and suspicion flooded into the worn places. Had Czenlyn discovered him and got him out into the open merely to turn him over to them?

He scanned the horizon, noting the broken peaks in the near and far distances. The sky was a mild turquoise, unblemished by either cloud or helicopter. He checked the back roads again, expecting to see a plume of dust that signaled an approaching car.

But what could the doctor hope to gain by engineering his capture? Jackson wondered. Prestige? Power? Position? He shook his head wearily as he swerved to avoid a pothole in the middle of his lane. Reacting quickly, he turned a teeth-jarring impact into an unpleasant experience that tried to rip his intestines loose. He glanced into the rearview mirror to check on Lorenz, then tried to read the emotion on Czenlyn's face as the doctor tried to make his patient more comfortable.

Jackson believed Czenlyn's story about being from 2248, and believed the man had been slated for displacement before taking his future into his own hands and escaping into the past. He believed. But that was all. Buddha, had he forgotten how to trust?

Even now, Jackson wanted no part of Czenlyn or the man's problems. If a way of escape offered itself, he was determined to follow it instantly. For a month, he had resided in safe obscurity, living a menial existence that had gradually given him more happiness than the initial despair that had filled him after realizing he was stranded.

Yet, he had absolved all ties with that life once Czenlyn introduced himself. Why?

Did he really want to return to his present that badly?

He searched himself for the answer and kept telling himself that no, he didn't want to go back to 2250, to Suzanne, or to anything or anybody who could associate him with Temporal Projects. But every time he thought of Czenlyn's plight and how the man said he was unable to return to 2248, a coldness filled him, drawing from his stomach to form a small iceball between his eyes.

Being stranded was one thing, yes, but there was always hope of returning. Of going home.

But to be isolated as Czenlyn was . . .

Jackson didn't think he could mentally accept that and remain sane. Lester Wu and Rosito Alvarez hadn't. He had first-hand knowledge of that. And how many others?

"Turn left at the side road," Czenlyn said.

Squinting his eyes, Jackson tried to make out the road Czenlyn was talking about. Finally a thin ribbon of baked dirt that evidently served as a road separated itself from the rest of the desert.

Jackson jammed on the brakes and felt the big car tear itself loose from the street in a sideways skid that roiled dust behind them. Shrieking rubber burned into the interior of the Cadillac. Then the tires found traction again and he headed it down the dirt road.

Strands of barbed wire ran parallel to the road, marking property boundaries. Cactus flowers glinted canary yellow above and between the sharp spines.

"How much farther?" Jackson asked. He was forced the slow the headlong careen of the vehicle, sliding around the awkward twists and turns of the road as it scaled a high rising plateau. Scrub oak and arroyo brush cluttered the side of the hill, breaking the otherwise monotonous tedium of the landscape.

"We're almost there," Czenlyn said.

"Where?"

"Home."

Jackson scanned the horizon but still didn't see any sign of pursuit, aerial or ground. Had they been that fortunate? True, Czenlyn hadn't been sparing in the amount of fletchettes he'd used on the two Time Policemen, but Jackson had learned to expect nothing short of the impossible from them. Even in his worst childhood nightmares, he had never envisioned anything as implacable as the Time Police.

The Cadillac came to the end of the road, skidding to a stop against a blank wall of dirt and rock. To the left, a scenic panorama of the desert floor hundreds of feet below was presented for view. Jackson swallowed hard. If he hadn't been stopped by the sudden appearance of the wall, the luxury car might have toppled over the edge. He forced himself to turn loose of the steering wheel, feeling muscles unknot the length of both forearms. Buddha, only a few feet more and it would have been too late to stop at all.

Dust swirled over their backtrail, breezing over into stubby trees with leaves that seemed only to serve as an afterthought.

Jackson felt naked, vulnerable, against the sandy-covered rock of the plateau. They would be easy targets if the Time Police were in control of any of Mexico City's helicopters. Anger built in him as he realized Czenlyn's ploy had left him with nowhere to run.

He started to turn, to vent his anger at the doctor, then noticed the small electronic key in Czenlyn's hand.

A tiny red light blipped on for a moment, then just as quickly winked back out.

"Drive," Czenlyn said as he dropped the electronic key back into a jacket pocket.

Jackson turned back around and saw the yawning cavern that had opened up where the wall had been. Flicking on the headlights, he shifted and nosed the Cadillac through the gateway. He tried to be cautious, wondering if he was truly escaping or dropping even further into the mazes of time. A stasis field seized the car and it no longer responded to his control. The Cadillac slid into the waiting darkness, becoming weightless.

The cavern mouth was a framed rectangle of bright sunlight. Then it was gone.

CHAPTER SEVEN

Jackson leaned over the massive drafting table studying the map Czenlyn had given him, absorbed in trying to put together all the information he had been given during his trips through time.

Behind him he could hear the doctor puttering around with the coffee pot, putting in fresh grounds. A soft blues medley played in the background from the CD player built into the console of the ornate desk against one wall of Czenlyn's den.

Using a forefinger, Jackson wiped a stray bit of mustard from what Czenlyn insisted should have been the lower section of Oklahoma state. Instead, it was a part of the Republic of Texas, colored the same vile orange as the rest of the nation.

"Can you remember anything about Texas?" Czenlyn asked as he came back to stand at Jackson's side.

"I have a brother who lives there," Jackson said.

"In your time?"

"Yes."

"Do you remember if it was ever a state?"

Jackson shook his head and reached for another half of a ham and rye sandwich from the plate sitting on the desk. "Martin might know, but I was trained as a linguist. Give me access to a library and ample time at a 'ssette viewer and I can find out anything you want to know."

"You can't in this time," Czenlyn said. "The libraries in Mexico City and in the larger cities in this area all reflect the same thing you see there before you. In this time-line, Texas never became a state."

Something nudged the back of Jackson's mind but evaded his questing mental grasp like a scum-slick minnow. "What makes you sure it was a state?"

Czenlyn tapped his forehead. "Because I know, Jackson. I wasn't just a gifted surgeon and geneticist, I was also an amateur historian. I did a lot of genealogy research for friends and on my own family."

"Genealogy?"

"The study of family from a historical aspect."

Jackson nodded and bit into the sandwich. The mustard
was a bit too hot for his liking but the sandwiches filled

the empty spot he'd discovered after using Czenlyn's shower.

"Someone changed the political and economical structure of this part of what used to be the old United States," Czenlyn said as he sat behind the big desk. "But for the life of me, I can't figure out why."

Jackson flipped the map over with one hand, noting the area break-downs of different sections. In a lower corner was a legend with kilometers per inch, national highway markers, and international highway markers. Another corner announced that the map was published by Arcolo Printing, Inc. for Phillips 66 stations. "When did you notice the change?"

"Last week."

Jackson studied the international trading areas centered on the mouth of the Mississippi area. According to the information shown on the map, the Republic of Texas owned the area. And even though he was trained as a linguist and not an economist, Jackson knew the arrangement meant a lot of money for the Texan government.

If someone had altered the course of history concerning Texas' future, why? What could be gained from it?

Or maybe he was looking at the question wrong. What could be lost in the shuffle if Texas became its own nation instead of one of several United States?

The possibilities seemed endless and made his head ache. He still hadn't recovered from the encounter with the Time Police less than two hours ago, or from the stasis field inside Czenlyn's plateau hideaway over twenty miles away. The hunger that had almost consumed him when Czenlyn's daughter brought the sandwiches in a few minutes ago had been the first real feeling he'd had since leaving the Franco house that morning.

"Who is in charge of the Texan government?" Jackson asked.

"Robert W. Kelly. He's the forty-ninth President of the Republic of Texas." Czenlyn sat behind the desk with his fingers laced together over his stomach. His tie hung over the back of his swivel chair. An empty plate that once held sandwiches sat on the desktop beside his glasses.

"Does he trace forward to anyone in the 23rd Century?"

"I don't know. As I told you, I tried to get back to 2248 twice and failed in both attempts."

"What about dates shortly before then?"

"I didn't try those."

"Why?"

A uncomfortable look filled the big man's face. He shifted from the chair and went for the coffee pot. "Because," Czenlyn said as he poured coffee, "once I found the wall there, I didn't care to explore the range of my travel. I'm just getting used to the idea of being a prisoner here without finding out the full scope of my cage."

Jackson nodded, understanding. The coffee was too

hot and he sat it to one side to cool. He turned back to the map, hoping that if he let his mind rest and not continue to pick at every possibility, it would force something from his subconscious.

"And there is every chance that the future I find in whatever year I care to choose will be exactly like the pasts I have visited while trying to find answers."

"What do you mean?"

Czenlyn sat behind the desk again, running his fingers through his hair in obvious fatigue. "As I said, I'm an amateur historian. My grandmother instilled the love of it in me. She wasn't wealthy, but as a child she took me many places around here. She wasn't well learned, but she had read enormous amounts of literature about Mexico and Central America. Every summer she would take me places, tell me about the people who lived there centuries before and what eventually happened to them. Once I fled from Brelmer and the Time Police, I indulged myself, traveling back to all those places. The things I have witnessed could fill volumes of histories. I keep journals over the time periods I have visited. They are locked away, of course, and, if the problems with Brelmer and the Time Police are not resolved before I die, they will be destroyed. I do not want to leave any ties that will lead back here to this time, to my wife and daughter."

Jackson carefully folded the fragile map and slid it to one corner of the drafting table.

"In all of my travels, I have never once encountered a

past in which Texas became a nation instead of a state."

"What do you mean, 'a past?'" Jackson asked.

Gesturing expansively, Czenlyn said, "Surely you've noticed how the past seems to flow in all directions since the invention of the time machine."

"No."

Czenlyn got up from behind the desk and walked in front of the fireplace in front of Jackson. It wasn't hard for Jackson to imagine the doctor just so while lecturing a class.

"Picture this," Czenlyn said while holding up a clenched fist. "This is the present. Your present. Maybe my present, only two years earlier, is wrapped somewhere around the central core. Maybe your present, two years later, is wrapped around a central core two years before my time. I don't know exactly where all the breaking points are. However, my theory suggests that all history and future history hinge on the invention of the time machine. Possibly the actual event of the first time trip is the focal point. Whichever, the end results are the same. A crossroads of Time has been given birth." He shook the clenched fist. "This is the NOW that seems to be the most unshakable. Certain events have to lead up to the time machine being introduced into the world. Just as certain events have to lead from it. Now, from this, we can have several different histories." Czenlyn held his other hand up, fanning the fingers out to one side of the fist. "All of these are viable histories, each leading up to the same events that led to the creation of the first time machine. Yet each can be radically different." He wiggled his forefinger. "In one, you have history as I know it: that Texas became a state, not a nation." The thumb wiggled next. "In another version, this time-line came to life."

"What do you mean, came to life?" Jackson was puzzled.

"Are you familiar with quantum physics?"

"No."

Czenlyn sighed and dropped his hands. "There is a theory involving the possibility of alternate worlds. For instance, a world where Jackson Dubchek became a famous Senator of the Republic. Another where Jackson Dubchek, at the age of two, fell through a frozen pond and drowned."

A cold chill flashed through Jackson when he recalled all the close calls he had had during his life. How many deaths could he have died in those alternate worlds if what Czenlyn said was true?

"Confusing, isn't it?" Czenlyn asked.

"Yes."

"And frightening."

"That too."

Czenlyn held the fist and handful of fingers up again. "Now imagine these versions of the past as they were before the invention of the time machine. There. Existing side-by-side, but never touching. NEVER touching. Now, under Voxner's direction and the mus-

cle of the Time Police, I believe these once separate
strands of time are being twisted inexorably together, to
form a single time-line which can never be changed.
The time-lines that are not beneficial to the end result
that is wanted are being peeled away somehow, through
perhaps minute changes of their personal histories and
perhaps large-scale assaults." He wiggled the fingers.
"Can you imagine the turmoil and sense of loss some of
those time-lines are experiencing?"

Jackson could and he sat there numbed by the
thought.

"Of course, those would be the outer fringe
time-lines. The ones furthest from the actual core of
the history being sought after."

Mass displacement. The thought rolled into
Jackson's mind with physical force. For a moment he
thought he was going to be sick. Ana had been trapped
for while in some other time-line and unborn in this
one. So had Martin's children. At least Jackson had
been able to save them from the collapsing history
Czenlyn was speaking of. Hadn't he? He still didn't
know for sure and that was one of the questions his
mind had played with constantly during the past month
of recovery and working in the melon fields. "What
happens to these time-lines that have been stripped
away?"

"It is my belief," Czenlyn said softly, "that eventually, if not already in some cases, that they will wither
and die."

"But that could mean the deaths of millions of people."

"Yes."

The enormity of the postulation slammed into Jackson. "But there must be some way to stop this."

"I think there is," Czenlyn answered. "Your narrative concerning the future rebels lends more credence to my thoughts. Evidently someone in the coming decades has arrived at the same conclusion."

"The Mnemosyne," Jackson whispered as he thought of Irene and her compatriots at the Vandiver Court in Springfield.

"Who are they?"

"You've never heard of the Mnemosyne Historians?"

"No."

"But you must have," Jackson insisted. "They've been around for years. I met the first Tysonyllyn in 2183." The thought that had been nudging so steadily at Jackson's subconscious burst into full flower. "It was the Satan-faced Tysonyllyn who first told me Texas was not part of the Second Republic at that time. I remember him mentioning that now." He struggled to recall what else Vaughn Tysonyllyn had mentioned. "But he didn't think anything of Texas remaining separate from the Second Republic. To him it was a mere annoyance."

"Evidently, this fellow was in one of the time-lines closest to the core."

"It was also only sixty-seven years from the present. Which, according to your line of thinking, would lessen the severity of the time changes."

"True."

Jackson shifted on the drafting stool, trying in vain to find a more comfortable position. Giving up, he stood and felt the pinpricks of returning feeling flood into his legs. He still felt bruised and hurting from his fight with Luis in the melon field and from the earlier confrontation with the Time Police. His thoughts raced as he tried to put everything together. "According to this Tysonyllyn, two men figured into the final stages of keeping Texas as an independent nation. A man named Leclerc and another named Bernardo O'Higgins."

Czenlyn crossed the room to the massive bookcase filled with volumes of varying thicknesses and differently colored dust jackets.

Jackson limped after him.

"MacMillian's CONCISE DICTIONARY OF WORLD HISTORY," Czenlyn said as he pulled a massive book from a lower shelf. It appeared much thumbed-through and several of the pages were smeared. "My bible of time travel. I use it to look up thumbnail sketches of people and places I want to visit. Ah, here we are. Charles Victor Emmanuel Leclerc. I remember the name from studies I have made. Let's see what it says."

Jackson watched a growing frown spread across the doctor's face.

"This is wrong," Czenlyn said angrily. "It has to be."

Taking the book from the man's hands, Jackson read the information. There were two Leclercs listed.

"What is wrong?"

"Everything. That book shows an elder and young Leclerc. A younger never existed. Leclerc was Napoleon's brother-in-law and died trying to put down the L'Ouverture revolt in Haiti. He never succeeded in reasserting white supremacy in that country, and he never returned to France to father a son that fought at the Alamo."

Jackson looked at Leclerc, the younger, noting in the brief biography that Pierre Leclerc had also been a deciding force in Texas' decision to remain independent as well as being a musician of considerable talent. Among his known acquaintances were Beethoven and Chopin.

Czenlyn moved away, eyes scanning the rows of books. "It's somewhere here, you'll see." He traced a forefinger down the multi-colored spines.

Flipping through the book, Jackson found a listing for Bernardo O'Higgins, discovering the man had led the Republic of Texas in major reforms that had brought the Irish immigrants into the country during the 1840s. He had also served as the third President. His beginnings stemmed from being a revolutionary leader in Chile in 1813 and was deposed in 1823 after his reforms were rejected. The dictionary didn't say how, but O'Higgins turned up in the Republic of Texas in 1828.

"There." Czenlyn removed a book from the shelf.

Jackson laid the dictionary to one side and flipped

through the battered copy the doctor shoved into his hands. The title was LONE STAR, written by Ferenbach. The covers were loose and showed the fabric webbing used to bind the pages.

"Look at the index," Czenlyn said.

Jackson flipped to the back of the book.

"Look for any mention of Leclerc or O'Higgins."

Jackson did. Then looked again. "They're not listed."

"No," Czenlyn said triumphantly, "because my history did not happen the way it appears to be now."

"But why would the dictionary contain conflicting information?"

"I bought the dictionary while I was here," Czenlyn said. "That must be the answer. The book you hold was one of the few personal things I brought with me from 2248 the night I escaped Temporal Projects." The doctor took the book back and opened it to another section. "See. In this book, Texas became a state. Not an independent country."

Jackson looked at the section, seeing the words but not reading. He remembered his encounter with John Reed in Geneva. The writer had been a part of the current history who had written a book at the behest of the Time Police. Yet Reed had also been aware that time had somehow warped itself around him while other people didn't know.

Jackson looked at Czenlyn. "How do you know your version of history is right?"

The doctor closed the book and tapped his forehead. "Because I know, young man. I remember. That is one thing the Time Police can never take away from us. We can make ourselves remember if the desire is great enough, no matter what kind of sweeping changes Temporal Projects pushes on us. How did you know your sister-in-law actually existed?"

"Because Martin remembered."

"Exactly."

Buddha. The complications of the problems he was facing left Jackson cold and tired. Why did it seem like he was inexorably drawn into the maelstrom of Time Temporal Projects had created? Why couldn't he be simply left alone and allowed to live out his life in peace?

"Jackson."

Looking up, Jackson discovered Czenlyn staring at him with concern on his broad features.

"Are you all right?"

"Yes." Jackson lied without hesitation. He left the bookshelves and crossed the den to stand in front of the fireplace, letting the heat soak into his body. "You say you've tried to go back?"

"Yes. Several times to ascertain the actual events concerning Texas' decision to become an independent country. But each time I discovered nothing wrong with the time-line I was in."

"Yet that time-line, the one Temporal Projects engineered, has to exist somewhere."

Czenlyn nodded.

"Why couldn't you reach it?"

"I don't think it existed when I first jumped back from 2248. The new time-line had to have come into being after my departure. I guess you could say I am a time orphan, Jackson. Cast out by my own future because there have been enough subtle changes in that present to phase it out of existence; and, since every man has to have a past of sorts, I have those pasts that were and are real to me."

"But what you're saying is that you don't belong here, in this time, either."

"I know." Czenlyn shifted, walking back to the desk. "You've met my wife and daughter, Jackson. They both belong to this time, to this moment of now. For them, there has been no change. Time shifted around them, changed their perceptions of history and left them the same people they always were. They think I am being paranoid."

"Do they know about the time machine?"

"Of course. I hold no secrets from my family. Just as I am holding no secrets from you. They have seen me spend weeks away from them, studying the past, writing in my journals. But they believe I have become fanatical about the subject, that I am inventing ghosts and aberrations where none exist."

"But if your theory is true, if a central time-line is being created at the expense of all other time-lines, what will happen to you?"

Czenlyn shrugged. "So far, nothing. But I don't know. I am truly a man out of his time. I can flee into a past so far removed from 2074 that the ripples of the time change will never reach me. But my wife, my daughter, they belong here. They have never traveled through time. You've seen for yourself what that some-times does to people. I can't risk their sanity. And I can't just walk away from them either. They are my life now." The big man's voice broke.

Jackson looked away, not wanting the burden of Czenlyn's despair added to his own. Yet, it settled on him just the same.

"I thought I was so clever in escaping Brelmer and the Time police in 2248," Czenlyn said when he had recovered control of his voice. "I was happily lost in the assorted centuries, enjoying the experience, taking a piece of existence here and a chunk of living there. I was a parasite of Time then, Jackson, living off of but never giving. Not until I met Elena and we had my daughter. Then I settled here and gave what I could of my skill and knowledge to the people nearby. As you can see by this house, and by the different escape routes I have to and from this house, I am a very wealthy man. I can have anything I want. Yet, because of Voxner's machinations, I stand to lose the only two people that mean my life to me. Can you understand how I feel, knowing I have no choice but to sit here, in this now, and hope for the best?"

Turning to stretch his hands toward the fire, Jackson

said, "Do you think I will be able to reach those pasts that have been altered?"

Visible relief showed on Czenlyn's face. "Yes," he said in a hoarse whisper that was almost reverent. "Yes, I do. Otherwise I would not have been so intent on finding you."

Jackson studied the yellow and red flames licking at the blackened log in the fireplace, wondering why the heat seemed too hot to his skin but didn't reach inside him. "And once I reach this past or pasts, what do I do then?"

"I honestly don't know, Jackson."

Thinking of the Time Police that would undoubtedly infest the era, Jackson thought that merely staying alive would be a good opening move.

CHAPTER EIGHT

Ronald Ruel Voxner, Senator of History, moved through the halls of Temporal Projects' recovery area and grinned inwardly. White-suited medtechs and nurses scattered before him like the fuzz from a wind-blown dandelion, intent, no doubt, on trying to summon someone of rank worthy enough to meet the power behind TP.

Even Brelmer would not have been able to accrue the amount of fear he saw visible on the faces of the recovery staff. That thought left him warm and pleased. As Praetor and head of the project, Brelmer had more access to these people than he did. It made Voxner happy to see their fright was well-placed. And it blended well with the harmony extended by the very spirit of the Second Republic. In this life, a citizen was guaranteed a job and security from most wants. But there were no guarantees about where that citizen would have that job or of what level of success would go along with it.

The antiseptic smell of the floor was a necessary bother and Voxner accepted it as such. So was the quietness. But he was used to that. Most rooms fell silent like the hospital quietness of this floor when he entered them on business. Even other Senators often quailed when he was in their presence.

Voxner thought of himself as an old and wily lion, but not so old that the frequently sent-for sex kittens went away unsatisfied. He was still a virile man, even for one in his early eighties, thanks to the genetics experts he kept on staff for his personal health. Of course, with the life-span near the one hundred-forty mark as it was now, he was only a little past middle-age. At fifty-some-odd, Brelmer was still just a pup. An insolent pup, at times. But Voxner had Brelmer on a short leash and the Praetor knew it. Tonight that leash was going to grow noticeably shorter.

The old and wily lion intended to flick one of his claws tonight and draw blood. Blood that would taint Brelmer with the duplicity that Voxner had been negotiating for years. No longer would Brelmer's vague attempts at standing up for the rights of the past intrude on his plans.

Voxner allowed himself a small smile as he thumbprinted the door open to a private room. Down the dimly lit corridor, he saw a nurse and male orderly watching him. The two quickly turned away, immersing themselves in whatever projects they were supposedly engaged with.

Power.

The feeling surged through Voxner like a drug.

Power.

There was nothing else like it.

No other stimulant, including Capricorn, could thrill the Senator's nerve synapses in quite the same way. And he deserved it. He had worked long and hard for the position he held now. Had given up so many of his dreams to barter himself into the Senate seat he occupied with so much authority now. In the early days, he reflected as he stepped inside the open room, he had had to align himself with other Senators whose goals had closely matched his own. He had had to make concessions. Even had to give up true love to marry a woman he despised to make his position more solvent. Still, thank the gods there had been no children. Perhaps later, when the time came for him to produce a heir. But by then there would be a legacy to pass on, and, hopefully, a title as well.

The room was in semi-darkness and Voxner didn't have Brelmer's crystal eyes to help him penetrate the gloom. Blackness gathered into a solid knot that appeared to be sitting on the whiteness of the bed sheets.

"Who is there?" a voice asked.

Voxner could sense the youthfulness in the voice and tried to figure out how old the man would be now. But the figure eluded his questing mental fingers as dates swarmed into his mind. Things were very confusing at times, trying to remember all the years that were involved with Project Clio. O'Higgins in 1836. The Medici woman in the Renaissance period in Italy. The Spanish ship sometime in between there? He pushed the computations out of his mind. They were not necessary now. He had the plan outlined at his Moscow office, under locvaul that would only answer to his thumbprint. "It's Senator Voxner."

"Hello, sir." The voice was more wary, more tactful now.

Voxner tried to peer through the gloom but it resisted his attempts. He thought the man was sitting up but was unsure. "I understand you underwent surgery not long ago."

"Yes, sir. This morning."

"And how are you feeling?"

"Well, sir." The tiredness in the voice belayed that fact though.

"Should you be sitting up? You are sitting up, aren't you?"

"Yes, sir, and I find it more beneficial than lying down, sir. At least this way I can manage to give my muscles a chance to remain loose and not tighten up.

I'm more sore than I was told I would be."

"Yes. I understand the augmentation and implants, plus the genetic alterations can be quite painful."

"Quite."

"Would you like for me to send for a nurse to get you a pain-killer?"

"No, thank you, sir. I can manage most of the pain on my own and I prefer to keep a clear head."

"Very well." Voxner shifted, feeling his way through the darkness to the chair against the wall. "Do you mind if I switch on a light?"

"It's fine with me, sir. They still have my eyes bandaged."

"I see," Voxner said, then called for the lights so he could.

The man on the bed was young and lean, with a shaved head already showing dark stubble from returning growth. Gauze bandages bisected his head and face, covering the eyes and ears where the crystal implants were made. His chest and arms and the one leg showing from under the bedsheet showed scars from the previous morning's surgery. They would be faded at a later time, Voxner knew, but for now they gleamed like fat white worms under the artificial light.

Relaxing in the uncomfortable chair and wishing for the more padded ones from his own offices, Voxner compared his memory of the man sitting before him with the visage before him now. The man was handsome. Had been, the Senator corrected himself, and would be again once the surgery had been completed. "Does it feel better to be a free man?"

The man smiled. "I can't tell the difference so far, sir. To me, it seems like I have traded one prison for another. Only in the first, I knew my way around. No one took my eyes away from me or shackled me to this." He held up his left wrist, showing the bracelet of IV tubes and monitoring equipment.

"I understand how you feel, Corbin, and I assure you this is only a temporary arrangement."

"I know, sir." Corbin put his fingertips to his temples.

"Are you having pain?"

"A little."

"Do you want me too . . . "

"No!" The answer came out too sharp and too explosive.

Voxner knew the man's composure was much more fragile
than he had anticipated. Maybe it would have been better to wait until later to see Corbin. But the young man was an important facet in the overall success or failure of Project Clio and Voxner had seldom had patience to wait to initiate any of the different branches of the plan. He bit back his own anger, mollifying himself by thinking of the ways Corbin would benefit Clio.

"I'm sorry for the outburst, sir."

"It's quite all right, Corbin," Voxner said, surprising even himself by his magnanimity. "I guess I can't really say I understand what you're going through, but I do empathize."

"It's not quite the emotion one should show to his benefactor," Corbin said.

"No," Voxner agreed, "but neither is it unacceptable under the present circumstances."

"I want to thank you again, Senator, for believing in me and for getting me out of prison."

"Thank you. I only wish I had been able to do more. You're going to be in pain for a few more days before the surgeons here at TP are finished with you, though."

Corbin managed a weak grin. "Still, days are much easier to handle than years."

"Would you care for something to drink?"

Corbin shook his head and hooked a thumb in the general direction of the medequip bank behind him. "I can't take any liquids or solids until the medtech checks me over."

"I'll see if I can't push the surgeons on it."

"Thank you. In prison you get used to getting three meals a day at certain times. My stomach has been reminding me of that constantly since I awoke."

Shifting in the uncomfortable chair, Voxner said, "I suppose you've been wondering why I've given you so much of my attention."

Corbin moved his head, evidently trying to get an audible fix on Voxner. He was only a little off, facing a spot a little to the Senator's left. "I wasn't going to ask, Senator."

"Still, you must have been curious. You're a learned man, Corbin. You don't find many men such as yourself in prison."

"I know." The young man's voice rung with the lonely desolation Voxner remembered from his interview with Corbin in the prison.

"That in itself was one of the reasons," Voxner said. "Your education. I find it much too valuable to waste. Your professors spoke highly of you."

"You talked with my professors?"

"I talked with a lot of people, Corbin. Including the arresting officers who testified at your trial three years ago."

Corbin's lips compressed into a thin, hard line. "And?"

"I think they were telling the truth. At least, as far as they knew it. They appear to both be good men."

"But they were wrong! I didn't kill anyone!"

"Easy, Corbin. I still believe your story. Otherwise I would not have optioned you out of prison as I have."

"I was told Temporal Projects recruited many prisoners."

"Not many," Voxner corrected. "Actually, only a select few. No known murderers."

"I am not a murderer."

"I don't think you are. Yet, I can't prove otherwise. Still, I have an enormous amount of power right now, and I can do what I want to for the most part. One of the things I wanted to do was free you from that hell-hole and get you back into a field you were trained for."

Corbin was silent, staring at the spot over Voxner's left shoulder.

Voxner let the silence build for a moment. Silence was the ultimate tool when you were in a position of authority and he knew it. And he could wield it with the precision of a laser-scalpel or with the punishing force of a machete. He had put a lot of time into Corbin's recruitment, had initiated much of what the younger man had been able to do with his life. Had made sure no one harmed him in prison. The young man had been raped on more than one occasion, and had been attacked and bullied even more. All those moves were designed to off-set the gentleness of his upbringing, to nudge Corbin up on the high-wire of sanity where the winds of madness could whip at him with ice-fangs. But in the end, Voxner felt sure the younger man would prove a valuable tool. A most valuable tool. The price had been dear, true, but Voxner had not paid it. And that would be a final valuableness that was priceless.

"Sir?"

"I'm still here, Corbin."

"I'm sorry for the outburst, sir, but for the first time in three years, I'm on the verge of being able to consider my future again. I find that more than a little unsettling."

"I know."

"I just want to know what I have to do to repay you."

Voxner let his grin spill out onto his face, knowing his captive audience wouldn't be able to see it. Power. And this was it. Power over individuals that rippled outwardly over events till even they were within his grasp. "I need a bright young man in my organization, Corbin, and I think you'll fit the bill. That is the extent of my repayment. I think you were unjustly convicted of the murder of your step-father, but I can't prove it. I still have a team working on that end of things, but for now I can offer you a shelter of freedom under the umbrella of the Time Police corps. I'm sorry it's not more." Voxner worked to put genuine sorrow in his voice. It was an imitation he had become very adroit at while working at the Relocations Office of the Department of Employment while telling different people they and their families were about to be uprooted and flung around the world.

Corbin seemed satisfied with the answer and remained quiet.

"I just wanted to take the time and visit you myself," Voxner said, "now that the surgery's been completed. I'd talked with Hoban, the chief surgeon, earlier and he said you were doing as well as could be expected."

"How do I look?"

Voxner considered the question. Corbin had understood the intricacies of the operations required to convert him to a Time Policeman. And had understood as well that there was no way the operations could be reversed. Did the young man have any qualms about the choice to become a member of the Time Police? That possibility didn't exist in Voxner's plans. He had to own this man body and soul. "You look fine," the Senator said, though he would not have wanted to be in the young man's shoes. Corbin had been an extremely handsome young man. He would never be that again. Which would, in time, ferment into another of those ice-fanged winds which threatened to whip him from that high-wire of sanity.

Pushing himself to his feet, Voxner asked, "Is there anything I can get for you? Or have the staff get for you?"

"No. Thanks."

"I'll be seeing more of you in a few days, then?"

Corbin nodded.

"Would you like me to turn the light out?"

"Please. At least that way it's easier to understand not being able to see."

Voxner cleared the lights with a vocal command and thumbprinted the door open.

"Sir?"

Voxner looked over his shoulder, catching a glimpse of the gauze-stripe slashing Corbin's face. "Yes?"

"I just wanted to say thank you again, Senator. And I'll try my best to fill whatever position you have for me."

"I'm sure you will," Voxner said. "I'll be taking a personal interest in your development. Perhaps we can accomplish much, you and I. Good night."

Voxner stepped out into the hallway as the door hissed shut behind him. Dr. Hoban occupied a doorway on the other side of the hall. A narco-smoker dangled loosely in the surgeon's hand.

"Good evening, Senator," Hoban said without the trace of rancor Voxner expected.

"Doctor."

"Was anything wrong, sir?"

"No. I found young Corbin to be in exemplary shape. You do good work. Of course, if you didn't, you wouldn't be at Temporal Projects."

Hoban was clearly trying to consider how he was supposed to take the statement. He inhaled another hit off the narco-smoker.

"How is Suzanne Brelmer?"

"Well as can be expected under the circumstances."

"And her father?"

"The Praetor is taking it pretty hard, sir."

Voxner waggled a finger and had Hoban fall in beside him as he swept down the hallway. "Were there any indications of violence that would corroborate Friz's tale of kidnapping?"

"Maybe."

"Come, come, doctor. I know this project pays you well enough to gainsay any fence-sitting."

"She has a recent bruise on her jaw, Senator, which I think also induced the small concussion she has. And there are other indications that she has been roughly handled."

"Enough to clearly indicate she was indeed kidnapped as Friz insists?"

"There is also the matter of the drugs in her system. Any of those could have been used to keep her under sedation."

"You think it was a kidnapping, then?"

"I think it would be unfair to rule the possibility out, sir."

"More fence-sitting?"

"No. It's just that I do medicine here, Senator, not mysticism."

Voxner halted, spinning on his heel and pinning Hoban to a stop in the corridor with a jeweled forefinger. He kept a small smile on his face but knew the anger he felt blazed forth from his eyes. He put a hard edge in his voice. "Don't ever forget where your loyalties lie, Dr. Hoban. There is a sole power at the root of Temporal Projects and it lies with me."

Hoban's gaze dropped away as he discreetly checked to see who was seeing the obvious exchange of unpleasantries. "Yes, sir."

Voxner flicked the man away with his forefinger, dismissing him with a threat-filled glance. He walked alone, taking the elevator up to his suite of rooms near the time labs. Once inside, he keyed on the lights, wishing he could drink some of the bourbon the staff kept on hand for his infrequent visits. But that would have made the time jump he had planned even more unpleasant. His stomach rumbled at the thought of getting anything digestible. It had been over twelve hours since he had eaten or drank anything more substantial than water.

Crossing the plush room filled with copies of his favorite paintings, Voxner voiced the fireplace into being and made himself comfortable on the huge couch. He felt tiredness pluck at him with dulled talons but ignored it.

"Vid," he snapped at the room.

A vid separated itself from the wall, spinning into a translucent globe that would tri-D anyone he talked to.

Voxner called for Friz Brelmer's private exchange at home. A recorded holo answered, showing the Praetor's wife, June. June Brelmer had once been beautiful. Voxner could tell that by the bone structure of the woman's face, as well as by the way she cared for herself now. Her prematurely gray hair showed white highlights under whatever light had been present when the holo had been recorded.

"I'm sorry," the holo said, "but Friz and I are unable to come to the vid at the moment. Please leave your name and number after the image and we'll get back to you."

The vid changed to a holo of an ancient pencil poised over an equally ancient notepad.

"Anti-vid scan lock in," Voxner intoned to the floating vid before him. A black ring inscribed the inner surface of the whirling globe. "Mrs. Brelmer, this is Senator Voxner."

A holo of a more vibrant June Brelmer interfaced into the globe. "Hello, Senator." The voice that accompanied the image was anything but jubilant. "To what displeasure do I owe for this vid?"

Voxner smiled, knowing the woman would see it. Gods, but she had a sharp tongue. How had Friz managed to put up with it for so long? Even now, trapped as she was by the machinations he had put into play, she showed him an insolence no one else would have dared. Including her husband. "Merely a social call, Mrs. Brelmer."

"Nothing is mere with you, Senator. You are a man of absolutes. Very few of which are charitable."

Voxner scowled. How could the woman taunt him so? Didn't she realize he held her very life in his hand? Then he checked the sudden anger, remembering she had not yet had time to get accustomed to the new role he had cast her in at the party only a few hours ago. "I just called to inquire if the prescription I gave you was adequate."

"Yes. Just as you knew it would be."

"Must we talk like this, Mrs. Brelmer? Really, I find fencing behind this ridiculous facade of your recorded holo most inconvenient."

"I'm quite comfortable, thank you." The holo was still smiling.

Voxner would have even sworn the eyes were twinkling. "Are you decent?"

"Of the two of us, Senator, I am probably the more

so."

Voxner's scowl deepened. "Clear," he commanded the vid.

In response, the vid seemed to invert itself as the black ring exploded in the globe's confines. It only took the vid connection a few seconds to pulse through the ether and seize a picture.

June Brelmer sat facing the vid from her dresser. She wore a white bath robe and her hair was damp. Even in the poor lighting of the vanity light, Voxner could make out the crimson dots high on the woman's temples.

Goat's horns, the street peddlers called them.

A sure sign of a Capricorn user.

And, as everyone in the Second Republic knew, Capricorn, or Capricodone, was illegal.

Even for Voxner's connections, the drug was costly. But money always converted quickly into power. It was the lever the Senator used when muscle or threats weren't necessary or applicable.

"Are you sure of the dosage you're using?" Voxner asked. Real concern touched his voice. It would be hard to replace a spy inside Brelmer's own household. Especially one who he owned as thoroughly as he did June Brelmer.

"Believe me, Senator, I've been dealing with the betrayals of my body for longer than I care to remember. I'm quite sure of what I'm doing." She applied a facial cream to her forehead and temples, obviously trying to mute the telltale of the drug.   "Why did you call?"

"To alert you to the possibility that Friz will be in a very tense mood when he arrives home tonight."

"This morning, you mean."

"Yes."

"Why call me?"

"To make sure you're awake enough to fulfill your part of the bargain."

"I'll be a good little informer, Senator. I promise."

hardening his voice, Voxner said, "I believe you will, Mrs. Brelmer, otherwise I will cut off your supply of Capricorn and make sure your husband knows he has an addict for a wife." He broke the vid connection, noting with satisfaction that the woman appeared visibly shaken. He exhaled loudly, working the anger from his system.

So many variables, he thought as he pushed himself up from the comfort of the couch, scattered across decades. Across centuries, in fact. Yet each of them had a part to play and each required attention on a regular basis. The O'Higgins plot, the Medici clan, Corbin, Mrs. Brelmer, and all the others. Yet, if everything went as planned, he told himself as he scanned the night lights of the city through the window, Project Clio would only be a pale shadow of the coup he had set into motion.

Power.

The pulse of it breathed fire through his veins.

And Senator Ronald Ruel Voxner was very, very glad that his drug didn't have telltales like June Brelmer's goat's horns.

CHAPTER NINE

Brelmer stood in his daughter's hospital room quietly, waiting for the shakes to pass. He focused on Suzanne's breathing in an effort to calm his own. In. Out. In. Out. Slow. No force. A natural movement. But even though he got his breathing slowed to a more normal pace, he could still feel his heart thudding inside his chest.

Reluctantly, he moved away, giving one of her hands a final squeeze.

The laser attack had unnerved him to a degree, coming on the heels of events he already had trouble dealing with. There was no doubt in his mind that Voxner was at the bottom of the toothless attempt.

Whoever had squeezed the firing stud had undoubtedly held him in the weapon's crosshairs for a time before using the recorded holo to illustrate the nearness of death.

But did Voxner fear him that much?

Brelmer couldn't believe that. The Senator had no qualms at all about having whoever was in his way displaced. Rosito Alvarez and Lester Wu were prime examples of that. As was Jackson Dubchek.

But Brelmer had agreed in Dubchek's case. After all, despite Suzanne's protests to the contrary, there had been the list of names Slye had come back with. And Dubchek's had been at the very top.

It had bothered him at first, he remembered as he passed through the doorway into the corridor. Realistically speaking, it would have seemed that Dubchek's duplicity in the past would have been discovered before it was. Yet, by the same token, it was amazing that the incidents were discovered at all. The past, filled with shadows of itself was becoming more and more dangerous.

Things changed.

History altered now of its own accord.

Brelmer had tried to tell Voxner that but the Senator refused to listen to all the paradoxes the Praetor had discovered. Some of them were natural outgrowths of action they had put into play, true, but some of them weren't.

It was hard trying to plan for every eventuality.

Equally hard to foresee every twist and turn the timestream would take now that the banks were slowly being eroded.

According to the Christian Bible, God had destroyed the world once before by flood. Would it now end again as a tide of centuries swept away the present?

Brelmer didn't know.

It stood to reason that his present would survive since there were the Time Rebels from the future.

But would it really?

And what exactly would his present consist of?

A coldness, initiated by the coolness of the hospital recovery floor, crept down the Praetor's spine as he walked toward the elevator banks.

Another possibility nagged at him too. What if Time became so unhinged that the present, his present, the present in which the time machine had been invented, became a whirlpool? Sucking Time into it from both ends?

The captured Time Rebel held in solitary confinement had induced this new line of thinking. She was Suzanne's great-granddaughter, according to the genetics scan. And she hated him. Hated everything Temporal Projects stood for. According to the girl, Brelmer occupied a very ideal spot in the Time stream. Somewhere in the middle where all time flurries were less effective, less threatening and only slightly disconcerting. But how long would that last?

And if some sort of Time whirlpool developed, as

Brelmer was afraid would happen, how ideal would that position be then?

He turned his thoughts away from the conjecture, marshalling himself for the meeting with Voxner which was only minutes away. He had not had much time after the assassination attempt to guess at the Senator's reasons for this impromptu time jump and knew it was often useless to speculate on the intricacies of the man's true plans.

Above all else, Brelmer respected Voxner's abilities as a tactician. He had seen the man snatch prize after prize in the Senate with every means imaginable. Honor, integrity, you didn't find those concepts much in Voxner's vocabulary. But they were tools the man used against his foes. Tools inside the other person, man or woman, that made them vulnerable to whatever method Voxner chose to dismember his victim with.

So Brelmer respected those abilities just as he feared them.

Tapping his shoulder-com, Brelmer ordered a com-connection with Costuming.

Paress Linnet answered.

Brelmer was amazed at the tiredness in the woman's voice. "There was a package I requested earlier," Brelmer said as he turned a corner and passed through a set of double doors. He spotted Hoban down the hall, loitering near the nurses' station and vaguely wondered what the man was doing out of bed again.

"Yes, Colonel. It was a little late because I wanted to

take care of it myself. Julian is on his way up with it now. I think you'll be happy, sir. It was very considerate of you, if I may say so."

Brelmer permitted himself a slight smile only because he knew the woman would not see it. "Thank you, Paress."

"Sir?"

"Yes."

"Were you aware that Senator Voxner requested my presence on the jump you and he are making?"

Brelmer considered that, trying to find a connection for Paress Linnet in any of Voxner's convoluted plans. "No. I was not."

Hoban caught his eye but the surgeon stayed where he was, inhaling deeply on the narco-smoker he held.

Brelmer felt vaguely annoyed at the man. Hoban knew of Brelmer's dislike for any narcotics, even the legal ones you bought in the credit machines. He could scent the familiar minty smell of Earlsboro Elegance. The same brand Brelmer's father had smoked.

"Do you know why I would be assigned to the time jump?" Paress asked.

"No, but if I do, I'll let you know."

"Thank you, Colonel. I'm nervous about this. I've never made a trip back before."

"Have you eaten?"

"A few hours ago, but aren't you supposed to go on an empty stomach?"

"Precisely my point, Paress. When you get a moment

from your sewing machines, you might make a jaunt to the women's lave and stick a finger down your throat. It may help."

"Yes, Colonel."

Brelmer closed the com-link and closed in on Hoban. "Is anything wrong, doctor?" he asked in a voice only he and Hoban could hear. Had something happened to Suzanne earlier? The medequip had looked fine but Brelmer felt a small worm of anxiety squirm against the top of his stomach.

Hoban put the smoker out against the bottom of his shoe and stored it in a pocket of his lab smock. His eyes were red-rimmed and bright with a concealed emotion. "Suzanne's doing fine, Colonel. One of my other patients received a visit from Senator Voxner a few minutes ago. A nurse alerted me and I got out of bed again. You just don't see Voxner in this building all that much. Especially on this floor."

"Who was the patient?"

"A young man named Corbin. I did the augmentation and genetics on him yesterday morning."

"Why would Voxner be interested in him?"

"I don't know, sir. But I do know it was the Senator who paroled him from prison for assignment in the Time Police."

"Which is even more mystifying," Brelmer said to himself.

"Yes, sir."

New ingredients in the stew? Brelmer wondered as

he stared at the blank face of the door. Or other avenues of Voxner's planning that were just coming into play? He made a mental note of Corbin's name. When he returned from whatever trip Voxner had planned, he would take a look at the man's past himself.

"I suppose he asked about my daughter as well?" Brelmer asked.

"Yes, sir."

Brelmer glanced at the doctor and saw apprehension etch worry lines across Hoban's forehead. "I won't ask you about the conversation, doctor. I can figure out the gist of it on my own."

"Thank you, sir." Hoban was clearly relieved.

"But I would like to know if Voxner indicated how he had found out about Suzanne."

"He didn't say, Colonel."

"Care to guess?"

"I haven't a clue, sir."

Brelmer stared at the surgeon, wondering how true the statement was. It was no secret that Voxner had an active grapevine within the concrete and steel walls of Temporal Projects. What Brelmer hoped was secret was the handful of men he had culled from the ranks of the Time Police and staff who were utterly loyal to him. "When do you think Suzanne will regain consciousness?"

"It's hard to tell, sir. Her system has had quite a shock and there is the baby to consider as well."

Brelmer felt as though an icespike had been driven

through his heart. "Baby?" he said in a voice so soft he almost didn't hear it himself.

"Yes, sir." Hoban stared at him. "You didn't know, did you?"

"No." Brelmer made an effort to grab the composure that had slipped away from him. A baby. Suzanne's baby. He thought of the Time Rebel held captive who was Suzanne's great-granddaughter. Was the baby Hoban spoke of the link that connected the generations? And whose baby was it? Dubchek's? Shiva. It had to be. Brelmer had known about his daughter's other affairs, though there had been few. Two he had interfered with, without Suzanne's knowledge, of course. One without even her male acquaintance knowing. The other had taken an open threat to dissuade. But all of this had been before the promotion to Temporal Projects. When he had had the time to watch over Suzanne.

Hoban looked away, clearly embarrassed. "I thought the scrub-techs might have told you, sir. The fetus showed up on their scans."

"It was on the scans?"

"You were probably looking at it while we were in the medvault, sir. You just didn't know what you were looking at."

Reaching deep inside himself, Brelmer grabbed a double-handed grip on the iron will that had sustained him throughout his life. Ripples. He had often thought of the ripples that took place in the time stream that were now able to wreak untold havoc with events. Was Suzanne's baby destined to be one of those unpredictable ripples? Then he thought of the Time Rebel again. Or had it already been?

"Chances are, sir, that your daughter doesn't know she is pregnant either."

Brelmer nodded, analyzing the information in the small, rational part of his mind left. Suzanne's baby. His grandchild. Flesh of his flesh united with Dubchek. Fury swept through him with hurricane force and he kept it shackled under the unbendable iron will he had nurtured every year he lived. "How far along is the pregnancy?"

Hoban shrugged. "Only a few days. Perhaps a week at the most."

When does life begin? Brelmer asked himself. There were still so many theories, so many arguments to sway the listener in a choice of directions. Only the technology of being able to detect the pregnancy had advanced since the 20th Century. Yet the arguments of when the fetus assumed its own mantle of life remained unchanged. "Remove the fetus," Brelmer said, surprised at the coldness in his own voice.

"You mean abort it?" Hoban seemed incredulous.

No. He could never kill anything that belonged to Suzanne. But this child had to be Dubchek's. Perhaps it had even been fathered back in the past for some reason not yet fathomed. Until he was able to weigh out the repercussions of the child's conception, he would remove it from Suzanne's life. It would be one less guilt she would have to live with.

"No," Brelmer said. "Keep it alive, but in an artificial womb."

"But why?"

Brelmer glared into Hoban's face coldly, backing the man down from him. "Because I think she was raped by Dubchek when he kidnapped her. Because I know the kind of woman my daughter is and I don't think she should be forced to make a decision about this now. Not until she's had time to recover."

Hoban seemed about to say something, then noted the intense look Brelmer gave him, and decided against it. "Yes, Colonel."

"And this had better remain our secret, doctor," Brelmer said. "I want the scans from earlier erased and I don't want the fetus extraction taped at all."

"Yes, sir."

"You will keep it safe-guarded until my return or I will make sure you never existed."

Hoban's hand twitched for the narco-smoker in his pocket. "Yes, sir."

Without saying another word, Brelmer strode from the surgeon and homed in on the elevators. The doors met in front of him and erased the nurses' station from his view. He let two floors drift by, then punched the emergency stop button. His hands knotted into fists as he leaned against the wall. Blue veins made thick ropes around his wrists.

How had his life turned into such a landslide of living? He had always managed himself so well before. Promotions had seemed to court him, falling gracefully one after another at his feet. Success had never been elusive. Had, instead, always been a companion on whatever adventure or conquest he had chose to pursue next.

And now?

Brelmer shook his head.

Suzanne.

Shiva, if he faced any downfall whatsoever in this life, it would be through his family.

Suzanne. A mother.

He forced himself to think of her that way.

She had only been a gamin-faced little girl a handful of years ago. Still uncurious about boys. Wanting nothing more than to follow in his footsteps.

A mother.

If he had not ordered Hoban to take the fetus from her. Yet, in a way the responsibility was seductive. Having a child would ensure Suzanne stayed more wary of her involvement with Temporal Projects' affairs. She would be more protective of herself. And of her child.

But what if he was right? What if Dubchek had gotten her pregnant to fulfill some other scheme whatever band of Time Rebels he was coordinating his activities with had concocted?

In his heart, Brelmer knew he'd regret his decision to take Suzanne's baby away. Even later, if everything turned out to be all right, Suzanne would hold his interference against him. Maybe she would even consider him to be the soulless monster many other people who had worked for and against him believed him to be.

But he couldn't take the chance that it was a plot. Suzanne would be even more hurt then.

Regaining control over the maelstrom of emotions swirling inside him, Brelmer punched the elevator back into operation, shooting back up to Voxner's office.

"Come in, Friz," Voxner's voice said.

The door sheared away and Brelmer stepped into the luxurious office/living quarters of TP's most illustrious and infrequent guest.

Voxner lay on the huge couch in a semi-prone position, eyes focused on a hovering tri-D vid.

Nothing but the best for the time program's benefactor, Brelmer thought sarcastically. He made himself at home on one of the anti-grav O-G-Boy recliners, feeling it slump automatically as it adjusted for his weight. Then the anti-grav units pushed him back up to the acceptable height and an attached foot-rest swung up under his feet. The chair also began a warming and vibrating cycle that the Praetor found entirely too relaxing. He manually shut the features off and turned his attention to the vid.

"Have you met Senator Lisa Ky?" Voxner asked. He waved toward the vid.

Brelmer faced the whirling globe and made a pleasant face, unsure if he shouldn't have remained standing. He had assumed the woman was another of the many courtesans Voxner employed.

Senator Ky was of Oriental extraction. Brelmer found that quite evident in her natural yellowed ivory coloration as well as the slight slant of her eyes. Just as he found her reserved beauty quietly arresting. Dark hair cascaded down her bare shoulders, an ebony wave that rippled past the emerald green evening gown she wore. Her eyes were richly brown, with a warmth that spoke of a passion for more than politics. "I am pleased to meet you, Praetor. I have heard much about your past work and hope to hear more about your present project as it is declassified."

"Thank you, Senator," Brelmer said with a small nod. Clearly the woman had been one of the guests at Voxner's party yesterday evening, but why was Voxner contacting her at this late hour? Or was the macho thinking Suzanne often complained of blinding him to the possibility that Senator Ky had contacted Voxner?

Diamonds glittered from the rings adorning Senator Ky's hand as she drank lavender liquid from the goblet she held.

Brelmer watched her slender throat pulse as she drank and felt a momentary surge of desire that was quickly displaced by guilt. He had enough things occupying his mind at the moment without adding adolescent whimsy to the list.

Sitting back in his seat, Brelmer listened half-heart-edly as Voxner's and Ky's conversation turned to the dealings of Senate. Some names that were brought up were familiar to him. Many of the others were not. The fact didn't surprise him. He made sure he kept himself sequestered away from people who didn't have to do with his post or next promotion in any way. All too often, those political superstars had a tendency to pick apart people they didn't understand. And Brelmer intended to never let himself become carrion for a Senate investigatory body to pick over.

After a few more moments of conversation carried on in a political short-hand Brelmer could not grasp at all, Voxner blanked the vid and swiveled his massive head.

"What do you think of her?" Voxner asked.

"She seems to be an impressive lady," Brelmer said.

Voxner grinned. "For that, I intend to take vast amounts of credit. I've been grooming her for years. Although she is not truly aware of it. Now, it seems as though those years are going to pay off."

Brelmer remained silent, knowing the Senator would get to the heart of the discussion when he chose to.

"You've heard the post of Premier is about to be vacated?"

"Not for certain," Brelmer said. "I'd heard Patryce was considering stepping down for health reasons."

"Well, it's more than rumor now. Patryce is finishing out the next two months, then he is out of politics. Beats the hell out of me what the man is planning to do with the rest of his life. Would you like a drink?"

Brelmer said no thank you.

Voxner made himself a bourbon, neat, at the wet bar in the corner and retreated back to the couch. "His position has two serious contenders vying for it. One is Lisa Ky. The other is Auqua."

Brelmer snorted in disgust. "Doesn't the Senate realize that Auqua would break the power of the Second Republic? If that man had his way about things, we would all still be conducting business from meetings in separate town squares."

"True. Which is why I want to see Lisa Ky fill the position."

Brelmer doubted that was all there was to it. Voxner only did something for the good of the majority if he happened to be in the majority.

"Lisa Ky is of Vietnamese heritage, which will be a point in her favor with all the Third World Senators as well as with Pope George Ringo. And she is pretty and vivacious and incredibly intelligent. Her sole fault lies in the fact that she is also a Dunker. Twice-dunked, in fact." Voxner grimaced.

Brelmer understood the grimace. Dunkers were a conservative religious group that believed in only one god instead of the official Bahai pantheon. He searched for the Dunkers' real name and remembered with some difficulty. Rock of Rome Church the Savior. Being twice-dunked was the real catch, though. Dunkers ritually dunked their children between the ages of ten and twelve. The second dunking was after the individual had come of age and was only done by choice. Normally the strong ties of the Licinians backing Auqua would have been interested in someone as conservative as Lisa Ky. But being twice-dunked would make them wonder who she was going to serve first: her country or her God?

"I can't stop her from being a Dunker," Voxner explained, "because that would require too many adjustments. But I will dissuade her from being dunked the second time."

Brelmer looked at the Senator wordlessly, putting it all together in his head. Costuming's mention of the Dunker clothing. Voxner's questioning of Hoban so Brelmer would know; an implied threat. Perhaps even the voided laser attack as well.

"How do you plan to prevent that?" Brelmer asked, though he was almost certain of the answer.

Voxner beamed brightly over the rim of his glass. "Oh, come now, Friz, it's not like you to be defeatist. Surely we will think of something."

CHAPTER TEN

Jackson sat in the darkness pooled under the veranda, holding his knees in his arms against his chest. The sky over the barren land spreading out from the back of Czenlyn's hacienda was filled with stars, looking like a black handkerchief covered with diamond dust. A cool breeze swept in from the broken plain, carrying the faint odor of dust, washing over him as it ruffled the silk clothing Czenlyn had purchased for him during the past week.

Anxiety filled him, channeled along on cloven feet. For the last week he had fearfully considered what this coming morning would bring. Now a restlessness that would not be denied kept him from sleep.

Did his present still exist and therefore, hopefully, a future?

Or would he find some invisible wall as Czenlyn had?

In either event, what would happen then?

An endless number of possibilities seemed to confront him, just as Czenlyn proposed that an equally endless number of pasts and futures beckoned. He could go his own way once he returned to 2250, disregarding any promises made to Czenlyn, and hope the Time Police would forget about him. Or he could research the past as he and the doctor had talked of for the last week. Each moment of Time had become a way station in his mind, thanks to Czenlyn's interpretation of events, and Jackson couldn't shake the thought that perhaps he wasn't as in charge of his future as he believed.

Even in his own present, the problem he was currently considering was a thing of the past. And somewhere, his life was a thing of the past as well.

The thought left him cold and barren, as if the nothingness that thrived out on the desert before him had been funnelled inside his soul for a frozen moment.

Buddha, what was right? Czenlyn had risked his life to save Jackson from being stranded. But there had been a selfish reasoning behind it. Czenlyn had done it to achieve something he wanted. Would it be wrong for Jackson to do the same? To use the time machine Czenlyn would be giving him for his own purposes?

Escape?

Or further entanglement with the plots of the Time Police?

He felt guilty when he thought the intelligent thing to do would be to take the time machine and flee. Czenlyn had brought him into this house and made him welcome. There had been no undue pressure on Jackson to make the trips in Texas' past. Only a handful of summary issues Czenlyn had felt were important to the development of the state's history. How could he betray that trust?

Feeling sudden anger at himself and the way he was pitying himself, Jackson closed his eyes tightly and tried to force the confusing questions of loyalties away. When he opened them again, Rachel Czenlyn was standing before him.

The girl was wearing tight jeans and a frilly white blouse. She was barefooted and had her long black hair tied back so it could drift down her back. "Peso for your thoughts, Jackson," she said in a soft voice.

"You'd be overspending," Jackson promised sourly.

"Mind if I sit down?"

"No."

Rachel sat beside him, crossing her legs before her in lotus position.

An interesting bit of cleavage drifted in front of Jackson's eyes for a moment as the white blouse resettled, letting him known the girl wasn't wearing a bra. The guilt that drifted over him this time was even more demanding. It wasn't enough that he was considering shirking the commitment he had made to Czenlyn, now he had to entertain thoughts of seducing the man's daughter as well.

"You should be sleeping," Rachel said. "You will need your rest before tomorrow."

I have rested.Maybe that's what is wrong."

"You can't sleep?"

"No."

"I can get Father to prescribe something."

Jackson shook his head. "It's something I'll have to deal with on my own."

"Is it easier to deal with the side-effects of macho pride or do you just like doing things the hard way?"

In spite of himself, in spite of the mood he found himself in, Jackson smiled at the girl. He guessed that there wasn't a handful of years between them but their passage seemed to reward Rachel with an intensified beauty. He had noticed pictures of the girl at different ages in Czenlyn's study while he had been studying the LONE STAR book during the past week. She had been no ugly duckling even then, but her beauty now touched on a bit of regalness that seemed to fit in perfectly with the immensity of the hacienda. She reminded Jackson of Racquel Welch of the ancient holos. A very young and impressionable Racquel Welch. "I don't know. Maybe it's just because I'm hungry again."

"We could fix a light snack," she suggested.

Jackson rejected the idea instantly, though the idea of sharing a candlelit midnight meal with Rachel was certainly appealing.

"We ate dinner at a very early hour. Father insisted we eat with you." She smiled. "I'll be very honest. I'd intended to raid the refrigerator myself when I came downstairs. Then I saw you out here and wondered if anything was wrong."

"Go ahead," Jackson said, ignoring the hollow spot in his stomach. "I'd rather put up with a little hunger than succumb to the full effects of time travel sickness."

Rachel made a face. "Father said that can be pretty draining."

"He's right."

"Isn't there anything you can take for it?"

Unwillingly, Jackson's mind returned to when he and Suzanne made love the first time they jumped to Mexico and how there had been no sickness during the time traveling immediately following. Perhaps there was something he could do to prevent the after-effects of time travel, but he wasn't going to explore the possibility here. "No."

"Are you afraid?"

The brashness of the girl's question made Jackson look at her more intently. She pulled a few strands of hair from her face and returned his stare. Her eyes were dark pools above high cheekbones. Jackson looked back out at the desert. "Yes."

Her hand closed softly on his forearm. The warmth seemed electrifying. "It's all right to be afraid, Jackson," she said. "Or is that primitive macho hang-up you have denying you access to understanding your own psyche?"

"Primitive?" Jackson looked back at her unbelievingly. "I was born one hundred fifty years from now."

"And you nurse a belief that should have died in the Stone Age, Jackson. Don't you think I've noticed how you've deferred to my femininity? Remember when we went riding these past few mornings at my father's insistence? Remember how you would hold my horse's reins till I was in the saddle even though it was immediately apparent you'd never ridden a horse before?"

"I remember your father telling me the exercise would help loosen up some of the muscle injuries I've received the last few days," Jackson said. "And I remember I almost couldn't walk the second day we went riding."

Rachel grinned. "Sometimes Father forgets not everyone loves horses the way I do. He has been riding with me since I was a little girl. He says the experience has served him well in some of the pasts he has visited."

"Some of the pasts," Jackson echoed. He studied her face in the darkness. "Have you ever jumped back in time with your father?"

"No."

"Why?"

She looked away and grinned a crooked grin. "Because I'm afraid, Jackson, and I'm willing to admit it. Father would have let me, perhaps, if I insisted on it. I can control him to a degree. But I have seen the things that have happened to him. Mom and I have pulled him from the time machine more than once when he was burning up with fever from some disease that died out centuries ago. He's come back to us within that 9.6 hour time limit looking totally emaciated. Father is a big man. You've seen him. But can you imagine him weighing only a little over a hundred pounds? Less than I do now?"

Jackson shook his head.

"Well, I have. When I was fourteen. He had been researching the Apache Indians up North and had gotten captured. They used him for a slave, doing menial work around the tribe, and named him Dog. It was months before he could escape and return to the time machine. The ironic thing was, he had gone back to that particular point of time to research the rumors of a white man who had spent time with the Apache. A white man who had known enough to keep those Indians alive despite some of the worst circumstances they had ever faced. Once he got there, with the rawhide thong around his neck that he wore the whole time he was their prisoner, he realized he was the man he had gone back to research."

"An experience like that didn't make him shy away from time travelling?"

"No. And when he encountered members of the Time Police in the past, he still refused to stay away from it."

"Why are you telling me this? Is this supposed to

encourage me about climbing into the time machine tomorrow?"

"No. I just wanted you to understand, Jackson. My father is driven by something different than you. He seeks to understand, to know everything there is to know about what Temporal Projects has done to the world. To Time."

"What do you think drives me?" Jackson asked.

"Many things. You are a very complex person, Jackson Dubchek, pushed by need and desire and fear. That's not to say that my father is not a complex person. It's just that he has had time to come to grips with the twisting reality that is granted him by the time machine. You haven't."

"What makes you think that?"

She looked at him and he felt the warmth of the penetrating dark eyes. "I have watched you these past few days, Jackson. I've seen you smile and sing and scheme. But there is a detached part of yourself that slips over your face when you think you are alone. You spend a lot of time trying to justify your involvement in this thing."

"Maybe I'm just trying to forget a lot of what I've had to do since I was sucked into this."

"So you wall off a portion of yourself in order to handle it?"

Jackson didn't reply. Didn't look at her. Her observations were striking too closely to home.

"Do you intend to keep sacrificing small bits of yourself every time something goes wrong?"

Jackson shook his head. In the past week, while recovering from the beatings he had sustained from Luis, the field hand, and from the Time Police, he had enjoyed Rachel Czenlyn's company. She was young and vibrant and alive, and the daydreams she had been the catalyst for had been all to pleasant. He remembered her best on horseback, galloping, with her dark hair flowing behind her. He wasn't used to hearing the fire in her voice as he was now. Especially since it was directed at him. "Why are you mad at me?"

Rachel glanced away. "I'm not mad at you."

"Then why are we arguing?"

"We aren't arguing."

"Yes, we are."

"No, we're . . . " Rachel caught herself. "Okay. Maybe we're arguing. But I didn't want to argue."

"Neither did I."

She squeezed his hand in hers. "Look, I just see something different in you than I see in my father. He has become accustomed to whatever it is you and he face every time you strap into that damned machine. But you . . . Buddha, Jackson, you should see your face when Father talks to you about things or when you go look at the time machine. You act like you're on the edge of an abyss with a wind at your back. Like you're being forced."

"Maybe I am being forced."

"By Father?"

"No, Rachel. I want what your father wants. I just don't know if I'm the man who can get it for him. There are a lot of people who have believed in me and I feel like I've let them all down in one fashion or another." Suzanne Brelmer had believed him when he had said he would stay away from Temporal Projects. Irene of the Mnemosyne had believed he would help them despite his protests.

"Then walk away from it, Jackson. Stay here with us. With me."

Jackson looked at her, noting the wet gleam on her lower lip, wondering how her mouth would taste. An ache filled his groin. Then an image of Suzanne Brelmer's face superimposed itself on Rachel's features and neutered his sexual feelings toward the girl.

Leaning forward, Rachel kissed him.

Jackson felt her tongue flick delicately into his mouth
and he responded, pulling her toward him. Her arms wrapped around his neck as she bore him to the ground, straddling him. There was no way she wouldn't notice his erection pressing up against her. She pulled his face to her blouse and he smelled the heavy musk of her breasts, scented lightly with a delicate fragrance. Desire became a raging torrent inside Jackson's head as his hands cupped the girl's buttocks, feeling their firm softness despite the denim material.

Hooking his thumbs into her belt loops, he slowly pushed her away.

A hurt look of confusion filled her face as she rearranged her clothing, searching his face for some clue as to what she had done wrong.

"It's not you," Jackson said. "You're very attractive and desirable."

"Is it because you're friends with my father? He never interferes with my relationships."

"No. It's me, Rachel. I just know that it's something I can't do. At least not now."

"You seemed able to me."

Jackson felt his face flush, amazed at the girl's straight-forwardness. "You're asking me for a commitment, Rachel. A commitment I can't give."

"No, I'm not."

"Then why this? Why the questions?"

"This is what I'm talking about," Rachel said. "You don't just live your life anymore, Jackson. You've started searching behind everyone and everything involved with the Time Police."

Jackson held back a scathing retort. How the hell else was he supposed to feel? How could she say she wouldn't feel the same way in his shoes?

"Did you ever think, even once, that I said what I said and did what I did because I care about you?"

Watching her leave, Jackson felt the emptiness return, washing over him with tidal force.

Jackson studied the winking lights of the time

machine's control board. There seemed to be no difference in Czenlyn's machine and the ones he was used to. It was odd knowing the machine was over twenty actual years old, according to Czenlyn, yet only two years old in design from Jackson's present.

If that present still existed.

A cold feeling chugged down Jackson's throat, drowning the bile gathered there.

Are you all right?" Czenlyn asked.

Swiveling his head, Jackson looked at the big man standing in the open doorway of the time machine. "Yes." He tried to make the word sound certain.

The time machine was housed in a second basement under the Czenlyn hacienda. The spatial coordinates had been logged in the machine's computer memory under Ur, which had been the first city in ancient Sumeria. The beginning. A simple effective code.

Jackson, dressed in a too-big Temporal Projects uniform that once belonged to Tyrell Czenlyn, buckled the final straps across his chest. They had decided on the TP uniform in case the time machine was somehow drawn to the Time Police building. It would at least provide a brief camouflage.

Nausea bubbled inside Jackson's stomach. But this time it was from his own nerves rather than the time machine. That would come later, he knew.

Czenlyn blew on his glasses and cleaned them on his shirt. "Are you ready?" the big man asked.

Jackson nodded, not trusting his voice. He could feel

his hands quiver and locked them around the seat grips before Czenlyn noticed. In the seat next to him was the doctor's tattered copy of LONE STAR. They had tried to photocopy it but the machines they tried had refused to print out the information contained in the book. Every copy they had received had been the duplicate of the Ferenbach book in existence in this now of 2074. The book Jackson took with him was an anomaly. A very precious anomaly that could not be duplicated and would be the only signpost he had on the journey he had undertaken.

"Are you sure about your first jump?" Czenlyn asked.

Jackson nodded. "The first thing we need to know is if I can still get back to my present. And if it has been changed in any way. While I'm there, I'm going to check with Irene and see if any of her oral historians can help me with anything we might have overlooked."

"I'm just worried about when you might end up if you hit the same barrier I've encountered."

"I know. But I've got the POES," Jackson said, referring to the Portable Ovshinsky Energy System, "so I'll be able to charge the time machine no matter where I end up."

Over Czenlyn's shoulder, Jackson saw Rachel enter the small room. Her face looked freshly washed, devoid of any make-up. She wore jeans and a tee shirt that showed off girlish curves.

Jackson stared at her, not knowing what to say or do. He had stayed up most of the night, trying to analyze his feeling about the upcoming jump and searching for something to say to the girl. Or woman? He wasn't sure which applied. He wanted to explain about the confusion in his mind about Suzanne, to tell Rachel about the time he and Suzanne had shared the motel room, but he was afraid his words would fall on deaf ears. He had hurt her and he knew it. Unwillingly, true, but it was hurt just the same. He couldn't help but wonder if she would tell her father and what the outcome of that would be.

Buddha. Suzanne and Rachel both shared that one factor: a strong, dominant father they resisted but who took his daughter's welfare personally.

"Are you ready?" Czenlyn asked.

"Ready as I'm going to be," Jackson said. He pulled the helmet on and attached a facebag to the special clips. The Veritas knife was a heavy weight in its sheath across his heart and one of Czenlyn's fletchette pistols was tucked securely between the seats of the time machine. He was returning, but this time he wasn't going unarmed.

Czenlyn backed out of the time machine, securing the door behind him.

Jackson read his lips through the crystal windows. Buddha watch over and guide you. He nodded, then looked up at Rachel. He waved, feeling lighter of heart when she waved back, thinking maybe the rift between them wasn't so very far after all. Then he wondered if that wouldn't just create more confusion in his life later.

Damning himself for channeling his thoughts in such convoluted loops, Jackson hit the ignition switch and held n as the time machine seemed to come apart.

Massive arms reached for Jackson, picking him up with pile-driving force, whirling him through the air in a flying mare, then dumping him down, bringing him hard, splitting, shredding, shattering him across the extended knee of Wrestler Time as an explosion of oranges and ammonia ripped through the interior of the time machine, sinking fishhooks into his conscious mind as his subconscious walled itself in from the unending darkness between this moment and the next.

CHAPTER ELEVEN

A black hawk's wings swept away the stars like brilliant pinwheels of multi-colored lights, chasing a dark void outward from Jackson and the time machine in all directions till nothing and nothingness remained.

He felt himself swell inside the time machine till it seemed his flesh pressed against the hull, but his eyes told him the glittering array of dashboard lights never moved from in front of him.

Perspiration dripped off of him as invisible pincers wrung him out. The droplets cascaded down his face, smelling like oranges and ammonia and coffee grounds.

To his left, a green warted frog riding a pink pig in a mini-skirt passed him, flailing away with the riding crop it held in one green fist.

Jackson stared after the duo, fascinated, absorbed in the way the blackness of no-space/no-time seemed to stain the pig's feet and tremble as it passed.

He closed his eyes, waiting for the nausea.

The time machine skipped like a flat stone across a smooth lake. Only upside down.

Then it turned.

Twirled.

Righted itself.

And fled across whatever it was that existed in nonexistence.

What if he didn't make the jump? Jackson wondered. What if, instead of being rebounded as Czenlyn had been, what if he hung here? Frozen. Trapped as surely as a fly in amber. Would he become one of the unusual sights seen by future travellers? Or past travellers? But wouldn't he have passed himself all ready if that was going to happen?

Or would he be frozen now and pass himself later, in the past? Would the memories stretch across his personal history till he remembered that it HAD happened even though it was only happening now?

He blinked his eyes open, forcing himself to watch.

Nothing.

Buddha, nothing.

No sensation.

Was he moving?

Panic welled up inside him and he forced himself to

leave the restraining straps alone and not disengage them.

A rectangle drifted into view from whatever distance was possible in the middle of nothing. It flipped. Turned end over end as it twirled around. Somehow the time machine became a mirror image of its movements, tracking onto a collision course.

The rectangle turned, flipped, twisted slower. Slower. Slower. Stopped.

It dwarfed the time machine, as tall as a three-story building. An interior light flared from somewhere within/behind it, casting garish shadows over the rectangle's faces. Two faces. One at either end of the rectangle, presented profile. One face was clean, unmarked. The other, scarred. Two halves of an uncertain whole.

A number of gravities pressed Jackson back into his seat. He tried to move and succeeded in wiggling his fingers.

Recollection of the double-faced rectangle preyed on his mind like a caterpillar nursing at a tobacco leaf. Methodically chewing through memories.

A playing card, Jackson told himself. It's just a playing card. It will pass.

The caterpillar in his mind seized another leaf and masticated happily.

Recognition haunted Jackson. The two faces were from the crystaled picture he had taken from the street punks in 2250 who had been paid to kill him. The picture had been of Jackson, but a future Jackson. One who had been horribly disfigured and mutilated.

The bottom face smiled at him, still in profile. It was his face, Jackson realized. The face he wore now. Unmarred. Whole.

The top face leered at him and madness seemed to jump from the single eye. The ear presented in this profile was a burned and twisted lump beside a starburst scar that sent scattered and broken spider's legs across the face. The right arm ended abruptly, a shard of bone gleamed from bloody flesh.

"I am you," the bottom face said.

"You am I," the top face said.

The giant card spun as the voices continued to chant.

Jackson screamed but couldn't hear himself over the voices of the spinning faces. He still had the crystaled picture from whatever maybe/possibility/eventuality that it had come from. Despite its threat, despite the feelings of hopelessness and despair it brought, he had been unable to release it or even tell Czenlyn of it.

"I am you," the bottom/top face said.

`"You am I," the top/bottom face said.

The giant card folded itself neatly and spun till it was presented edge first to Jackson. For a moment he could see only a darker line drawn across a darkest darkness. Then legs stepped out on both sides and pulled the rest of the body with them.

The giant stood on nothing, facing Jackson, wearing both of Jackson's faces. It was dressed in the doublet and armor of the Jack of Hearts, carrying the shiny sword in its left hand.

"I am you," the left side of the mouth said.

"You am I," the right side of the mouth said.

Without warning, the giant brought the double-edged sword up. A thousand suns gleamed from the polished blade as it reached the apex of its swing. Then it came down.

Cutting.

Slashing.

Crashing.

Biting.

Into the fabric of Jackson Elgin Dubchek's soul. He felt himself sheared in twain. Burning hot and cold. Shapeless and shaped. He screamed, knew he screamed, but heard nothing except the unending chant.

Then the darkness unfolded octopus tentacles and pulled him in close. He tasted hot lizard breath in his nostrils, then fell into nothing.

The time machine jolted into a present that was filled with a darkness only a little less oppressive than the one Jackson had just left.

He tried to check his surroundings through the crystal windows in between bouts of severe wretching but couldn't keep his eyes open. Gasping mouthfuls of sick air jetted between his lips as his stomach reached for something that wasn't there. He grabbed his stomach and leaned forward as he fought to find a way around the cramps.

Gradually, the seizures lessened and allowed him control over his body again. He ripped the mask bag from his face angrily and used the adhesive seal to close it. Buddha, why did it have to be so bad each time? You would have thought he could get used to it after awhile.

Still shaking, he glanced out through the darkness again, knowing the time machine's security system could protect him from most everything short of being run over by a tank.

He blinked his eyes and studied the concrete wall on the other side of the crystal window. If he had jumped to his programmed coordinates, the wall was supposed to be there. Unless the time machine had malfunctioned again and dropped him somewhere, somewhen else. He checked the readout again. 2250. Near the end of the 9.6 window he had open for his return. He was home if everything had went as planned.

Unless the time machine had dropped him in Wheeling, West Virginia again.

Buddha, please don't let it be Wheeling.

Anxiously, he peered through the other crystal windows after releasing the seat restraints. He felt relieved when he didn't see the stacks of wrecked automobiles that were a signpost of Wheeling, West Virginia, 1968-1969.

Instead the blank emptiness of a bunkerlike reinforced-concrete parking garage stretched out behind the time machine. He had been there one time before. With Bryan, the future Time Policeman who had died helping Jackson and Suzanne procure a time machine from Temporal Projects to attempt Rosita Alvarez's rescue.

Cautiously, Jackson pushed the time machine's door open and stepped out. The musky smell of the enclosed space flooded his nostrils. A gentle gust of wind pushed leafy sailboats across the concrete ocean of the parking garage, making tiny scratchy noises to mark their passage.

Feeling reluctant, but knowing the penalty if he was caught, Jackson left the fletchette gun locked in the time machine. The Second Republic had harsh laws concerning any automatic weapons in the hands of citizens. He resettled the Veritas dagger across his chest, making a mental note to ask Irene if her costumers couldn't come up with a suitable sheath for the knife instead of the make-shift one he had. The cloth rigging he had thrown together had chafed at him during the times he had worn it during his stay at Czenlyn's hacienda.

The knife was important to him, representing many things. For one, the most obvious and most distasteful, it was a weapon. Double-edged matte finish with a polished black handle. It would fit in with any culture, any time. The dagger's only distinguishing feature was the maker's mark just below the hilt guard in the form of a tiny crane. It also served as a reminder that Jackson had friends and compatriots hidden in the folds of Time. The female Tysonyllyn had given it to him and had surprised him by knowing some of his history even though she had been in the past. Finally, it was a tool to help ensure his survival. With it he could fashion many other things. He had had no specific training in woodlands survival, but he had encountered many ideas for carving fish hooks, bows and arrows, as well and building shelters in much of the literature and biographies he had studied during his lingual training, as well as during his tenure at New Ninevah.

Jackson closed the door and pressed his face and hands against the window of the time machine, engaging the security system that would protect it while he was gone. No one would be able to use it. Unless they brought along his face and hands. Shivering at the thought, Jackson walked to the back of the machine and pulled the charge cord from the access port and walked to a yellow and black striped support pillar toward the center of the garage area. He located the electrical outlet and plugged the charge cord in, hoping the building was still tapped into some power source. The blue light on the charge cord flared into quiet life, indicating the connection satisfied the time machine's 120 volt 60 cycle demand that would bring the batteries back to full power within five hours.

Tucking the LONE STAR book under his shirt, Jackson walked through the parking garage's open maw. Staying within the shadows of the surrounding buildings and the trees, he made his way to the street.

He could barely make out the carved marble head with the elaborate pseudo-Greek headdress just over the awning. The rows of broken lights over the double doorway hadn't been replaced since his last visit here.

How long had it been since he had last seen Irene? Jackson tried to remember and found it almost impossible. His sense of time had been running at different speeds than the old woman's. No more than two days, he felt sure. Three at the most.

Feeling naked and vulnerable and exposed, Jackson trotted across the street, noticing the light rain for the first time. The street felt slick and unsure under his shoes and he had to move slower than he wanted to.

He took the stairs leading up to the Landers Auditorium and Vandivort Center for the Preservation of Live Performance Arts two at a time.

What had happened in the short time he had been gone from the Mnemosyne? Brelmer had been so close behind him in Mexico. Was it possible that someone had uncovered the hiding place the historians had picked out for themselves?

Trying to ignore the prickling fear that trailed across the back of his neck, Jackson opened one of the doors and took the right-hand stairway, ignoring the left. He wasn't sure exactly where it led. His previous visits to Irene had been insanely rushed things and there had been no time for social amenities or exploration.

The hallway at the second landing was dark but a distant beat drew Jackson to a side door. He opened it slightly and peeked in. At least two dozen dancers gathered in the large room, circled around an area of the floor that glittered with multicolored lights. In their center, a young man dressed in a white three-piece suit preformed gyrations that would be considered clearly sexual in most cultures Jackson had studied. The surrounding men and women, dressed in outlandish antique costumes as well, clapped their hands in time to the upbeat music.

Regretfully, Jackson closed the door quietly, making sure the lock made no noise as it snicked back into place. Idly, he wondered if he would have been able to follow the music with Odar'a, his dulcimer. Recovering Odar'a, even if he learned nothing at all from Irene, would mean a lot to him.

He turned in the darkness of the hallway and trudged up to the third floor landing, thinking it would be just like Irene to schedule late-night practices and keep the lights off in the building. But it had been dark last time too, he remembered. He dismissed the thought, thinking it was probably a reflection of the tight-fisted control the woman held over the Mnemosyne. A Fedcredit saved is a Fedcredit earned. He could hear her all ready.

Without warning, a figure separated itself from the stairway wall, stepping forward toward Jackson. There was no mistaking the inherent threat in the approach.

A broken shaft of light splintered across the figure as

the right arm swept upward. The heavy machete blade gleamed brightly. The dulled ivory of the hockey mask, dotted with black holes that somehow echoed the features of an insane face, flared to unholy life.

A Time Policeman? Jackson's mind screamed at him. But he ignored the question, turning to bolt down the stairs.

"Hey, wait," a young voice said.

Jackson paused, his legs trembling under him with the urge to make the mad dash back to the time machine. He looked over his shoulder, hands braced on the stairway railing to hurl himself over to the next landing.

The figure lowered the machete and raised the hockey mask. "Hey, it's okay. I didn't mean to scare you."

The face under the mask was young, freckled, showing only embarrassment.

Jackson peeled his fingers from the railing, feeling his heart still thudding painfully inside his chest. It was only then that he recognized the hockey mask from one of the old holo horror films brother Martin had always insisted on renting from the vid store. He tried to remember how many sequels the horror character had been in and failed. The only thing that stuck out, besides the nightmares, had been the ghoulish way the killer's body seemed to get progressively worse in each film.

"Sorry about that," the teenager said. He held the hockey mask and machete in his left hand and stuck out his right. "Terry Jones. I'm an actor here." He gave Jackson a lop-sided grin. "I specialize in fright holos."

Forcing a smile he didn't feel, Jackson stuck out his hand. "You're very effective, Terry Jones."

"Thanks." The boy lowered his eyes to the hockey mask ." The boy lowered his eyes to the hockey mask in his hand and touched it reverently. "I'm glad somebody appreciates what I can do."

Thinking that he never said he appreciated the boy's performance, Jackson said, "I'm here to see Irene. Do you know where I can find her."

"Sure." A troubled look filled the boy's face. "Look, you're aren't going to tell her about this, are you?" He indicated the hockey mask and machete.

"No."

The boy smiled. "Good. Irene wants me to spend more time with Shakespeare and less time with these things. But I feel the horror holos need to be preserved as well. There's nothing like the thrill of watching something gory and obscene happen right before your eyes. It gets you over your daily troubles and creates a menace you can deal with on a purely physical plane. No stress, no menial chores. Just a fight to live."

Remembering his first impression that the hockey mask covered the altered features of a Time Policeman, Jackson agreed about the fight to live part. It was easier to react to a threat from Brelmer and his Temporal Projects counterparts than it was to seek retribution against intradepartmental strife at New Ninevah

Library.

"But Irene doesn't see it that way," the boy said dismally. "She has her own ideas about things and it's hard to get her to change her mind. You know what I'm talking about?"

Jackson nodded. He knew. He was about to challenge the woman's iron will again himself. He followed the boy up another flight of rickety stairs, not surprised to find they were headed for the main classroom. It was where he had seen Irene most, and where he had met her the first time, marshalling her acting students like a general preparing for war. Though, in a sense, Jackson knew that simile wasn't far off-base. The Mnemosyne Historians were at war. Fighting the vague memories of half-history that wended their way through the time barriers as well as eluding capture or conviction by the large resources at Temporal Projects.

So far, Irene and her cohorts had only been proven guilty of being insufferable at Senate hearings during which time they disputed various historical events and lobbied for the right to investigate the past for themselves. There had been no mention of involvement with Jackson Dubchek as yet, thank Buddha. Even though Irene was willing to risk herself and her people, Jackson knew that once it could be proven that the Mnemosyne were travelling into the past and were fighting against operations ordained by the Second Republic through Voxner, the operation here in Springfield would be shut down. If not "accidently" conveniently bombarded with an aerial shipment of toxic waste.

Jackson wondered if Irene had mentioned that possibility to her followers. Then decided she probably had not. The woman was the present Tysonyllyn, leader of the Historians, and was responsible for more than just the lives of the people who believed in their movement. She lived with the knowledge that memory of the past could be ripped away from them all, even as she knew that it trickled through her fingers at a constant flow. There was no damming the tide of loss, she had told Jackson before. The best they could hope for now was to slow it. Until some new safeguards were put on Temporal Projects and Senator Voxner and Brelmer were ousted from control.

The boy left Jackson at the door, pointing toward Irene, and discreetly disappearing.

Feeling like a schoolboy late for class, Jackson rapped softly on the wooden door leading into the room.

Irene swiveled her head, changing her attention from the dark and empty stage before her to Jackson. She sat in the front row, her posture correct with no sign of tiredness to betray her. Even across the distance of the room Jackson could feel her presence, demanding and unyielding.

"Jackson," she said, "come in." She patted an empty chair to her right.

He moved into the room, wondering what thoughts she had been chasing while sitting in the darkness.

A vocal command from her caused two electric torches, positioned on either side of the curtain-covered stage, to spring into glowing life.

Even though he had talked to her a number of times now, Jackson still had a hard time believing such a sense of presence could radiate from such a small person. Though less than one meterpointeight himself, he was a giant when compared to Irene. She was thin and dark haired, a reed that refused to bend to any breeze.

"How long has it been, Jackson?" Irene asked.

Jackson sat, uncertain of himself the way he always was in the woman's presence. "I don't know. I was about to ask you the same thing."

"For me, less than three days." She reached up to smooth away his hair.

It was the first personal interest Jackson could recall the woman taking in him and he wondered what it would cost. Her fingers felt cool and cruelly thin, brittle, yet possessing steel marrow.

"I can see by the way you hold yourself that it has been far longer than that for you. These old eyes are used to watching body movements, Jackson, so don't act so surprised. Acting is both an art and a way of life, and each is reflected in the other till there is no way to be certain which originated which."

"Over a month," Jackson answered.

"And did you find out about the Holocaust?"

"Yes."

"It existed?"

Jackson nodded.

Irene straightened the dark green dress she wore. "Why did you spend so much time there?"

It wasn't there and it wasn't by choice," Jackson said. In brief terms, yet striving to make the woman feel some of the fear and uncertainty he had experienced, he told her of his trip back with Suzanne Brelmer and his eventual displacement in Mexico.

"I've heard of Tyrell Czenlyn," Irene said when he was finished, "but the history we have of him is tangled and uncertain, like most everything else we have been able to salvage from the past. I recall that he was a brilliant surgeon but had disappeared in 2248. I had not connected him with Temporal Projects. That adds another wrinkle to the mosaic Voxner and his bullyboys are weaving of our history." She glanced at Jackson again. "He has been gone all that time and no one from TP has been able to locate him?"

"Yes, but that may change now. Two Time Policemen tried to apprehend us within the last week of his time line. I wouldn't be surprised if he was identified."

"He was," Irene said idly.

Fear prickled along the back of Jackson's neck. His voice was hoarse when he spoke. "What do you mean he WAS?"

"In one of the versions of history we have, Dr. Tyrell Czenlyn organized a revolt against the Second Republic in 2074 and was killed."

The woman's flat, emotionless words rolled over

Jackson, tearing at the fabric of reality he had so carefully wrapped around himself during his time jumps.

CHAPTER TWELVE

Jackson gave up trying to hold back the anger surging inside him. He pushed himself out of the folding chair, aware that Irene had not moved. "Why the hell did you have to tell me that?" he asked. His words echoed the length of the classroom.

"Because you needed to know," Irene said. She sat still, focusing those piercing eyes on him, keeping her hands folded on her lap.

"Why did I need to know?"

"I don't want you clinging to Czenlyn, Jackson," the woman said. "I can tell from the way you talk about him that the man has made an impression on you. You're all ready talking of going back there."

"You're wrong about the revolt," Jackson said. He stood before her, anger giving him the strength to meet Irene's withering gaze.

"I can show you in our archives if you wish."

"Damn you, Irene, I don't want to see. Right or wrong, I don't want to see."

"Don't be foolish, Jackson. You are a man alone at this moment, cut off from friends and family. You are hunted everywhere, in any decade you think you can escape to. I've recently learned that Praetor Brelmer has issued new orders concerning you. If found by a Time Policeman, they are to check you for a scar on your shoulder and, if it is found, you are to be shot dead at once."

Jackson involuntarily reached for the scarred shoulder, massaging it, even more aware of the nerve-deadened spots on front and back than ever.

"Information is the best defense you have now, Jackson," Irene said. "And the safest harbor you'll find in whatever year you find yourself in."

"You're wrong about Czenlyn and the revolt," Jackson said. "I just left him. Czenlyn is in hiding. He has no intention of challenging anyone."

Irene said nothing.

A shadow darkened the doorway to the main classroom and Jackson watched the woman wave it away without looking to see who it was.

"Why do you do this?" Jackson asked.

"Do what?" Irene asked.

"Give me half-truths, twist things around when you tell me about them."

"I have never lied to you, Jackson."

"And you've never told me quite the whole truth either, Irene."

The woman said nothing.

"Damnit! Listen to me. You're so involved in straightening out the history we've been given to live with that you're forgetting Brelmer and Voxner and the past aren't the only enemies the Mnemosyne have. The future is still out there, Irene. And it's waiting with bared fangs. At least some of it is. Buddha, there are Time Rebels who are attempting to find a way to control the flow of the past even as much as Temporal Projects is. Only we, you and I and Brelmer and Voxner, we are all the past to them. We are accessible. They are not. The event that wiped out my brother's wife and children was triggered by some faction of those future rebels, working for whatever grand design they think will preserve their present."

"I know that," Irene said. A hostile edge hovered in her voice. "Remember, Bryan worked with us."

Jackson refused to back down from her, feeling a warm red haze threaten to engulf him. "Bryan died for you, Irene. Hell, I've killed for you. For whatever dream you and the rest of the Mnemosyne have been chasing. You sit here, in this antique building filled with dead arts, with children who have yet to even taste the thrill of life, and you program them to be recepta-

cles of a history that may be nothing more than a fairy
tale. You weave your webs just as surely as Brelmer
and Voxner do. And people die as a result."

"You can't compare me to them."

Jackson leveled a finger at her. "I can. I've been
there. I've worked for the Mnemosyne and Temporal
Projects and I can tell you honestly I can't find a difference."

Silence filled the dark classroom. The weak glow of
the electric torches illuminated the pinched planes of
Irene's face.

Jackson breathed in through his nose and out through
his mouth in an effort to calm himself. Never had he let
his anger take control of him so fiercely.

"There is one difference between us and Voxner's
minions," Irene said after a moment. "We are not trying
to track you down and kill you."

"But who was largely responsible for turning me into
a rabbit for the Time Police greyhounds?"

"You were all ready there. I just elected to utilize
your involvement to the best advantage for all of us."

"You sought me out, Irene. I didn't come looking for
you."

"Bryan wasn't the only one knocking on your apartment door that night, Jackson. Chances are he saved
your life then."

"And perhaps the Time Police Brelmer sent were
there to only frighten me some more."

Irene flicked her dark eyes into direct contact with

Jackson's. "Is that how you want to live your life, then? Frightened?"

Jackson's voice was calmer, more steady. "I'm frightened now, Irene. I was frightened the whole week I spent contemplating coming here. I spend almost as much time looking over my shoulder as I do looking forward."

Irene pushed up out of the chair and Jackson felt an almost physical intensity bump into him, testing. "You've changed, Jackson."

Jackson didn't say anything, waiting, blowing on the embers of his anger, determined to voice his own mind this time.

"You are frightened, yes, but you don't let it rule you anymore."

"Don't play games with me, Irene. You used me."

"There aren't many options left in this world we share, Jackson. I'm not proud of what I did to you. Just as I'm not proud of some of the other things I've been forced to do to preserve our history. But I've had little choice. I'll have to live with the things I've done to other people a long time."

"At least you'll be living."

Irene ignored the sarcasm. She turned away from Jackson and stared at the curtained stage area. The electric torches were reflected from the scattered sequins sewn into the heavy velvet drapes. "Why did you come back?"

Jackson softened his voice. "To let you know about

the Holocaust and to get your help."

Irene stared at him, arching her eyebrows. "I thought you didn't trust me."

"I don't. Not wholly. You exist to serve your search for a correct version of history, Irene. I intend to do things on a more personal basis."

"What kind of foundation is that to build a working relationship on?"

"Not good," Jackson admitted, "but it's more honest than any we've had before."

A small, sad smile touched the woman's thin lips, quickly winking back out of view. "You have learned while you've been away."

"I've been given no choice." Jackson slipped the LONE STAR book out from under his shirt and held it out. "Czenlyn gave this to me. It details the history of Texas the state rather than Texas the nation. When I encountered Vaughn Tysonyllyn in 2183, he was aware that the history concerning Texas had been altered. I wasn't sure if you were aware of it or not. Czenlyn said Texas had been a state when he left in 2248."

Irene crossed the wooden floor, taking the book reverently. "There are conflicting stories about Texas," she said as she turned the pages with care. "We've held to the statehood theory, but this confirms it."

"I tried to get it copied in 2074 but the machines wouldn't copy this version."

"So you are going to investigate this matter?"

Jackson took a deep breath, feeling as if the firm

stance he had taken with the woman had just been turned to quicksand. "Yes."

"Will you let me know what you find out?"

Jackson hesitated, thinking of what Irene had told him about Czenlyn and the revolt. If things went as she predicted, someone still needed to know, and, at the moment, his life was an insubstantial thing to record on. "Yes."

"I suppose you'll be wanting this back?" Irene asked, indicating the book.

"Yes. I promised it back."

"Let me have it long enough to get it copied."

"A machine may not do it," Jackson warned.

"If it doesn't, I'll have some of the documents staff hand write it. They can get the job done in an hour or so with the amount of people they have here tonight."

Jackson nodded.

"I'll have Cheryl fix something for you in the kitchen while Ray brings your things."

Jackson thought about the nausea that would plague him during the upcoming time jump back to Texas, balanced it against the fact that he had not eaten for the previous twelve hours and that he might not be able to get a meal in Texas when he got there, and nodded.

Irene tucked the book under her arm and said, "I wish it didn't have to be this way between us."

"I wish it didn't either," Jackson said honestly. "But that's not my decision."

"Inferring that it is mine?"

"You're still using me, Irene, and you'll continue to use me whenever you get the chance. You and I both know that. I'm the only person you know who can come and go through the past."

"You make it sound like I am some ice-hearted witch."

"No. I just know you are blinded by the destiny you think you are serving."

"There is no way I can convince you otherwise? You could be a valuable asset to the Mnemosyne. We are more closely connected than you think."

Jackson took the crystaled picture of his future self from his pocket and handed it to her. "Then tell me about this."

Irene glanced at it then quickly handed it back. "I can't. I'm sorry."

The anger returned, threatening to consume Jackson. "This is my life we're talking about, Irene. I may become the mad, scarred thing in that picture unless you tell me what you know." He paused, waiting for an answer, not surprised when it didn't come. "Damnit, Irene, I know that somewhere in your phalanx of historians there has to be a person that can tell me about my involvement in the past. You produced that picture of Suzanne and me with Rosita Alvarez easily enough, knowing the shock value of it alone would make me take the trip. I know there has got to be further mention of me and the things I have done in the past. For all I know, this happened somewhere in the past."

"Perhaps even in the revolt I told you about," Irene agreed.

Stung, Jackson looked away. Was that why she warned him away from going back to see Czenlyn once he had some answers about the Texas situation? Or was she putting him onto a false trail? Buddha, he had already dug a grave for whatever line of logic he chose to follow. He had no doubts that Irene knew that.

"What would you have me do, Jackson? Promise you invincibility as you meander through those twisted trails in Time? Promise you that you'll never die if you never reach the year 1492? Don't you understand that history is being rewritten even as we speak? This book should underscore that fact. I could tell you what we know but that would only serve to influence whatever decisions you make. Even the picture I showed you the first time we met would have vanished from existence if you had not made the decision to go back. I took a chance that it would tip the scales in our favor. In favor of the correct version of history."

Jackson said nothing, knowing the woman was right.

"I'll see you in an hour," Irene said as walked through the door. "I really am sorry things can't be better between us, Jackson."

Jackson glanced up at her, noticed how ramrod straight her spine was despite the burden he knew she carried, and said, "Me too."

Hoban was waiting for Brelmer in the transmission rooms. An unhappy look flirted with the surgeon's face but disappeared entirely once the man saw the Praetor. A stainless steel and plastic box hardly larger than a small suitcase sat at Hoban's feet.

Brelmer strode through the doorway, working to keep his features passive. Anger still seethed through him from his visit with Voxner. He had known it would come to this sooner or later. Shiva, he had known and had closed his eyes to the possibility. Yet, he had not expected Voxner to be so damned flagrant about it.

Unnameable power over events and individuals flowed through the glascrete and steel walls of Temporal Projects. And Voxner was not the man to have been placed in charge of TP. It was like letting a fox guard the henhouse.

But who was Brelmer to inform? He had carefully guided his rise to his present position by currying few political favors. Chances were, he had been virtually unknown to most members of the Senate until his assignment to Temporal Projects. Now he had to bear the stigmata of being Ronald Voxner's handyman in Time.

Even if he could tell someone about the scheme Voxner was concocting and carrying out tonight, Brelmer knew he could never protect his family from the Senator's wrath. An aide had told him of Voxner's singling June out at the party last night, though the man had had no idea of why, and Brelmer had felt the foundations of personal security crumbling around him. Suzanne was all ready in a precarious position if Voxner wanted to bring charges. The kidnap case Brelmer had logged against Dubchek was only flimsy at best. Nothing that would keep away the legal dungbeetles Voxner kept under his thumb.

Brelmer glared at the silver box at Hoban's feet.

As if everything else wasn't enough, he now had this to contend with too. A baby. Only days conceived, and all ready it could be used as a lever against him.

But it was Suzanne's baby. His grandchild. And another liability. One more pawn to play in the chess games Voxner made of personal and political life.

Unless he was able to spirit it away and reclaim it at a time when his family life had started to settle.

Suzanne didn't need the additional responsibility at the moment. It would have been too much for her to deal with. And Brelmer had an idea of how to make things much easier for them all. At least for awhile. As a father, it was the least he could do.

At his approach, Hoban reached down for the clasp of the silver box and took it from the floor.

"Are you ready, doctor?" Brelmer asked as he paused for a moment in front of Hoban. He swept his gaze around the facility, watching the jump team preparing the chamber for Voxner's entourage that would be arriving in only a few short minutes. They were crack operators and talk was kept to a minimum.

"Yes, Colonel."

The dispirited tone in the surgeon's voice grated against the thin skin guarding Brelmer's ire. "Is something the matter, Dr. Hoban?"

Hoban looked away, shifting the silver case gently to his other hand.

"I asked you a question, doctor. I expect the courtesy of an answer." Brelmer put an edge in his voice that underlined his words.

Hoban fidgeted and almost reached for the narcosmoker in his smock. "I don't feel right about this, sir."

"Why?"

"What if something happens to the baby?"

"When I asked you earlier, you seemed sure another time jump would leave the fetus unharmed."

"You asked me how it survived the first time jump, Colonel. You didn't say a thing about subjecting the child to a second jump."

"Then you don't trust your own judgment?"

Hoban visibly squirmed. "Yes, sir. I do."

"Perhaps you just don't like having your theories tested."

"What about your daughter, sir? Doesn't she need to know about this?"

"She will when the time is right," Brelmer said. He started toward the time machine on the left, noticing the surgeon fall in behind him. He opened the door for Hoban and watched as the man carefully belted the box to a seat. "Crismeyre," Brelmer called.

One of the time techs looked up, noticed Brelmer for the first time, and brought a package over. Paress Linnet's neat handwriting adorned the upper left hand corner, addressing the contents for Praetor Centurion Lieutenant Colonel Brelmer's use only.

Brelmer accepted the package and got in the time machine on the other side. He tapped the shoulder-com and ordered a com-connek with Costuming. He talked as he strapped in, noting the grayish caste of Hoban's face. "Paress?"

"Yes, Colonel."

"I received your package. Everything was in order?"

"Yes, sir."

"How are the Dunkers' costumes coming?"

"We finished with the last of them a few minutes ago. They're ready for you to pick up."

"Good." Brelmer fitted the helmet over his head, feeling the coolness of the inner lining kiss his bare scalp. It took a moment longer to adjust the face-mask over his beard. "Make sure the delivery of those costumes is delayed for another fifteen minutes."

"But, sir, Senator Voxner made it very clear that this was a rush order."

"It is, Paress. I want those costumes in fifteen minutes and not one minute later." Brelmer tapped the shoulder-com off and reached for the systems initiation switch. A small glow of satisfaction dawned inside him when he saw Hoban flinch and grab for the sides of the seat.

Fifteen minutes wasn't much time, Brelmer thought as he felt the machine start to shimmy and shake under him, but that was all the time it took to open a doorway to forever. Or at least, a doorway to a hiding place for Suzanne's unborn baby.

Still fighting the residual effects of the time jump, Brelmer walked down the dark corridor of the building, using the infra-red optics of his crystal eyes while Hoban followed uncertainly behind him. The silver box containing his grandchild was a light weight at the end of his arm and swung easily with his stride. A mini-Matthews rode his right hip under the suitcoat that had been one of the garments Paress had forwarded for this solo journey.

Using a forefinger, Brelmer flicked on the reception unit tucked neatly behind his right ear, feeling the microphone pulse into quick life against his neck. "Wells?" he called softly. His voice echoed the length of the subterranean corridor.

"Here, Colonel."

"Have you got a fix on me?"

"Yes, sir."

"I'm bringing along a passenger and a case, Sergeant, and I want security kept tight. This is strictly a need-to-know operation."

"Alabama, Colonel."

"Are the perimeters secured?"

"Yes, sir. You came in clean as a whistle."

"Any backwash along this time line?"

"Not that the machines could pick up, sir. I'd stake my life that you arrived unaccompanied."

Thinking of Voxner and what the Senator might do if he found out the reason for this jump, Brelmer said, "You might be doing just that, Sergeant."

"Yes, sir. The recovery team is standing by."

"Very good, Sergeant. Execute recovery." A slight hiss sounded behind Brelmer and he turned his head, watching two dark shadows separate themselves from the walls and approach Hoban.

The surgeon looked panicked and held his hands up before him. "Colonel?" His voice held a note of hysteria.

"Purely precautionary, doctor. You have nothing to worry about."

The two Time Policemen closed in on Hoban. One of them put his arms on the man to restrain him while the other pressed a hypo-spray to Hoban's neck. A swish of pressurized gas signalled the release of the anesthetic. Hoban slumped forward and would have fallen if the Time Policeman hadn't caught him.

Brelmer stepped through the opening he had deliberately passed while leading Hoban. One of the guards shouldered the surgeon's inert form. "Take him to my office," the Praetor said, "and make sure he stays there."

"Alabama, Colonel."

Brelmer led the way through the underground maze, navigating through the ability given him by the crystal eyes. A steady drip of water echoed in the narrow walkway. Brelmer had had the leak installed the day he converted the building's lower chamber into a command chamber for himself. It masked the noise the false walls would make if the outer security wall was breached. Gradual shiftings would take the intruder through a long trip to the other side of the building. If the person wasn't identified as a substantial threat and disposed of accordingly.

Above ground, the structure was the Lester Dent Building, located in New York City of 1939. It was Brelmer's favorite place to visit when he felt a need to escape the pressures of Temporal Projects. The Dent Building overlooked the World's Fair and was only minutes away by cab. The marvels introduced at the Fair were incredible by the standard of 1939, even for decades later for some of them. But for Brelmer they were creations of historical importance, outdated and outmoded. Still, while walking the hallways and through the exhibits, he never failed to feel some of the awe that had gone into their arrangement.

Brelmer had spent hours wandering through the fairgrounds, putting the problems of paradoxes and Voxner behind him when he could. He had discovered the World's Fair quite by accident while securing the Manhattan Project from any Time Rebel tampering. An ad in a local newspaper had drawn him to the affair on

May 2.

The sight of the Perisphere and the Trylon drew him into the heart of the Fair. The Perisphere was a golf-ball shaped globe two-hundred feet in diameter that had jets of water shooting up from its base so it looked like it was floating. The Trylon was a seven-hundred foot steel needle. A frail looking metal ramp squirmed around the Perisphere and connected to the Trylon. It wasn't until Brelmer had stood in the center of the ramp and looked down over the rest of the gaily colored Fair that he felt the enormity of this particular position in Time. So much discovery lay ahead of the people around him. In only thirty years the moon would know the imprint of its first astronaut's boot. So much knowledge in so many short years.

And standing there, with the chill winds whipping around him, Brelmer had envied the scientists of this century. So much was within their grasp. So many new things lay waiting to be discovered, found out, guessed at. All the sciences would make tremendous leaps in the coming decades. It wasn't like being given control over a project that knew no controls.

Shaking the thoughts from his mind, Brelmer took a fresh grip on the silver case containing Suzanne's baby and laid his palm on a section of the wall he had arrived at. He had often wondered if Voxner really knew about the cubbyhole he had put together and maintained here. Just as he had often wondered if he truly had the loyalty of the people stationed here or if they belonged to the

Senator.

Well, he would know soon enough, Brelmer thought as he entered the opening left by a section of the wall sliding away. He just hadn't been aware that the stakes would be so high.

CHAPTER THIRTEEN

Jackson found Irene in the same classroom they had talked in earlier. He felt sleepy and satiated, a little too full and he knew he would regret it soon enough. But the food had seemed to bring back his strength as well as a more positive mental attitude.

"Feeling better?" Irene asked. She sat in the same seat she had before. The LONE STAR book and a sheaf of papers were stacked neatly in her lap.

"Yes. Thank you." Jackson sat a few seats down, not feeling comfortable with a close proximity to the woman. There had been too many hurtful words and too many unresolved differences of opinion.

"The book contained a lot of valuable information,"

Irene said. "Some of the things we found in there interlocks with a lot of theories some of my people have advanced but have never been able to prove."

"Good. Were you able to copy it?"

Irene nodded. "Apparently, this is still a viable subject in our present."

"Why couldn't I get it copied in 2074?"

"I couldn't tell you, Jackson," Irene said. "Judging from what you've told me, there must be some physical laws at work that we know nothing of as yet that prevents an anomaly to exist. The 2074 you were stranded in may not touch the time-line that gave birth to this book."

Jackson nodded. "Czenlyn mentioned that. He said he thought that was what Voxner and Temporal Projects was gradually doing: peeling away time-lines they didn't want until only a central core remained."

"We've hypothesized that, but we've never had proof."

"Yes, but that would mean Czenlyn is an anomaly as well."

"The book can exist in that time, Jackson, but it can't be copied. Therefore, it is reasonable to assume anomalies can exist. This book, Czenlyn, yourself. All are anomalies and all exist in that 2074. Even the influence of Bernardo O'Higgins and him compatriots in the march toward nationalism for Texas instead of statehood is an anomaly. Only that anomaly is backed by the considerable forces of Temporal Projects and the string of incidents Voxner has engineered over Buddha only knows how many years."

Jackson turned the thought over in his mind, wondering which end of it to consider first. It was like the old question of which came first? The chicken or the egg? And, as always, the answer depended on which perspective you chose.

"In your journeys," Irene said, "you may find that more anomalies exist in the flow of Time now than bits of real history."

"I know," Jackson replied, focusing on the electric torches on either side of the curtained stage. "It's so easy to get lost along the way."

"So which will it be, Jackson?" Irene asked.

Jackson looked at her, feeling the pressure of her piercing gaze.

"Will you continue your quest for information to help Czenlyn in what will be, I promise you, a fruitless chase? Or will you stay here to help us?"

"Either way, Irene, I'm going to end up risking my life."

"I know."

"The problem is, I get the feeling you all ready know what my decision is. Somewhere in those files of yours, you have information that has told you what path I'm going to choose and what is going to happen to me once I do."

Irene remained silent.

"That's what I hold against you, Irene. You know

something of my future, at least the part or parts of it that lie in the past, and you refuse to tell me about it." Jackson stood, shouldering his pack, feeling the neck of the dulcimer tap against the back of his leg gently. "That's what keeps me from believing in you and the Mnemosyne movement. You're a hard woman. Buddha knows you have to be in your position, but I could never work with you without wondering every time you asked me to do something. I know, without a doubt, that you would willingly send me to my death if it would advance the cause you are groping so blindly for."

"I wouldn't have to grope so blindly," Irene said in a level voice, "if you would stay and help."

"I can't, Irene. Buddha knows I would have a few months ago if for no other reason than the sense of duty you attempt to foist off on me so readily. But, like you've said, I've changed. I've seen too much, had to deal with too many things. I think better alone now." Jackson gave her a crooked grin. "Like Siddhartha, I'm going to have to find my own path to enlightenment."

Irene nodded and stood, holding the book and the sheaf of papers out. "I put together some notes on Bernardo O'Higgins. I had Cathy assemble a chronology of O'Higgins's life, highlighting the discrepancies from the history of Texas nation when compared to your book. Perhaps, they will be of some help."

Jackson accepted the book and papers without looking at them, keeping his eyes focused on the woman's face. "You knew I would choose to go back in Texas's history?"

Flinching away from the answer, Irene turned her back to him.

Jackson forced his anger away, knowing the woman would not bend before him. Nor would any of her staff inform him of anything if she did not wish it. He bit back the scathing remarks he had on the tip of his tongue and turned to go. At least now he had Odar'a to help him think his troubles through.

"Jackson."

Turning, Jackson saw Irene facing him once more. She tossed a bag toward him and he caught it deftly, amazed at the weight of it.

"You're going to need that," the woman said. "It's gold coin. You'll find a page in those papers I gave you that details the worth of each one. Be careful about spending it, though. Our research indicates that the periods of Texas history you'll be visiting were lawless times and money of any sort was scarce."

"Thank you." Jackson tied the leather bag to his belt and dropped it inside his pants pocket.

"You'll also find some clothes for that time period by the door."

Jackson spotted the small suitcase and hefted it. He felt confused, guilty for the harsh words he had subjected the woman to. He looked at her. "Irene . . . "

Brightness sparkled in her hawk's eyes and her voice was husky. "Don't say anything, Jackson. Trust me, it would only make things harder for us both. It's like you said: we both have our destinies to follow. And we'll have to do that to the best of our abilities. Any kind of life outside the rule of the Second Republic is hard, and filled with choices. You'll find yourself weighing friendships and futures constantly as you approach the swirl of madness that erupts like some kind of pestilence from Temporal Projects. Each year is an open wound waiting to suck you into it if you give it the chance. And each year seems to deserve your attention. Or it will seem to when you get there. The only problem is, people like you never develop the calluses necessary to lead others through the morass because you refuse to sacrifice even one follower."

Was she speaking from experience? Jackson wondered. Or was it from some knowledge she had of his future in the past? The questions settled on his mind like spiderwebs. Downy soft, yet deadly; filled with a tensile strength that wasn't readily apparent.

Irene's smile was sad and small. "If you should find your Bo Tree, Jackson, do me a favor and let me know what you discover beneath it. And, if at any time you need a safe port to recover your strength, remember that you'll always have that here."

Jackson nodded and left, shouldering his confused emotions toward the woman with his travel bag. He hurried down the stairs as if trying to evade the guilt that hovered over him.

Was he being selfish? he asked himself. Would it

have been better for everyone if he had agreed to stay with the Mnemosyne and check out the various leads they had on history? But if he had done that, wasn't he breaking the promise he had given Tyrell Czenlyn? Would it matter? Irene said the man would die soon anyhow? Why should he continue risking his life for a corpse? Was that any more realistic that pursuing the dreams that Irene held true?

He let himself out the lower door, grateful no one had seen him leaving. All of Irene's followers were full of life, radiating whatever art they pursued, young as well as old. Yet, Jackson could not look at them without seeing them as soldiers trapped in the invisible war between the Mnemosyne and Temporal Projects. How many of them would be reduced to ash and scattered across the seas within the coming year?

The chill wind whipped into him, crowding the bleak thoughts from his mind as he clasped his arms around himself. The leather sheath of the Veritas dagger was cool under his shirt, heavy with the weight of the blade.

He was about to cross the street and reclaim the time machine when he spotted a public vid. Acting on impulse, he jogged to it and asked for a connek to his brother, Martin. The vid flickered three times before a picture blocked into the blank screen. The vid showed a recorded holo Ana had made.

His sister-in-law gave a brief message that the family wasn't able to come to the vid at the moment and to leave a message after the beep.

Jackson declined the opportunity, knowing his reappearance would create even more questions for Martin. And, after all, it had only been a few days since he had spoke with his brother, according to Martin's personal time-line. It was enough for Jackson to know that the effort he had made back in 2074 to correct the assassination had at least gone well enough to preserve his brother's history.

He blanked the vid and was about to go.

Then slipped in the Fedcredit chit from his travel bag and keyed in Suzanne Brelmer's home number. The memory of Suzanne lying so still over her father's shoulder had haunted him for several nights. He still did not know if she had been somehow wounded in the assassination attempt.

Her recording was all business, no-nonsense.

Jackson was captivated by the look of her, remembering all too well the blonde of her hair, the sea green of her eyes, the taste of her lips. His attention turboed to sudden life, flashing danger signs in his head when the recorded holo jumped track for just a moment. Knowing someone had tapped into the vid connek, Jackson released the vid, blanking the screen and gathering the travel bag from its place at his feet.

He forced himself into a run, staggering slightly under the weight of the bag. He had no doubt that the Time Police were monitoring Suzanne's vid. Their last escape with a time machine hadn't gone entirely unnoticed.

He ran, putting everything he had into the effort, amazed at how well his body had started to perform. The extra weight he had carried around while at his job at New Ninevah Library had long since dropped away. He had never been fat, but neither had he been exceptionally athletic. Now, however, he felt like he could give Chrys Calvino a race for her money.

Pounding into the abandoned parking garage, Jackson saw the darkness gather around him and had to tell himself that no one was waiting on him. There was more to worry about from whatever ground forces Temporal Projects might summon to investigate the public vid.

He pressed face and hands to the time machine's exterior and heard the hiss of the lock releasing. Grabbing the handle, he pulled the door open and clambered inside, chagrined that he would think of the time machine as a place of safety instead a device that repeatedly threw him into danger.

Belting himself in, grimly aware that the Time Police could come into the garage with flashing lights blaring onto him at any moment, Jackson flipped open the file Irene had given him. He switched on an interior light and dragged a finger down the columns of the chronology on Bernardo O'Higgins's life. Locating the first date listed that showed O'Higgins's arrival in Texas, Jackson set the date on the time machine.

His thumb tapped the initiation switch and it felt like the time machine sprouted dragon's wings that clawed into the whirling winds of Time, dragging him afterwards like a kite's tail.

Clothed in hospital sani-dress for the second time in the same night, Brelmer watched Hoban open the silver case they had brought back with them.

The surgeon had complained of the lack of proper medical facilities but Brelmer had ignored it. Artificial insemination was something he was familiar with from working with the Time Police. For awhile Voxner had considered pushing a program through to clone Time Police. Brelmer had verbally rejected the idea, saying the field operatives needed to have an ingrained basis of knowledge and logic to work with. Too many things happened in the past once TP opened the door. Clones were possible, true, despite the Senatorial ban against their usage for replacement organs, but it took five years to mature one to the point of being able to carry out simple tasks. And brain overlays weren't entirely successful. In the end, it was the cost of the program that eventually blew it out of Voxner's consideration.

Instead, the Senator had reached for the floodgates of prison, for those people who simply didn't fit into the structured life the Second Republic offered.

The room was cleared of everyone except Brelmer and Hoban and the young woman lying on the table. Sterilization units sat around the operating area, culled from the station's own protective measures from the viruses plaguing 1939.

The woman was a Time Policeman, as her altered features readily bore out. Black hair cascaded across the surface of the table, almost covering the pointed ears. She kept her eyes fixed on the ceiling.

Her name was Cassandra Ross, Brelmer reflected, and he had thought of her immediately after deciding what had to be done with the fetus. She was intensely loyal to Brelmer as were all of the Time Policemen assigned to this post. The thing that rankled the Praetor's sense of fairness was that the woman was only a little older than Suzanne. Yet, here, surrounded by people he trusted, Cassandra Ross would be much safer with his grandchild than Suzanne would be in the present.

When he had outlined what he proposed to do only an hour ago, Ross had shown only a little hesitation. He had not told her that the child was related to him, only that it was very important that the fetus be kept safe. As compensation, she would be taken to the time period of her choice to bear the child. If it came to that.

Brelmer was hoping it didn't.

But how could he approach Suzanne later to return her child? Making the allowances in time travel, it was conceivable he could return the fetus only minutes, or hours, after taking it away. But that was according to the fetus's personal time clock. Not Suzanne's.

Brelmer had to face the possibility that involvement in Voxner's schemes might delay returning the fetus for months.

What could he say then? What excuse could he give for doing what he had done?

In Suzanne's eyes, he had done what she had accused him of doing ever since she first got mixed up with Jackson Dubchek. He had played God. He had played God and, what was even worse, he had done it with her life.

But in his eyes, he had had no choice. Not really. He wanted to spare Suzanne the agony of having to deal with the situation for the time being. And, perhaps, there was a bit of selfishness in there as well, because it delayed the inevitability of dealing with Dubchek himself.

Hoban opened the silver case at the foot of the table.

Ross raised her legs at his command, still focusing on the ceiling, naked under the light sheet that protected her from the chill of the room.

"Well, Corporal Ross," Brelmer said, "have you made your decision about where to spend the pregnancy?"

"I have, sir," Ross said.

An acti-skel arm elevated from the silver case. Fluid gleamed dully from the hollow spot inside and Brelmer couldn't help looking for the fetus, knowing he wouldn't be able to discern it even with the enhanced vision his crystal eyes afforded him. When did life begin? The question had continued to hammer at him ever since Hoban had told him of Suzanne's pregnancy.

"And where would that be?" Brelmer asked.

Hoban's voice was a dull monotone, controlling the acti-skel arm.

"London, sir, near the turn of the 20th Century."

"Why that particular choice, Corporal?"

"It was a favorite period of mine while I was studying history at graduate school."

"I see." Brelmer noted the smile on the young girl's face, remembering how Ross had initially been rejected from Temporal Projects because of her knowledge of history. It was also one of the reasons Brelmer had gone back and authorized her appointment to the ranks of the Time Police. Which was why she had become so loyal to him. The men and women comprising the small cadre of TP people Brelmer had confidence in were selected from those whose loyalties were not easily swayed and had a sense of personal and moral obligation. Only a few of those had been recruited from prisons but more often than not Brelmer found those people to be political activists than killers or rapists.

"Sir?"

"Yes, Ross."

The girl grimaced as the insemination process began. "Would I be out of line if I asked you to hold my hand, Colonel?"

"Not at all," Brelmer said softly as he stepped forward to take the girl's hand.

Within minutes after the insemination operation,

Brelmer arrived back at the outpost in New York City of 1939 ten days later. He could have waited the time out, he knew, but wanted to remain infused with the sense of immediacy Voxner's project had instilled in him. True, he had all of forever to deal with his personal problems and still arrive back in his present within the fifteen minute limit he had established for himself. But he didn't want the Senator to sense the change in him. Brelmer had been tired and frayed around the edges when Voxner had last seen him. He would be even more so, he decided, when they met again.

"How is Ross?" the Praetor asked once he entered the portion of the outpost he had ordered sectioned off for Corporal Ross.

"She is fine," Hoban said. He sat in a straight-backed chair puffing on an Earlsboro Elegance. He hadn't shaved the entire ten days he had stayed with Ross to monitor the pregnancy.

Shelving the anger he felt toward the surgeon, Brelmer closed the door behind him and waited for Ross. Hoban would definitely be a liability when they returned to the present, Brelmer knew. A liability he intended to take care of at his earliest convenience. "There were no problems?"

Hoban stubbed the narcosmoker out. "No, sir. Everything went quite well. Except that I've felt like a prisoner the entire time I have been sequestered here."

"Careful, doctor," Brelmer warned. "Insubordination at this point may lead to an extension of that feeling."

Hoban nodded quietly.

The door opened behind Brelmer and Cassandra Ross entered the room, dressed in her Time Police uniform.

There was something about her, Brelmer noted. Something more ALIVE, more VIBRANT about her. Then his flagging memory synapses closed a circuit and he remembered. His wife had looked the same way when she was pregnant with Suzanne. "How are you, Corporal?"

She smiled at him as she snapped off a quick salute. "Fine, sir."

"And today is your big day?"

"Yes, sir."

"Has Sgt. Patilla provided you with everything you'll be needing for your stay?"

"Yes, sir. A cover identity was pieced together with my help, and clothing and money were easily retrievable from the past."

"Very good." Seeing the smile and feeling the enthusiasm that was evident in the girl took away some of Brelmer's guilt for using her as a receptacle for his daughter's child. Ross would not go unrewarded for her sacrifice, no matter how long the time actually turned out to be, but it was good to see that she was looking forward to her chosen post.

Ten days had passed since the insemination, though only an hour or so for Brelmer. It made him feel good. In those ten days nothing had happened to the fetus. Evidently Ross's body had no problems accepting the child and had not tried to abort it.

Even more promising, however, was the fact that Voxner had remained unaware of the whole procedure. In a way, by setting the events as he had, Brelmer had used the past of the previous ten days at the outpost to safeguard the future he would return to. According to theory, if Voxner hadn't learned of the baby during those ten days and sent someone back to retrieve it, then the Senator wouldn't find out about it when Brelmer returned.

According to theory, Brelmer reminded himself. But that wasn't including the possibilities of the paradoxes that Temporal Projects had unleashed. Those were still immeasurable forces that touched every past, present, and future that had, did, and would exist.

Despite the surface appearance that everything was going according to plan so far, a chill passed through Brelmer.

CHAPTER FOURTEEN

A harsh wind swirled through the narrow, dirt streets of Nacogdoches, whipping red sand into stinging flurries.

Jackson took cover behind one of the thick posts supporting the eaves over the wooden boardwalk in front of saloon. He checked his chron again, sliding back the sleeve of the flannel shirt Irene had packed for him. It was 2 PM. According to the file the Mnemosyne had cobbled together, the stage coach carrying Bernardo O'Higgins would be arriving in twelve more minutes. Across the street the green chalkboard in front of the stage line office advertised that the stage was due in at 12 PM.

How could any transportation medium allow their service to be ran so shoddily and stay in business? Jackson wondered. Surely an official from the Assistant Secretary to the Secretary of Public Transportation's Office would have reacted to the complaints the travellers would have surely voiced by now.

He rubbed sand from his eyes again, knowing the effort was in vain because the wind would hurl it back over him again. All ready his shirt and jeans were covered with a light red dust, and some of it had worked inside his shirt, feeling as abrasive as sandpaper.

His legs still ached from the long walk into town, but he had found a good hiding place for the time machine under a stand of brush. He had left the Veritas dagger sheathed across his chest despite the evident fact that men in this time period went openly armed with both knife and pistol.

Lifting the flat-brimmed hat he wore as protection from the sun, he ran his fingers through his sweat-slick hair, grateful for the cooling breeze.

The batwing doors of the saloon squeaked open behind him.

Resisting the impulse to look, Jackson scanned the street again, marveling at how primitive the town was. Yet, according to the information contained in Czenlyn's information, it was a booming metropolis compared to many other towns in Texas at the time. The buildings were clapboard, with garishly painted signs that were all ready cracking and peeling with age.

He read them with interest, only knowing what some of them offered. The Diamond Hotel. Jim Preston, Blacksmith and Livery. Hansen's Feed and Grain. Sheriff's Office. From the star painted over the building, Jackson assumed the last had to do with the law enforcement agency in 1836.

He glanced at his chron. 2:05.

"Waitin' for somebody, cowboy?" a deep voice drawled behind Jackson.

"I'm waiting for the stage," Jackson replied, glancing over his shoulder.

The man that stood behind him was huge, dwarfing Jackson. The man wore a flannel shirt that hung outside his pants and a vest that looked at least two sizes too small for the barrel chest. There was a hole in the right knee of the Levis the man wore that still had a patch fluttering from it. The man was broad and beefy, with arms inches too long for the shirt he wore. But the arms ended in huge hands covered with scarred knuckles. The only piece of equipment on the man that appeared to be given any attention at all were the two massive pistols hanging from the belt fastened over the shirttails.

"You been waitin' a spell," the man said.

Jackson was undecided over whether to take the statement as fact or as a question. When the man kept staring at him as if expecting something in return, he assumed it was a question. "Yes, sir. I'm waiting on my uncle." The eyes beneath the heavy brows were ice-blue, like those of the arctic wolves Jackson had seen pictures of as a boy in Springfield. He got the impression those eyes could see right through him but made himself face the man just the same.

"You been aroun' these parts long, boy?"

"No."

The man nodded. "Didn't think I'd seen you aroun'. What brings you here?"

"I came to get my uncle." Jackson got the feeling he was being boxed in but couldn't figure out why. He hadn't done anything against this man. He checked for the telltales of the Time Police and saw nothing.

"How'd you get here?"

"I walked."

The big man nodded, squinting up against the sun. "Mighty long walk to here from anywhere. I reckon it would take a man on foot, if he was to walk real hard, at least a handful of days to get here."

Jackson nodded, not knowing what else to say. A flash of green drew his attention to the window of the saloon behind the big man. A woman, looking only a few years older than Jackson, stood there watching. The emerald dress she wore was low-cut and her breasts threatened to spill out at any time. Her red hair was piled up on her head, contrasting sharply with the bright ruby lipstick she wore. When she saw that Jackson had noticed her obvious interest, she spun away from the window, the dress billowing up to reveal smooth muscled legs.

"I figure that walk would be most distressin' on a man," the big man said. "And wouldn't wear well on his clothes neither. But them clothes you got on look store-bought new." The look in the blue eyes was flinty hard.

"What do you want with me?" Jackson asked. "What right do you have invading my privacy?"

The big man grinned. "I got lots of rights, boy." He flipped a corner of the stained vest back, revealing a star that vaguely resembled the one painted over the Sheriff's Office down the street. It flashed dully in the mid-day sun. "I'm the marshall of this here town and it's my job to 'invade people's privacy' when I think they may be courting the wrong ideas."

"But I haven't done anything wrong," Jackson protested.

The sheriff tipped his hat forward and scratched the back of his neck. "No, son, no you haven't. And I aim to keep it that way. But I been watchin' how you been starin' after that stage while I was havin' my dinner inside the saloon. 'Pears to me, a boy your age, especially if he was waitin' on an uncle and not some gal friend, would be inside the saloon downin' a few beers and tryin' to put the make on a few of the saloon's girls. He wouldn't be out here puttin' up with the heat and all this sand. Nosir, I just can't see that happenin'. So, I thought to myself, there must be some other reason. Once that thought made itself home in my head, I just couldn't get rid of it and enjoy my beer. So I moseyed

on out here to find out what was goin' on for myself.
Now that I seen you up close, I figure you strike me as
somebody I should know. What's your name?"

"Jackson." A sinking feeling in Jackson's stomach
urged him to run but a glance at the guns belted at the
sheriff's waist told him he wouldn't get far.

"Named after the President, are you?"

Not knowing what to say, Jackson shook his head.

"You got a last name, Jackson?" the sheriff asked.

"Martin," Jackson replied after a moment's hesitation. From the way the big man nodded, he was sure
the sheriff hadn't let the hesitation go unnoticed.
Thoughts tumbled through his head as he turned away
from the sheriff. The big man's presence at his back
wasn't easily forgotten and the threat he exuded was a
physical thing.

Jackson considered leaving, trying to make his way
back out of town, but knew the sheriff would stop him
if he did anything to further raise suspicion. He waited,
no longer wishing the chron would spin faster. Instead,
he willed Time to slow down, to allow the sheriff ample
opportunity to "mosey" somewhere else. He felt as
tense and tight inside as the support post he was leaning
against.

A dust spot at the south end of town gathered volume
as it neared.

"There comes the stage now," the sheriff said.

Jackson heard the big man shift on the creaking
boardwalk behind him and tried to keep his imagination

from running wild.

The stage looked like a huge wooden pumpkin on wheels to Jackson. A layer of red dust overlaid the worn and weary woodwork. Six horses pulled it into town and stopped in front of the stage office. Two men sat on top of it. One held the reins controlling the horses and another had a shotgun.

The driver tied the reins up and dropped over the side. Jackson watched the shotgunner clamber down on the other side, pausing long enough to shoot a stream of tobacco into the dirt under the body of the coach. He opened the door and said, "Everybody out. This here's the end of the line."

Jackson studied the people getting out of the coach, not knowing what to expect. There had been a picture of Bernardo O'Higgins in the package Irene had sent, but it had been hand-drawn and photocopied from years past. O'Higgins was all ready living a life that wasn't his, and Jackson wondered if the man would look the same.

The first man out was slim, dressed in business attire that drew curious looks from the passersby who had gathered to see the coach riders disembark. He stood to one side of the coach, looking out over the crowd in a manner Jackson recognized clearly as being a security measure.

Bernardo O'Higgins was next, looking more like his hand-drawn picture than Jackson would have thought possible. Like the first man, he was dressed in a three-piece suit that drew attention to the fact that he wasn't from anywhere nearby.

The third man to get out was a dead man Jackson had never expected to see again.

Laszlo Slye.

The name thundered through Jackson's brain, creating more of a flight response in him than the big sheriff at his back. Memory flooded over him like an undammed river. Slye had been the person responsible for initially displacing Jackson in 2183. He had also been the man who had discovered the list of future rebels who would and were fighting Temporal Projects' attempts to change the past. But what was the man doing here and now? Jackson had shot him in Prague, in 1968, and there had been no doubt but that the man had died.

Slye was dressed in Western fashion, complete with a big cowboy hat and a tied down handgun. A long rifle filled his left hand as he stepped from the swaying coach. The hard planes of his face absorbed the shadow from the hat clamped down tight on his head.

How could anyone even think the man belonged to the human race? Jackson wondered.

Slye towered over most of the other men around him, looking like a misplaced giant. He turned to the driver, who had climbed back on top of the coach, and motioned for the luggage. The driver tossed it down and Slye caught it easily.

"Can you show me an uncle in that crowd?" the sheriff asked.

"No," Jackson answered, feeling his throat tighten in response.

"Didn't think so," the sheriff said. "Let's go, boy."
A heavy hand dropped on Jackson's shoulder and pushed him forward, out onto the street. He started to run, then felt the octagonal barrel of one of the sheriff's pistols prod his right kidney painfully.

"Don't try it, boy. I ain't in no mood for a damned foot-race. I'll blow a hole in you big enough to drive cattle through."

Making himself relax, Jackson glanced back at the stagecoach, sweeping his gaze across O'Higgins and his Time Police escort. He had proof now that Temporal Projects had brought O'Higgins to Texas, but how could Czenlyn hope to use the information? Evidently the plot had started before now. But the years before O'Higgins's arrival at Nacogdoches were a blank. Even to the Mnemosyne.

Assuming he had all the answers as to how the transportation was set up, doing anything about it would mean taking on a contingent of the Time Police. Jackson didn't want to do that. Yet, what choices were left? He wasn't versed in history well enough to counter-plot the machinations Voxner had used Brelmer to set into motion.

The sheriff's gun prodded him into a faster pace.

Feeling helpless, Jackson kept walking toward the Sheriff's Office. Before he could look away, Captain

Laszlo Slye's eyes locked with his. Something stirred in the darkly evil depths.

Jackson hoped it wasn't recognition.

The jail cell was small and square, situated in the rear of the Sheriff's Office, seemingly overpowering in a stark sort of way due to the bare bones of the iron bars.

Jackson sat on the thin bed chained to the stone wall, trying to figure a way out of the mess he had landed in. He was still confused as to why the sheriff had locked him up. The man had mentioned things like "a gut feelin', boy," and "a lawman sort of senses when he ain't bein' told the truth." He had started to protest when the man herded him into the cell, saying he had rights.

The sheriff had said, "I'm the Law aroun' here, boy, and I'll do the decidin' about who has rights an' such." Then he had turned the big key and locked the door.

At first Jackson had been afraid Slye or one of the other members of the Time Police force Brelmer had stationed in this time-line had arranged for the sheriff to arrest him. After all, if Slye had recognized him, Slye could have told Brelmer about the encounter and a trap, acting through the sheriff, could have been laid. But, if that had been the case, wouldn't Brelmer have all ready known about Jackson's capture in 1836? Laszlo Slye had died a year ago. Wouldn't he have known Jackson Dubchek had been apprehended in 1836? Or was that one of the underlying reasons Slye had dumped Jackson in 2183 and accused him of being in on the Persian ambassador's assassination?

The thoughts formed a Moebius strip of convoluted thinking too quickly and made Jackson's head hurt. There was no telling for sure where the true beginning was anymore. No line of demarcation to show a difference between what had once been and what is, leaving only a garbled and perilous path toward the future. And the operative word was TOWARD because there weren't even any guarantees of getting TO anything. He grasped the iron bars of the cell's only window and pulled himself up.

A scattered handful of men and women plied the streets, seeing about the business that had brought them to town. Recalling some of his studies concerning the time period, Jackson remembered that most families still lived outside of town, tending farms and cattle.

A buckboard rattled to a stop in front of a general store in back of the jail. A little girl, dressed in a gingham dress and wearing a bonnet, sucked on her thumb and stared at Jackson with wide eyes till her father took her up in his arms. It reminded him of Mateo's little sister in 2074.

Are you going to continue to sacrifice a piece of yourself here and a piece of yourself there? Rachel Czenlyn's words came back to haunt him in intense fury.

Pushing himself away from the wall, Jackson's foot

tangled in the single sheet covering the stained and smelling bed and nearly spilled him to the hard floor. He recovered his balance in time to keep from smashing face-first. When he pushed himself back up, he saw the woman from the saloon standing before his cell.

She still wore the green dress he had seen her in but had put on a short-waisted cloak that failed to hide her cleavage. Her beauty was startling.

"What's your name?" the woman asked as she reached for the big keyring hanging on the wall opposite Jackson's cell. She seemed tensed, hurried.

"What are you doing?" Jackson asked.

She gave him a sarcastic look as she fitted the key in the doorlock. "What does it look like I'm doing?" The door creaked open. "Now get a move on. We ain't got much time afore the sheriff gets back."

"But then I'll be guilty of breaking jail?" Jackson held back. It was one thing to escape from certain death, but he had no reason to run from the sheriff. It had all been a mistake that would surely straighten itself out. If he ran now, the sheriff might stop him with a shot rather than a shout.

"Do you like it in there, mister?" the woman demanded. "Because if you do, I can surely arrange it." She stepped forward and raked Jackson's sleeve back, exposing the chron. "Look, I saw you checking that while you were waiting on the stage. I know what it is and I know what it means." The guttural accent had dropped from her words, creating even more questions in Jackson's mind.

Jackson followed her through the hallway leading to the main sheriff's office. She motioned him down as they approached the door. They ducked together and a man walked by, casting a momentary shadow on the frosted glass of the door.

"When we move," the woman said in a soft whisper that Jackson found sexy despite the circumstances, "go toward the back of the building. I've got a room above the saloon and you can stay there till Kanter and I figure a way to get you out of town."

"Why are you doing this?" Jackson asked. He was aware of the woman's strong perfume tickling his nose, drawing out secret thoughts he hoped didn't show on his face. Or anywhere else on his body. Her physique seemed electric with sexuality, tempering every movement she made.

She looked at him and he discovered her eyes were a lighter green than the dress. "You aren't the only person to have been displaced in Time, guy."

Jackson recognized the 23rd Century inflection in her speech now, though it was more coarse than he was accustomed to.

The woman stood again, easing white and tapering fingers around the doorknob, turning slowly.

Jackson paused, flattening against the wall till he reached his backpack hanging from the coatrack. He gathered the straps in his hand and followed the woman out the door.

She ran as lithely as a deer once they made the corner and Jackson was hard-pressed to keep up with her. She held her dress up, out of the way, and her legs flashed sunlight.

Even with his heart thudding in his chest, knowing each breath might be his last, Jackson was almost hypnotized the bare flesh.

They circled behind the two-story saloon and took the stairs leading to the upper floor. The woman took his hand at the bottom of the stairs when a man appeared at the top of the landing still buckling his pants.

"Afternoon, Miss Joy," the man said as he stumbled down the stairs.

"Afternoon, Otis," the woman said with an accent that matched the man's.

Jackson felt himself pulled closer to the woman as the man passed, realizing she was attempting to keep the man from seeing him. His face skated along the softness of her breasts and he had to steel himself against responding. How was it, he asked himself, that he had been able to put Rachel Czenlyn off the night before he left 2074, yet found himself so incensed with the woman he had just met?

Before he found an answer to the question, he found himself shuttled down a carpeted hallway and pushed inside a small room that seemed to be nothing more than a bedroom.

The woman locked the thin door behind them.

"Sweet Buddha, that was close," she said.

Jackson stood in the center of the room, taking in the low ceiling, the cloying smell of rose-scented perfume, the brightly colored curtains covering the window overlooking the street in front of the saloon. A handful of dresses as daringly styled as the one the woman was wearing occupied a narrow closet beside the door. A small bathroom with a claw-footed tub sat behind a half-open curtain.

"Not much to look at, is it?" the woman asked with a sad lilt in her voice. "Not when you're used to vids and sonic showers and the other taken for granted luxuries of a normal life."

Jackson looked at her again, noticing for the first time that she was only a little older than he was. Tiny crow's-feet had started eroding the corners of her eyes but age had only filled her body out to complete robustness.

"How long have you been here?" the woman asked.

"Today."

"You can put your things in the closet," she said, indicating the bare floor under the dresses. "You'll be staying here till I can figure out how to get you away. The easiest way would be to wait till dark and sneak out then. Kanter can help you then."

"I can't stay here," Jackson said. "What if the sheriff finds out?"

"He won't," the woman said, "if you just chill out a little." She approached Jackson and put her arms around him. She took a deep breath. "Buddha, you would not believe how long it has been since I've smelled a clean man. And so young." She kissed him.

Jackson kissed back, wondering if he had jumped from the frying pan into the fire. The woman knew he was a time traveler. In fact, she assumed he was a dis- placed person, traffic, as she was. But why would she befriend him? And who was Kanter, the man she said could help him? If Brelmer was setting O'Higgins in power in this time-line, why would the Praetor people it with displaced persons?

The woman ran her fingers through his hair.

`Disengaging for a moment, Jackson held her at arm's length. She smiled at him lazily, as if she thought he was only teasing. "How do you know you can trust me?" Jackson asked.

Her smile was larger, more filled with humor. "Meaning, how do you know you can trust me?" She laughed. "My, my, how paranoia does set in once we get lost in time."

Jackson responded to her kisses again but still gently forced her away.

"What's wrong?" the woman asked. "Afraid I'll slip a knife between your shoulder blades?"

"The thought has crossed my mind," Jackson replied, though the thought hadn't. Now that it had, it made him more than a little uncomfortable.

"At first, when I saw you waiting on the stage, when I saw the chron on your arm, I figured you for one of the enemy. Then, when I saw the look in your eyes as you recognized Laszlo Slye climbing down from that coach, I knew we were on the same side."

"Which side is that?" Jackson asked.

"The side against the Second Republic. I was one of the volunteer squad from my time-line to attempt to keep O'Higgins from being brought to Texas."

"What happened?"

The woman shrugged. "Most of us were killed by Brelmer and his Time Police. We disguised ourselves as Indians and attacked them in the forest earlier this year. Evidently our commanders underestimated their strength. Despite the attack holos we had, Brelmer's forces made their way through us. Since then we've gathered around this town, waiting for O'Higgins to arrive and finish him off. You need to get out of your clothes."

"What?"

"Your clothes," the woman repeated. "You need to get them off. The sheriff will recognize them easily. Buddha, but you're a tenderfoot about things. How long have you been on the Second Republic's displacement list?"

"I don't know," Jackson said truthfully. "It was pretty sudden."

"I'll say." She helped him take his clothes off, piling them unceremoniously in the floor. "Two pieces of advice I can give you. One: never mix it up with a drunk Indian; they're worse than a rampaging Time

Policeman. And second: stay away from Jackson Elgin Dubchek."

"Dubchek?" Jackson croaked.

"Yeah." The woman paused in taking off his pants. "Have you heard of him?"

"No."

"Well, you'll find that that guy pops up a lot in the past and he's nothing but trouble. My squad was given order to kill him on sight. The problem was, our hold on history was so shaky we could never get a picture. But we know he worked with Brelmer and Temporal Projects." She peeled out of her dress and dropped it on Jackson's clothing. Her breasts hung before her for a moment, staring at Jackson. Then she cupped them and smiled lewdly. "You never did say what your name was."

"Sid. My friends call me Sid."

The woman smiled as she herded him toward the bed. "Well, Sid, I'm going to be your friend." She laid on top of him on the bed.

Jackson felt her hand snake between his legs, then felt the coldness of her fingers. He couldn't shake her words from his mind despite her fingerplay. Kill him on sight. Buddha, it was bad enough knowing Brelmer and the Time Police were searching through Time for him without adding this.

"Loosen up, Sid," the woman said plaintively. "You're acting like this is rape or something." She grinned as she squeezed him. "And Buddha knows that definitely isn't the case if this is any kind of indication."

Considering everything the woman had just told him, Jackson figured she was lucky to have any indication at all.

CHAPTER FIFTEEN

Brelmer's mind felt fuzzy from the stim he had instructed Hoban to give him before returning to their present. He felt the time machine settle back into the transmission lab with a harsh bounce that filled his stomach with shredded glascrete.

Still fighting the nauseating sickness, he grabbed Hoban by the arm and powered him from the time machine. The surgeon doubled over, fighting a stomach cramp that wrote its intensity across his face, and nearly toppled Brelmer as well.

Brelmer retched again into the face bag, having nothing to give up but being tithed by the travel sickness just the same. Regaining his sense of balance, the

Colonel forced himself onward, dragging Hoban after him.

"Colonel?"

Brelmer looked up and saw Crismeyre looking at him, tapping a sheaf of papers in his hands nervously. He straightened up, forcing away the last of the violent retching, still tasting the sourness of it burning his throat, maintaining his hold on the surgeon. "What is it, Crismeyre?"

"It's Senator Voxner, sir. He's at the door demanding entrance."

"Do a full scan, Crismeyre. It will only take a few minutes and it will show our esteemed benefactor that our security measures are on the upswing around here."

"Yes, sir." The man was obviously unhappy about having to keep Voxner waiting.

Brelmer didn't blame him but the fact still remained that Hoban had to be cleared from the transmission lab. He wished the stim would leave his mind unfogged but knew that he was pressing his luck just to remain ambulatory.

Hooking one of Hoban's arms across his shoulders, Brelmer guided the surgeon toward an exit door that was keyed for his personal idents only. He leaned Hoban against the wall, noticing the pasty white moon that was the surgeon's face. At his touch and eye-scan, the door slid into the sheath of the wall soundlessly. A hulking Time Policeman stood there, hand hesitating over the butt of the large-scale Matthews holstered at his hip.

Brelmer glanced at the Time Policeman. "Vanish," he commanded.

"Alabama, Colonel," the man said as he padded away quickly down the narrow hallway.

The exit door hissed shut behind Brelmer as he grabbed a double fistful of the surgeon's smock and slammed the man up against the metal wall.

Maintaining his hold on Hoban with one hand, Brelmer ripped his face mask away, willing his crystal eyes to go dark. It was one of the personal touches he had ordered when the optics were implanted.

The vomit made a sick odor between them, curling, threatening. Brelmer let the smell sink in for a moment to remind Hoban how close they had been to death, then tightened his grip on the surgeon's throat.

Hoban coughed as his face purpled. A dry heave died unborn.

"Only you and I know of this, doctor," Brelmer said in a tight voice. "Only you and I and Ross, and I can trust her. Do you understand?"

Not having any other means of communicating, Hoban nodded, wincing as he gave in to the pressure of Brelmer's fingers.

"If anyone else finds out about what we have done, you'll have no time at all to regret it. Are we clear on this?"

Hoban nodded again.

Releasing the man, he stepped away, tripping the

security on the door to the transmission lab again. Hoban was dropping to his knees even as the door slid shut.

"Security confirms it is Senator Voxner, sir," Crismeyre said as Brelmer stepped back onto the lab floor.

"Let him in, Crismeyre," Brelmer said. He slid his polychromatic helmet off and set it on one of the protective railings around the transmission area. He had changed back into his regular clothing before he and Hoban had made the jump back. There was nothing about his appearance that should let Voxner know he had all ready jumped.

Voxner strode into the room, filling it with his presence at once. His voice, when he spoke, was an orator's dream: all rolling thunder and righteous indignation. "What in the nine hells of Abdigon is the meaning of this, Colonel?"

Brelmer had to admit that he had rarely seen the Senator in better form. Shiva, you could see the shark blood in the man roiling, nostrils flaring, seeking the scent of wounded prey. It was the kind of performance that had rocked the halls of the Senate many times, and had often proved to be the swaying factor in an argument. Voxner could threaten a room full of people by himself and get away with it, never having to lay his hands on a single person. Brelmer had often thought that talent was useful but had never mastered it, choosing instead to keep his confrontations, as with Hoban, confined to a more personal, one-on-one basis.

"Security measures, Senator," Brelmer answered, using the titular response because Voxner would recognize it as a concession toward him and the power he wielded. "After last night's break-in, I upgraded the system all ready in place and have placed a 24-hour flesh team in here as well. We're not taking any more chances, sir. Assuming the Time Rebs have been able to pinpoint TP, we're taking the initiative to arrange a full-scan bio profile and matching them against the computer records."

Voxner glared back. "Computer records can be tampered with, Praetor."

"Duly noted, Senator, but the highest level of TP, those people needing access to the transmissions labs, have been crystal-coded. You can't alter those."

Voxner harumphed and Brelmer knew the glare he spread around the lab was meant to reinforce his importance to the project and to let the gathered personnel know who the ultimate power in their lives was.

Inwardly, Brelmer felt himself relax. Once the Senator had resumed posturing he knew he could be fairly certain the danger had passed. The stim swam dizzily in his head and he was dreading the upcoming jump, wishing he could have arranged a short nap somewhere in his contortions of Time. But events had all ready been cut too closely. If he had made it back to the present even a handful of minutes later, it would have been too late.

For the first time, Brelmer noticed the gray flannel robe the Senator wore. The hood was tossed back, revealing Voxner's white mane of hair.

Dunker clothing for a gathering, Brelmer realized. Then remembered Voxner was traveling back to place an indelible mark on someone else's past. His mind captured the memory of Senator Lisa Ky's open and honest smile, and Brelmer wondered if he would ever see it again after they returned from Voxner's mission.

A light patter of rain fell across the park and Brelmer was glad the Dunker robes were hooded. Not only did the hoods help disguise the presence of himself, Voxner, Paress Linnet, and the half dozen Time Policemen they had brought back as guards, but it helped keep him dry as well.

A steady stream of bullets traveled slowly down the street beside the park, their tires wickering across the wet pavement.

"Colonel?"

Brelmer looked down, still amazed at the number of robed figures that filled the small park. He had had no idea the Dunker religion was so huge. "Yes, Paress."

The costumer shivered inside her robe. "Has Senator Voxner said why he wanted me along yet?"

"No."

"Oh."

Brelmer watched the woman's face disappear inside

the depths of her hood again. "You're more familiar with the ways of Voxner than I am concerning Temporal Projects affairs, Paress."

"I know. Voxner is a person who loves surprises, Colonel, and the nastier they are, the better. I have a feeling one of his nastiest yet has all ready been planned for today."

Brelmer silently agreed but didn't say anything. Perhaps it wasn't that the Dunker belief had a large congregation, he told himself as he looked out over the thousands of people spilling out around the outer edges of the park. Perhaps it was just that here, in Oklahoma City of 2228, there was just a greater concentration of them. Oklahoma state was locked centrally in the area that had been known as the Bible belt of America for years. The state had also been one of the last to ratify the Bahai religion that was adopted as the official religion of the Second Republic in 2183.

Memorial Park, a small sign had proclaimed at the end of the park where Voxner's directions had taken them. The park itself was totally unpretentious. It formed a shallow bowl, filled with a handful of tennis courts needing repair, a collection of children's toys, and a fountain that hosed a spray up at the rainclouds.

The Dunkers had formed an audience around the fountain, leaving room for the speakers and a long wooden pole which, when a believer was tied to it, would dip the person head-first into the shallow water while prayers were offered by the rest of the assembly.

Brelmer and Paress stood together under a tree all ready denuded by the coming fall. Despite the chances of lighting striking the tree during the light rain, Brelmer had opted for the shelter it offered. He knew Paress Linnet had chosen to stand beside him out of some need for reassurance. He wondered if she knew there was nothing he could do if Voxner willed it.

He blinked slowly, trying to wash away the haze of fatigue that fuzzed his vision. The stim was still strong in him despite the mile or so the party had been forced to walk from the time machines. His thoughts turned relentlessly to Suzanne and the baby and his wife, kaleidoscoping into a whirling feeling of guilt that washed over him with tidewater force.

"Well, Friz," Voxner's voice said, "can you feel it?"

Brelmer shifted, turning his head inside the hood till he saw the man standing beside him. Shiva. The stim must be making him groggy if he hadn't heard Voxner come up on him. The last Brelmer had seen of the man, Voxner had lost himself in the depths of the gray-robed crowd, trailed by two of the Time Policemen. "Feel what, Senator?"

A gloating smile covered Voxner's face. "The belief, Friz, the belief. Gods, you can almost reach out an touch it."

Brelmer looked back out over the crowd, noticing how many of the Dunkers had sat cross-legged on the wet grass. He tried to "feel" what Voxner was describing. All he was aware of was the quietness of the assembled people, the way even the children sat waiting on the speakers to start.

"Come, come, Friz," Voxner said. "Surely you must feel something."

Brelmer shook his head. The only impression he got was one of imminent danger. And that was radiating from Voxner in a five klaxon-alert that seemed to vibrate under Brelmer's skin.

Voxner waved an arm out over the proceedings. "Maybe you've been cloistered away too long in the ranks of the military and science, Friz, to truly appreciate what is sitting out there. Gods, the feel of it is like an elixir. You really don't know what you're missing."

Brelmer swiveled his head again and saw the mad gleam in the Senator's eyes.

"That is power out there, Friz," Voxner intoned reverently. "A power that is most startling when you can recognize it for what it is. The problem is that it is a fragile power. Extremely strong in its own right, of course, but lacking a tensile strength that will preserve it. Just as an egg is strongest at its ends and weakest in its center. That is the problem with all religions. They are entirely invulnerable when faced with their chosen foes, usually outside forces, yet easily fall apart when faced with something unexpected. Often, all it takes is a mirror, a glimpse of the idiotic trappings that bind their beliefs into a doctrine. And that is precisely what we are going to do here today: convince many of these people gathered here that the religion they are following is a vain attempt at whiting out the blackness that lies in the soul of every man and woman."

A coldness, inspired by the calculated tone of Voxner's voice, wrapped around Brelmer's spine, thin as piano wire and as fuzzy as a caterpillar.

"These people believe, Friz," Voxner said, "and that belief is the strongest thing here at this meeting. They believe in the man who is waiting to speak to them, who will speak to them of how he saved his soul from the very brink of the Hell each one of these people fear. He will speak and they will listen, hoping to glean some small kernel of fact from his address that they can use to preserve themselves from the damnation they believe in but cannot prove. They have built their own prison of their beliefs, tempered every bar with stories and doctrine till they are sure they are invulnerable, and spend the rest of their lives searching for some salvation many people can never believe exists. They are slaves to their own guilt."

Brelmer thought it fell along similar lines of the employees at Temporal Projects. Trapped by their jobs and by Voxner's influence, at the mercy of whatever paradox that confronted them from nowhere.

"Paress," Voxner called over his shoulder.

Brelmer heard the costumer's timid footsteps bring her to within their small conversation area.

"Yes, Senator?" Paress said.

"Do you see the man to the immediate left of the dunking pole?"

Brelmer changed points of interest, flicking the telescopic mode of his crystal eyes into play. Images
shuddered through his vision as each new magnification
locked into place.

"Yes, sir," the costumer said.

The man Voxner singled out was easily in his fifties,
Brelmer thought as he studied the Dunker. His slicked
back black hair was shot through with gray and silver,
and the folds around the hazel eyes weren't just the
result of genetics. Still, there was something about the
way the man carried his squared off shoulders that set
him apart from the rest of the speakers around him.

"That is Ngo Fan," Voxner said. "He is the leading
evangelist of the Dunker movement at this time. Fan
came to the religion and to these people late in his life
after living a good many of his years on the wrong side
of the law. His conversion was a media event seven
years ago and he has enjoyed a wide-spread following.
But, like many people who have rode the charismatic
tide of sudden popularity to a high position, Fan has not
seen to it that his position was cemented with his peers.
There are many in the Dunker religion who would like
to see Fan meet an unglorified end. Politically speaking."

When Voxner smiled, Brelmer thought he could have
found a warmer expression carved on the face of a
glacier.

"I have arranged for two of Fan's contemporaries to
come into possession of certain articles covering the

evangelist's past," Voxner said, "that will be nothing less than damning."

"I thought Fan had made a full confession when he joined the Dunkers," Brelmer said.

"Fan owned up to a great many sins he had been convicted of at an earlier time, as well as a few that had only been guessed at but never proven. The man is not stupid, Friz. The only problem is he is not as intelligent as he believes himself to be. He has maintained certain contacts to the black market and is managing to do quite well for himself there. That is one of the things that will be revealed today." Voxner turned his dark-eyed gaze on the costumer. "However, Paress, it will be up to you to set the sequence of events I have arranged into motion."

Brelmer saw the incredulous look on the woman's long face and felt the feeling echo inside him.

"Me, Senator?" Paress stammered, raising a hand to her throat. "But surely you can't expect me to take a part in this?"

"I do and you will," Voxner ordered. "What I did not expect is for you to aid Jackson Dubchek in getting into Temporal Projects last night."

A chilled fistful of talons locked into dangerous orbit around Brelmer's heart. Shiva. He had not known of Paress Linnet's involvement with Dubchek. Still, after a fashion, it made sense. Ever since Suzanne's first encounter with Dubchek last year, it seemed that the friendship between Suzanne and the costumer had grown considerably. Without wanting to, Brelmer found himself wondering what other secrets were locked in the woman's brain. But that was quickly washed away by the fear that flooded him. If Voxner knew Paress Linnet was involved in last night's compromise of TP's security, how much did the Senator know about Suzanne's own duplicity in the matter? And as further consideration: had Paress used Suzanne, or vice versa? He pushed the questions away, willing his face to remain unrevealing.

"You will do as I say, woman," Voxner said. "You made your choice last night. Today I have made mine."

Paress looked at Brelmer with frightened eyes.

Brelmer met her gaze with difficulty. How long had he relied on her, trusted her and her judgment? How long had he considered her as one of HIS people if crisis came to chaos? Yet she had been implemental in putting Suzanne in danger. How could he forget, or forgive, that?

"Don't throw yourself on the Colonel's mercy," Voxner said, "because you'll just be wasting your breath. Why should he hold any mercy for you? Without your involvement in Dubchek's activities last night, his daughter would never have been kidnapped nor almost killed."

So. For just a heartbeat Brelmer flicked his gaze from the silent impassioned plea in the costumer's eyes to Voxner's unflinching stare. So. That was to be the price of his complicity in the Senator's latest scheme.

A brief and fleeting respite from Voxner's vengeance at best. But hadn't Paress earned some kind of compassion from him as well? She had remained silent through the accusation, not saying what Brelmer was sure they both knew. Suzanne had not been kidnapped. Her vocal defense of Dubchek back in Mexico had proven that to him.

"I wouldn't have any feelings of kindness for the woman who endangered my daughter," Voxner warned.

Brelmer got the impression he could have reached out and touched the imprisoning net of unsaid words that the Senator had woven around him. Feeling trapped, he forced himself to think only of Suzanne, lying so quiet and still on the hospital bed. Shiva, he would not lose her. No matter what else his life came to, he would not let anyone take her away from him. Or cause her to be taken away.

Fighting with the mixture of strained loyalties knotting his stomach up, Brelmer turned away from the costumer and left her to Voxner's cold mercies. He felt Paress's hand fall away from his arm, as desiccated and frail as a dry leaf.

"It is only a small price to pay for so large a disloyalty," Voxner said.

The woman's voice was halting and lifeless. "What do you want me to do?"

"I want you to go down there and let the congregation know Ngo Fan fathered your illegitimate child." Voxner laughed without mirth. "I assure you, it is the

least of the man's sins, but it is one that will quickly
grab the attention of those people gathered here. Such
an act is one of the most distasteful in the Dunker religion."

"Why me?" Paress asked.

Brelmer exhaled a long, slow breath, feeling Voxner
step forward till he was once more in the Colonel's field
of view.

"As an act of contrition, of course," Voxner asked,
"to ensure your return to loyalty to Temporal Projects.
And because neither Friz nor I would be as convincing
in the role of accuser as you will be."

There was a moment of strained silence. Brelmer
was unsure of which way the argument would go.
Paress Linnet's sense of moral outrage would war
against Voxner's machinations, but how long would it
outweigh self-preservation?

Fallen leaves shifted and crackled behind Brelmer
only an instant before he saw the costumer's small form
drift into the sea of gray robed Dunkers in the park.

For an instant Brelmer thought she truly looked like
a lost soul among many others.

"I could have arranged this without you, Friz,"
Voxner said, "but I wanted you here. Out of everyone I
have working under me at present, you are the only one
who can truly appreciate everything we are doing here."

Brelmer didn't say anything. He felt numb inside,
almost as much the victim as Paress was.

"You and I," Voxner said, "we aren't that much different, Friz. We are both hooked on the powers and possibilities inherent in traveling through Time. You seek some way to contain and control it because that is your nature. It is a new and uncertain way for you to test yourself and your resources. It is a challenge. An obstacle to things neat and logical and orderly. As for myself, Temporal Projects is a challenge also. Only I cherish it for the lever it is: the power to move people and make things happen. For you, the paradoxes are a threat. For me, they are a random factor, exhilarating in their undependability. But neither of us, Friz, would have let this opportunity slip through our fingers without going for broke against it till we were broken or we mastered the game we play. We are not that different at all."

Depending on your point of view, Brelmer thought as he watched Paress Linnet threading through the packed parkground. Time travel could be either a blessing or a blight. Voxner seemed to have blinded himself to the negative aspects. For Brelmer the scales seemed to shift every moment.

"Do you see Lisa Ky?" Voxner asked.

Brelmer telescoped into the crowd but didn't knew where to begin his search. Surely Voxner had not waited until now to find the woman. Girl, Brelmer corrected himself. Over 20 years separated the Lisa Ky he searched for today and the one he had just met.

"Near the front," Voxner said, pointing.

Brelmer swept the forward ranks of the Dunkers, targeting in on the girl. She looked so young, so innocent, untouched by any of the political strife that had to have influenced her life in later years. Her unlined and rounded face spoke of living without compromise. Her black hair cascaded down her back, trickling over her hood as she sat bare-headed in the rain. A smile played across her lips as she shared secrets with the girl next to her and watched the speakers with rapt attention.

"Come on," Voxner said. "We don't want to be late getting into position."

Unwillingly, Brelmer drifted into the Senator's wake, surprised to find himself losing the larger man so easily. When one gray robed worshipper said, "Excuse me, brother," Brelmer picked the apology up quickly and used it to speed his progress through the crowd.

Low mutterings of disapproval followed Brelmer, coming from men and women. Children were an even worse obstacle. He found himself tripping over them while trying to keep Voxner spotted.

He was almost to the front of the crowd when a collective gasp seemed to pass through the audience and bring them to their feet.

Swiveling his head, Brelmer saw Paress Linnet at the forefront of the fountain. The woman's posture was aggressive and, even though he couldn't hear her words himself, Brelmer could tell they were effective enough to implement the desired effect Voxner had wanted.

Two of the younger members of the speakers darted forward, with the intentness of Dobermans at the charge, picking up the accusations where Paress had left off.

Brelmer saw the costumer whirl away, pulled into the bulk of the crowd by unfriendly hands.

Without warning Brelmer was sucked into the madness that gripped the congregation. A fist came from nowhere, turboing toward his face. He blocked the blow with an arm and followed through with a roundhouse kick that pitched his attacker violently backwards.

Cursing Voxner, Brelmer felt another wave of dizziness hit him, burning through the time travel fatigue, through even the effects of the stim, reaching down into the programmed centers of his brain for the self-preservation reflexes that had been fed into his nervous system. Burning jets turboed along his bloodstream and a wall of awareness smashed through him. His hands and feet moved automatically, weaving a vicious net of defensive and offensive moves that rendered him almost invulnerable from conventional hand-to-hand tactics. The system that had been overlaid into his subconscious fight/flight response during his military training had been impressive. But nothing like the complexity that was involved in the programming his central nervous system received when he had been promoted to Praetor.

Lashing out with a leg, Brelmer felt a man's face crack under his foot, heard the audible snap of bone breaking. The adrenaline flow draining into his body now would demand a huge payback later, he knew, but he could not relax out of the aggressive posture the comp overlay forced him into.

A fist exploded over his left ear. For a moment blackness shrouded around him as painful ringing took away his hearing. He could feel the adrenal surge rush through him, pushing the blackness away as the Y of his palm shot into his attacker's throat, driving the woman away.

"Friz!"

Not trusting his ringing ears, Brelmer reached a clear space and gazed around the mass of writhing bodies for Voxner.

"Friz, damnit! Over here!"

Peering over the raging congregation, Brelmer saw Voxner holding Lisa Ky protectively. All around them were a mass of bodies, torn and shattered by bullets Brelmer had never heard fired. The girl Lisa Ky had been talking to lay in a discarded heap at the Senator's feet.

"Friz, we've got to get her out of here before she gets hurt!" Voxner looked apoplectic.

Triggering the telescopic function of his crystal eyes, Brelmer spotted the three Time Policemen snipers standing on top of parked vehicles across the street, holding silenced Matthews at full extension, packed with 50-round clips.

Throwing himself onto the top of the crowd separating him from Voxner and the girl, Brelmer slid, shoved, and clawed his way into the clearing etched out by the corpses.

"She won't walk," Voxner said.

Brelmer gathered the girl into his arms, surprised at her lightness. He pushed the thought, the sight of the bodies surrounding the Senator from his mind, knowing they would haunt him far longer than Voxner. Shaking his hood back so he could be easily identified, he pulled Lisa Ky close to his chest and began the relentless staggering run toward the street, knowing every footstep he chose would trigger another death as the Time Police snipers shot down anyone who stood in their way.

A man lunged from the fringes. Brelmer lifted a foot, balancing all of his weight on his other leg. His boot connected with the man's face just as bullets from one of the Matthews ripped into the man, sending shudders down the length of his body.

A nightmare of swirling faces blinked into and out of existence in front of Brelmer like a faulty vid-recording as he powered his unsteady way to the safety of the street. Suddenly, there were no more bodies blocking his way, dead or alive. He took a breath and felt it burn its way deeply into his lungs. Only then could he feel Lisa Ky shivering and crying against his chest.

"Further, Friz," Voxner ordered. "We must get her further away from here. There's no telling how far this madness will spread before the law enforcement people can contain it."

A bullet honked warningly as Brelmer raced out onto the slick street.

A wave of fire from one of the Matthews silenced the vehicle, shattering expensive grille work in diamond-flashes that showered the street, skidding under Brelmer's feet. He felt the hard plastic shred and crunch under his boots. Struggling to keep his breathing even enough to let him continue running, he had nothing left to offer words of solace to the girl he carried. Blackness pounded at his temples but he forced himself to endure.

"Friz!"

Recognizing Voxner's strained voice, Brelmer slowed, then stopped, pausing at the side of a 7-Eleven. He released the girl but she seemed to afraid to step away from him. She hugged him and he knew the gray robe reassured her more than his presence.

The Senator was still fifty meters away, flanked by the six Time Police, but at least there was no sign of pursuit.

Holding the girl's head into his mid-section, Brelmer signalled the Time Policemen to put their weapons away before Lisa Ky or a passerby saw them.

Voxner panted to a stop in front of Brelmer, visibly straining to regain his lost breath. "Are you all right, Lisa?" he asked the girl.

Brelmer felt the girl's head turn slowly against his stomach. Even for him, who knew Voxner for the con-niving, ruthless man he could be, it was hard for Brelmer to see through the benign look that covered the Senator's face. Voxner looked like a kindly and concerned grandfather.

"Are you all right?" Voxner asked again.

The girl nodded.

Voxner stepped forward, hesitantly reaching for the girl's arms.

Brelmer wondered what her reaction would have been if Lisa Ky had known that Voxner was directly responsible for her friend's death. And if the Senator would have been able to manipulate her so easily.

"Remember, Lisa Ky," Voxner said softly, "remember that, like today, you will always have a friend in me should you need one."

Without warning, Brelmer felt the girl sag bonelessly against him. He tightened his grip around her before she could hit the ground. When he checked, the girl's eyes had rolled back into her head and her breathing was deeply regular.

"Relax, Friz," Voxner said. "I only gave her something to render her unconscious while we take our leave."

Brelmer looked at the Senator, watching as the man peeled a false fingertip from his left forefinger. Using the magnification factor of his crystal eyes, he scanned the small piece of latex and found the half-centimeter long needle in its center.

"She will sleep for a few hours," Voxner said as he stepped away from the shadows of the building. "She might have a slight headache but that is the extent of it."

Gathering the unconscious girl in his arms, Brelmer forced himself upright on shaking legs.

"What are you doing?" Voxner asked. His brows knitted together across his broad forehead and made a dark hood of   suspicion.

"I can't leave her here unattended," Brelmer said, knowing Voxner would recognize the inflection on the "I," knowing he was playing a dangerous game with the Senator's temper, yet needing some source of vindication after the sewer of death and deceit Voxner had prodded him through. Shiva, there had to be something of himself he could save in this. He had been unable to save Paress Linnet.

"Very well, Friz." Voxner waved him away and turned to go. But there was no mistaking the arctic chill of warning in his words.

Brelmer glanced at the captain leading their Time Police escort. "Captain Allen?"

"Sir?"

"The costumer?"

"She went down, sir."

"By our hand?"

"No, sir, though the Senator gave us strict instructions she was to go down with the first volley."

Brelmer fell silent, trying to find at least one end of the feelings that flushed rampant through him. Betrayer and betrayed. Voxner had managed to box him into both categories so neatly. And he lacked even the emotional strength to find a burning anger for himself. Or

Paress. Or any of the other dead left at the park.

"Sir?"

Brelmer looked back at the captain. "You won't tell the Senator, sir? That we missed the target? We were going to swing through the crowd, but there were simply too many of them."

Brelmer worked to find his voice, discovering it was almost as lifeless as the girl he held, hoping it wasn't as shaking and trembling as his arms. "No, captain."

A relieved grin spread across the captain's broad face. "Thank you, Colonel. That's why I wanted to tell you the truth. I knew you would understand."

Brelmer almost staggered under the girl's loose weight as he moved toward the doorway of the convenience store to leave Lisa Ky with the clerk till an ambulance could be summoned.

Understand. The captain's statement echoed through Brelmer's head, followed and punctuated by thoughts of what he had done these last few hours and in what times he had done them. Understand? He wasn't sure if he understood himself at the moment.

CHAPTER SIXTEEN

Jackson raised the window carefully, thankful it wasn't stuck and it didn't squeak. A quick glance over his shoulder let him know the woman Future Rebel was still asleep. Sheets twisted around her body, revealing slashes of nudity in the barren moonlight. Jackson wasn't surprised to learn the sight of one plump breast with its unwinking pink eye didn't even spark a twinge of desire within him. The girl was an expert and had mined every vein of the emotion from him. He had realized that only moments after they had begun their love-making. She could have taught Chrys Calvino a thing or two about prolonging culmination.

Gripping the straps of his duffel bag in one hand and

his boots in the other, Jackson swung a bare foot out onto the main roof of the saloon. The sheet metal felt cold and slippery. It wasn't until he rested the full weight of his body on his legs that he felt the dangerousness of the slope the roof.

But there was no choice, was there?

He couldn't stay there with the woman until her friends arrived. One Jackson Elgin Dubchek had all ready been declared a public menace in whatever century they hailed from. And, even if no one in the party was able to recognize him for who he was, there was always the possibility they would take the time machine away from him when they learned he had it. He couldn't stand the thought of being displaced again. Especially here, in a time he did not understand.

He closed the window behind him, checking once more to make sure the woman was still asleep.

Cautiously, aware that one misstep could send him sprawling out into the hard-packed dirt street running in front of the saloon, he started tip-toeing for the rear of the building and the stairway that would provide a safe descent. He trailed the boots in his right hand along the uneven surface of the sheet metal roof, leaning toward the trailing hand to help maintain his balance.

He turned the corner starting toward the rear of the saloon with difficulty, almost drifting over his center of gravity before he was able to find his balance again. A shadow jerked into life above him, accompanied by the skittering scrape of fingernails skipping along a holo projection pad.

Jackson lifted an arm to defend himself and lost his precarious hold on internal balance. He locked eyes with the black cat standing with bowed back on the roof of the saloon rooms, instantly glad the inhuman yellow lights glaring back at him belonged to a tabby rather than a Time Policeman.

His bare feet slid a few inches. Something sharp raked into the heel of his right foot, seeming to tear even more when he lunged forward to lock his fingers into the crack left where the roof butted up into the building. His boots clumped past him in an impossible and rolling gait, stepping off into air. Two dry thumps sounded only a second apart.

Still hanging by his fingertips, Jackson forced himself to relax and listen. Had someone heard him? The boots had landed in the alleyway at the side of the building. What if someone had heard and it turned out to be the sheriff?

The big man who had arrested him didn't seem like the type to believe Jackson had been rescued by a damsel who put him in distress.

Gritting his teeth, he put the pain in his fingers out of his mind, pulling himself back up. The duffel bag felt like an anchor in his other hand. Do it! he screamed at himself mentally. He pulled his knees under him, moving slowly because he didn't trust the fabric not to slither away from under him at the wrong moment. He slipped the strap of the duffel over his arm, sliding it down over his shoulder so he could use both hands to get to his feet.

Remaining hunkered down, he changed grips and wiped the blood from his cut fingers on his jeans. The sting of the lacerations was only a slight annoyance when compared to the returning feeling. He flexed the hand for a moment, then resumed the careful march toward the stairway.

Shadows played in a silent embrace on the last window separating him from the stairs. Writhing black grayness on a field of harvest gold.

Rather than chance another fall, Jackson ducked past the window, almost leaping for the stairway railing. He pulled himself over and felt relief when his feet rested on the landing.

Below, the street was quiet except for the tinkling notes of the saloon piano and the riotous voices of the various patrons. A horse snorted somewhere in the near distance, bringing larcenous thoughts to Jackson's mind.

He considered the animals he had seen tethered to the hitching post in front of the saloon. But they shot horse thieves in this time period, didn't they? The question brought a chill to him that wasn't born of the night air around him. Horses weren't just a means of travel in 1836, Jackson remembered from his studies, they were also considered one of a family's most prized and most expensive possessions. He had even read of where farmers in these years of Texas history had used their teams of horses and oxen as collateral at a bank.

Stealing one would be risky business, he told himself as he started down the stairs. But certainly less risky than being found out by the Future Rebs or being discovered by the Time Police.

He reached the bottom of the stairs without incident and gathered up his boots. Standing at the corner of the saloon overlooking the hitching post, he pulled the boots on. Eleven horses stood at the hitching post. Muted whickers reached Jackson's ears, punctuated by idle stampings of heavy hooves.

Jackson let the shadow of the overhanging eaves cover him. What would Joy do once she awoke and found him gone? She had no reason to suspect him of any duplicity, yet how else could she take his actions? How much longer would she sleep? Considering her sexual exertions Jackson thought she would be out for some time. For him, it had felt like swimming through a swamp of coma to reach an island of unfamiliar consciousness.

Just as he was about to step onto the boardwalk and make an attempt to reach the first horse, a man came staggering through the batwing doors. The man wore his broad-brimmed cowboy hat lopsided and weaved uncertainly to a support. Slinging an arm around the support wearily, the man rolled a cigarette and lighted it with a match.

Noting the big dragoon pistol holstered on the cowboy's hip, Jackson decided discretion was the better part of valor. Shouldering the duffel, he kept to the shadows clinging to the town buildings.

Even if he had managed to steal a horse, what then? he asked himself. If someone saw him take a horse that wasn't his, chances were he would be shot before he could ride out of town. An uncomfortable itch started between his shoulder blades and Jackson felt like he needed to hold something over the place for protection.

There were no other late night people walking the streets with him. Only the drunken cowboys gathered at the saloon kept the quietness of the evening from being complete. Jackson quickly realized that, even refraining from stealing the first horse he came across on this end of town, he would still be conspicuous to most citizens. Including the sheriff.

He stepped up on another boardwalk, wondering what he was going to do and even if there would be time to do it. Little pangs of guilt nibbled at him when he thought of Czenlyn. True, he had ascertained that the Time Police had been instrumental in changing Czenlyn's accepted view of history, but had he learned anything of consequence that would enable them to strike back?

Strike back?

Jackson wondered where the thought had come from. Czenlyn had never said anything about striking back at Temporal Projects if they learned something helpful. Yet, wasn't that what this whole reconnaissance mission was about? Probing the strength of the enemy for signs of weakness?

Damnit, Irene! You've got me dodging shadows.

Jackson pulled his light jacket around him more tightly, warding off the chill that had blown in with the night winds.

Czenlyn had seemed to only want to know for knowledge's sake. But it was evident the man had the finances and backing of the rural people in Mexico of 2074 to initiate a confrontation against the forces of the Time Police in his chosen time period if he wanted to.

And Irene had said forces of Temporal Projects had recognized Czenlyn while the Time Police were drawing closed the net they were using to search for Jackson. Sure, Jackson told himself, he had spent a week on Czenlyn's hidden ranch and nothing had happened. But that didn't mean anything wouldn't. Did it?

His boots clumped heavily on the boardwalk. He glanced across the dirt street to get his bearings and saw too late that he was directly across from the Sheriff's Office.

He felt his heart claw its way uncertainly to his throat and couldn't help staring through the single barred window facing the street. A candle burned inside and, hypnotized, Jackson almost paused to peer into the garishly lit interior to see if the big man was there.

Buddha, the way he was forced to live his life now was insane. The sheriff was probably a good man to the citizens of this town. Yet, if the man tried to apprehend him, Jackson would have to consider him an enemy.

Maybe even hurt the man in order to remain free. The possibility was frightening and morbidly fascinating.

Faces whirled around Jackson in the darkness of his memory. Buddha, when would the madness end? When would he know peace again? He had bitched at Irene for using him, yet she was probably more supportive of him than anyone else he had known. Suzanne had wasted no time in returning to the safety of her father's protection, knowing the blight Voxner was managing through the forces of Temporal Projects stretched across many centuries. She had turned away from him, left him displaced in 2074. There had been plenty of time for her to return for him.

The realization of the thought slammed into him, making him seem even more alone in the darkness of the building. He couldn't move his eyes from the window of the Sheriff's Office. She could have returned for him. At any time.

Why hadn't she?

Sagging against the building behind him, Jackson tried to force the line of thinking away. He had all ready dealt with the question before. Buddha knew, he had had plenty of opportunities and time to do so in Mexico City of 2074. He had arrived at several conclusions, drawn up dozens of hypotheses why Suzanne had not come for him.

More than anything else he had seen or been forced to do, Suzanne's treason cut into him deeply.

An answering ache started in his slashed fingers. He

focused on the pain, wrapping it gently around him like one of the simpler melodies he had first learned on Odar'a, playing it out till he found an echo of it flickering faintly in his tattered soul. He escalated it in his mind, changing breaks, adding extra rhythms, seeking. Seeking.

What?

Seeking what?

Salvation?

A savage memory of the woman, Joy, surging against him as they reached another mutual plateau of momentary ecstasy played through his mind, disrupting the concentration he had given to his pain. All his pains. He remembered the pain of his ejaculation into the woman, remembered the pain of the way the woman had bitten his lip at the moment of her orgasm. In his memory, Jackson blinked his eyes, first looking down on the woman's nakedness, then up into Suzanne's beautiful eyes as she gently mounted him and moved him toward a loving completion.

"Buddha," the word tumbled from Jackson's lips before he could stop it. He could almost see Suzanne standing before him. He raised a hand, aware that something was wrong but not knowing what. Then he realized he could see through her. See through the small smile she wore for him that was more honest than anything he had ever seen before. See through her and see the hard packed dirt of the Texas street behind her.

Jackson closed his eyes, feeling emotion burn at the

inside of them. He locked it in tightly, afraid to lose anything more of himself that made him human. The eyes, he thought. In so many religions, in so many beliefs, the eyes were the window to the soul. They scooped out the eyes of the Time Policemen, didn't they? Scooped them out with sharp silver spoons and . . . and . . . and did what with them? Spooned out their eyes (and their souls?) and dropped in globs of protein-based crystal that functioned even better than their original equipment.

New eyes. New windows on vacant lots. Soulless.

How the hell could you fight soulless monsters?

Fear gripped Jackson, suctioning into him through a thousand prickly tentacles.

No one had a right to expect him to fight soulless monsters in times that didn't even exist.

Yet, he had, hadn't he? Fought them and discovered they died. Just as messily as their own victims.

Now his hands were no longer clean either.

Jackson blinked, looking down, seeing the blood drip from between his clenched fingers.

Not clean at all.

Jackson could almost feel the thin line of insanity in front of him. Some force seemed to be sucking him forward, wanting to him take one last fatal misstep. The thin line so sharp and sour he knew if he ran his tongue across it, it would cut him and make his jaws ache with the taste of it.

Buddha, maybe if he embraced the madness, maybe it

would embrace him back and sweep him away from all the pain and suffering that ate at him as surely as acid rain.

He tried to fall forward, tried to force his shoulders from the building he stood in front of, tried to step inside the unseen Madness Falls surging in front of him.

He touched only the chill, dry wind that careened through the street.

Blinking, feeling the giddiness of emotions coming to a rest inside him, Jackson resisted the urge to curl into a fetal position. He scanned the darkness. He was still alone. Where had the madness gone? Buddha, it had seemed so real, its touch so whispery soft. Why hadn't it claimed him? Was that the way it was to be? Would even the time travel madness declare war on him as well? Or was the madness a fickle mistress, waiting for the rapture of the conquest rather than taking a willing lover?

Guilt shot through Jackson as he studied the obsession he had felt for the madness. He had fought so hard against it in Mexico City, in 2074. Why had his feelings toward it changed now?

He stood, clinging to the building for support, feeling perspiration pour from him despite the coolness of the weather.

Suzanne. He had been thinking of Suzanne when it came upon him. Thinking thoughts of betrayal. She had abandoned him, left him to be broken on the unsure shores of Time, left him to be murdered by the Time

Police.

No, he realized. It was betrayal that had triggered the insanity attack. But it wasn't her betrayal. Not Suzanne's.

It was his.

His betrayal of her.

Images of Joy riding him, slamming her hips into him again and again, greedily reaching for completion, tumbled nonsequential through his mind. He remembered the way the woman Future Reb had trailed her hair across his chest and stomach, licking her way down, down, down, d. . .

Memory of the love he and Suzanne had shared in the hotel room before doubling back on the assassination had been one of Jackson's most prized possessions. It had seemed so real, the feelings that had been freed in the room.

And Jackson had locked them away even then, determined not to let anything stand in his way.

How had Suzanne felt about that? Buddha, it had been like cutting off one of his arms to send her away. Or at least to make the attempt to send her away. But he had seen no other way. He hadn't wanted to take the chance of her getting hurt by one of the Time Police who hunted him or the Future Rebs he hunted himself.

Then, trapped in the past, he had used the memory to help him build a foundation that would keep him sane. How many times had he pulled those precious moments out to savor again and again? He had turned her into something more than human during those weeks.

Then defiled her memory by responding to the Future Reb's ministrations in bed.

Guilt, Buddha, the guilt felt so sharp, so heavy.

He had done it to himself, Jackson realized as he slipped the duffel into a more comfortable position. He had taken what he wanted of Suzanne's memory, of her relationship with him, and made it into something more than it had been; forged it through a time of want and need and fear into something so godlike. And so damned frail. It had become a chink in his armor after having sex with the woman over the saloon, festering away till the time madness could worm its way into his mind and try to steal lucidness away. He hadn't beaten it, but any draws were surely in his favor.

To thine own self be true.

The line from William Shakespeare's works dropped into Jackson's mind. Time travel was a mirror. It stripped away dreams, made you realize how delicate life really was. How very brief.

Jackson sucked in air, forcing his thoughts back to his present now, tracking his attention back onto his problems now. It was his own fault for letting his subconscious select Suzanne as his saviour, for getting him to compromise himself and that belief unknowingly and go through the resulting fall from grace that nearly let the time travel madness have him.

He couldn't depend on anyone.

Buddha, you would think he would have realized that

by now.

Hadn't that been what Irene tried to tell him?

You're alone, Jackson, he told himself. You've been that way most of your life. You were a loner even when you were working at New Ninevah Library. Martin married early, settled down and started raising children. What have you ever done to tie yourself to anyone or anything? To what cause do you owe allegiance? Czenlyn, Irene, the Mnemosyne, they fight the tactics of the Time Police because they believe in what they are doing. Why do you fight?

To survive, he answered himself. And for now, it's enough. And I'll keep telling myself that for as long as it takes till I believe it.

He pushed away from the building, walking toward the blacksmith's shop. He remembered seeing horses taken there from earlier in the day when he had been waiting on the stage. If he couldn't steal a horse and make a quick departure, perhaps maybe he could purchase one and enjoy a leisurely escape. There was no way he could make the walk back to the time machine on foot. Not the way he felt now.

The emotional pressure of fighting the time travel madness, of combatting the guilt he had unconsciously set himself up for (but who would have thought he would have to compete in a sexual marathon for his freedom?), and the physical weariness he had from traveling through time had left him barely able to care for himself.

He moved on through the darkness toward the black-smith's shop, turning frequently to make sure no one had noticed him. A shadow drifted across the window of the sheriff's office, causing Jackson's breath to catch in his throat for a moment, but no one came out of the building.

Light spilled out of the blacksmith's shop, throwing a yellow oblong against the dusty red of the street. Drifting sounds of unsettled horses reached Jackson's ears. The stamping, snorting, and snickering of the animals almost covered the bits of conversation that reached him as well.

Jackson paused across the street, wondering how many people were in the livery and who they were. The blacksmith also cared for the horses used in the stage line. He had learned that earlier as well. Still, what could be involved in caring for the horses? Then he remembered the way Rachel Czenlyn had checked the ones they had ridden, the way the girl had checked to make sure none of them had thrown their shoes or had injured a hoof. He had been amazed at the way she had handled the horses, pushing and making her demands known, all the while dwarfed by the huge creatures. Her hands had looked even smaller while holding a hoof up for inspection.

Reaching into his duffel, Jackson pulled out the bag of gold coins Irene had given him and chose two of the larger ones. He hadn't bothered to scan the sheet out-lining the value of the coins, but surely, for two of them, he could buy a horse and saddle.

He clasped them tightly in his hand and straightened his spine, trying to pretend he wasn't afraid, trying to tell himself he didn't think a Time Policeman might be on the other side of the double doors of the livery.

Shouldering his duffel again, he walked across the street. A horse, he told himself, any horse. He would be an easy sale. Surely there could be no problems.

He stepped around the open side of the double doors, marring the yellow oblong, creating twin shadows whose legs seemed to stem from the same source. Two coal oil lanterns hung on posts on either side of the building. The smell of hay and urine hung heavy in the air, shot through with a dozen different odors Jackson couldn't identify.

A horse snorted suddenly and startled him.

A man stepped out of one of the stalls, walking carefully, his attention riveted on what was happening in one of the other stalls.

The man looked too neat to Jackson, too well-kept to be someone whose financial existence depended on being able to move large horses by brute strength all day long. The man's suit was cut well, not at all like the clothing worn by most of the other people Jackson had seen in town.

"Hey," Jackson called, feeling the uncomfortable itch start between his shoulderblades again.

The man spun, too quickly, his nostrils flaring wide in surprise. A thick-bladed hunting knife filled his right hand.

Jackson raised his empty hands before him. "Look, I just came to buy a horse. I don't want any trouble."

A heavy sound rang out in the rear of the livery. Flesh on flesh. Jackson hadn't grown accustomed to the sound, but knew it well enough to recognize it for what it was. A figure came stumbling from one of the stalls, groping blindly for balance. For a moment Jackson thought the man might make it, then the man crumpled to the hay-strewn floor.

When the man rolled over, Jackson saw it was Laszlo Slye. The Time Policeman was bleeding freely from a cut over one eye and from his broken nose. Another man, larger than Slye, stepped from the stall the Time Policeman had staggered from, carrying a short length of 2X4.

"Time Police qwerk's head is harder than a Junqui-cursed coconut," the man with the 2X4 said.

Jackson's mind tried to grope with the situation. Slye here? Alive? The man with the club speaking 23rd Century English with a strangely twisted accent?

"Looks like you came to the wrong place to buy a horse tonight," the man with the knife said. Dulled madness gleamed in the bloodshot brown eyes.

Jackson turned, ready to give himself over to flight, seeing the third man behind him, noticing the way the man shifted his weight, lunging at him with a pitchfork. Jackson could see the sharp tines getting larger as they streaked for his face.

CHAPTER SEVENTEEN

For one frozen moment, Jackson thought the pitch-fork was going to slash his eyes out. Then the instinct for survival that had been honed so unwillingly during his evasion of the Time Police took over.

Without consciously willing it, Jackson found his body turning, dipping below the thrust. A burning strip of fire ignited along the top of his shoulder, letting him know the effort hadn't been entirely successful.

An unexpected force caught him from behind, yanking him from his feet. Rather than fight against it, he went with the sudden pull, using it to place himself even further from the man. The force seemed about to reverse itself when the pitchfork wielder yanked his make-shift weapon back. Jackson could hear the fabric of his duffel bag rip as the tines tore free.

The breath whooshed from his lungs as he hit the straw-covered hard-packed earth all wrong. A shadow, made macabre by the whispering lights of the lanterns, drifted into his field of vision stripping away the sizzling stars that screamed under his eyelids. The shadow jerked suddenly and a warning flare soared in Jackson's mind. He rolled away from the shadow, seeking shelter in the nearest stall.

The pitchfork buried itself in the spot he had just vacated, tearing small red clods from the ground.

Jackson kept rolling, scattering hay, losing the duffel bag somewhere, until he bumped in a horse's hooves. He grabbed for one of the legs without thinking, feeling the animal shy away from him. The stringy tail of the horse whipped across his face as a massive hoof grazed by his head. Realizing he couldn't stay in the stall with the horse without getting hurt, he threw himself into the next stall and tried to roll to his feet.

`Buddha, what the hell had he walked in on?

He almost had his feet under him when the man carrying the pitchfork whipped around the corner and lunged at him.

Jackson dodged to one side, stepping inside the man's reach without thinking. Self-preservation screamed at him, promising all sorts of grisly deaths if he didn't react.

For whatever reason, these men were willing to kill

him and he needed to accept that. Maybe they had all ready killed Slye. A brief flicker of memory reminded him of the Time Policeman's bloodied visage.

They killed Slye, the time travel madness cackled inside him, uttering a staccato of barking laughter that rang inside his head. They killed Slye and now you never did/never will.

Jackson felt himself on the edge of the madness again. Trapped. With no where to go. The tines of the pitchfork slid toward him in excrutiating slowness as the madness vertigoed inside him, speeding up his perception of events. How easy it would be to stand there, to let the sharp, long claw of the man rake his life away. There would be no confusion then, no questions of what is/what was/what will be.

Unwillingly at first, he felt himself move, shifting on the balls of his feet, changing balance. Then his hands were on the rough handle of the weapon, pulling in an imitation of the initial thrust. The man was caught off-guard by the act and came across the railing in front of the stall.

Slye, Jackson's brain hammered at him, trying to deal with all the complications of the still and unmoving body at the other end of the barn.

Dead!

Dead?

The man couldn't be, Jackson told himself wildly. Buddha, if Slye was here, it meant he hadn't killed the Time Police captain in 1968. But he had. He could still remember it. The incident still haunted Jackson in graphic detail. Slye's head had come apart when Jackson had pulled the trigger of the captured gun. No holo he had ever viewed had ever come close to the realness Jackson had experienced while killing the man. There was no way a med unit from Temporal Projects could have rescued the man. He and Suzanne had left the corpse there while they pulled Brelmer to safety and made the return jump in the time machine.

Which left it clear in the tangled logic running rampant in Jackson's mind that the Slye before him was from the Time Policeman's personal past. From a time before that last meeting in 1968. That event still lay in this Slye's future.

Lungs burning from the effort of trying to escape, Jackson seized a firmer grip on the pitchfork, holding it before him to back his attacker into the corner and into at least a temporary submission.

"Kanter!" the man yelled. He never took his bulging eyes from the pitchfork tines.

"Did you get him?" a man's voice asked.

"No."

Jackson lifted the pitchfork warningly, pressing it into the man's throat just below the bobbing Adam's apple. He tried to keep the images from his mind of what the sharp tines would do if he leaned on the handle with any real weight.

The man froze, stretched back across the railing of the stall behind him.

Jackson's mind spun, trying to keep up with every stray thought that flashed through it as he fought against the overload of sensory input from his adrenaline-enhanced senses for the sound of the two men left free in the barn. What if Slye was dead? Where did that leave him? His head hurt from all of the ramifications of the possibility. Buddha, life was so uncertain when you spent it on the outer fringes of Time. If Slye was dead, would that mean the time he had lived since the event back in the 1968 he remembered would become one of the orphan time-lines Czenlyn had hypothesized? How could what happened in the past NOW affect him in his future THEN? How could there be a NOW if there was not a THEN?

For a moment, Jackson considered the sweetness of having Slye dead in this NOW of 1836 instead of his THEN of 1968. There would be no displacement in 2183. No death on his hands. No head sick and full of what ifs and maybes.

And, if that were to happen, would that mean that this him, this Jackson NOW, would simply cease to exist and the other, younger Jackson would continue his life at New Ninevah?

Or would he die?

The question left him cold.

But what was death? he asked himself. Wasn't the way he was living now, constantly on the run and fearing any person who looked at him twice, wasn't that a type of death as well?

The uncertainty left his mind dazed and reeling from the explorations of logic that denied explanation. What was life when the IS of life depended on the WILL BE and could be lost so easily in the WAS?

Buddha! Slye had to be alive. There could be no other explanation. Circles within circles, each grinding inexorably into the other.

The rapid pulse of a Matthews in full roar swelled through the interior of the stable.

Jackson dropped the pitchfork and dove for the ground, scrambling for the next stall down, knowing the gunner would be expecting him to run the other way, toward the entrance. He didn't have time to give thought to everything, he told himself. Whatever happened, he had to play it out, sort through things later. If there was a later. Wood chips sprayed like heavy snow around him as the gunner raked the stalls.

The sound of bullets striking flesh sounded in Jackson's ears and he expected to feel the numbness of a wound at any moment, surprised when the feeling never came. He risked a look back and saw the corpse of his first attacker draped over the railing. A line of neat bullet holes stitched a bloody seam across the man's chest.

Jackson froze for a moment, taking cover behind the bulk of a dark horse with flaring nostrils. He ran his hands over its rippling flesh. Something had matted the horse's hair and he felt it smear across the palm of his hand. Glancing down, he saw the blood covering his skin, felt sickness knot at his stomach. He squelched the reflex with difficulty.

The horse stamped nervously. The matted hair jerked irritably at Jackson's touch. The animal moved suddenly in the small confines of the stall, brushing against Jackson with enough force to send him reeling into the railing.

The roar of the Matthews filled the still air again, chewing into the hard-muscled flesh of the horse. Jackson felt it stagger under the wave of bullets, felt something flick through the shirt he wore as he plowed into the ill-smelling straw lining the bottoms of the stall.

"Kanter, did you get him? Did you get the qwerk?" Jackson guessed the new voice came from the man who had

been standing over Slye. Was the man still there? Or had he taken up some new position? Buddha, even with both lanterns lit, it was so dark in the stable. He kept moving, working knees and elbows through the next empty stall. Sheltered by the shadows of his latest refuge, Jackson risked a look over the railing.

"No," Kanter yelled back. "I saw him moving over there. I killed the horse but I don't think I hit the guy."

"Did you see who it was?"

"I saw him when he first walked into the building but I didn't recognize him."

Jackson could see the big man still hovering over Slye's still body. Buddha, was the man dead? He ignored the question, focusing his mind on survival. Kanter was missing. The slender man with the brown eyes filled with mad passion had disappeared somewhere in the cluster of stalls.

Glancing overhead, Jackson saw the bottom of the second-story storage, wondering if it would be possible for him to reach the landing unnoticed. He reached inside his shirt and freed the Veritas dagger, holding it in his right hand despite the cuts from his earlier slide down the saloon. The double-edged blade glinted grimly in the poor light. It was darker here, and maybe it would give him the edge he needed. Buddha, it had to.

Survival.

That was the key thought centered in his brain. It surprised him how easily he could slip into the role of the predator. Like a familiar glove. But he hadn't slipped, he reminded himself. He had been goaded, forced and cornered.

Kanter. He rolled the name over in his mind, trying to remember where he had heard it before. Kanter. For a moment it slithered through his memory like a scum-slick tadpole but he held the thought tenaciously. Kanter was the name of the man the woman from the saloon had said would help him.

Kanter could have been an ally of sorts, as long as he didn't know Jackson Elgin Dubchek when he saw him. Instead, Jackson found himself backed against the wall by the very man who might have offered a hand in friendship, trapped by his intentions to save a Time

Policeman he had and would kill. The irony of the situation bit at Jackson with thorny teeth.

"Circle around," Kanter ordered from his hiding place. "The damned qwerk's got to be in here somewhere. He can't have just vanished."

The man standing over Slye nodded and moved cautiously toward the other end of stalls.

Realizing his time was swiftly running out, Jackson crawled under the railing into the next stall. A pair of horses shied away from him, moving toward the locked gate. Easing up, Jackson studied the gate, unable to fathom much of it in the darkness.

"Something has spooked those horses," Kanter called softly.

Peering between the railing, Jackson saw the slender man pause over twenty meters away, looking like nothing more than a black, vacuous two-dimensional figure leaning against a stall. Only the gleam of the stainless Matthews gave off any color.

Reconstructing the previous gates he had seen in his mind, Jackson remembered the sliding bar that kept the opening locked. Knowing it would take too much time and effort to slide it open, he concentrated his attention on the leather hinges that held the gate in place at the other end. He put the honed blade of the Veritas dagger against the top one and sawed it through, then moved on to the bottom one. When he felt the knife slide through the leather hinge, he stepped back, listening. Perspiration made his shirt stick to him. It would all be a matter of timing, he told himself in an effort to calm his racing heart.

Something snapped only a few meters away.

Without waiting to see which of his attackers had closed in on him so tightly, Jackson yelled suddenly and slapped one of the horses on the hindquarters.

Terrified, the animals bolted toward the gate, bowling through it easily. Their hooves drummed on the hard-packed ground and they whinnied in fright. Jackson could see the whites of their eyes rolling like albino marbles in the darkness.

Jackson sheathed the Veritas dagger and ran up the railing of the stall, grasping at anything and everything within his reach, clawing his way to the storage area that made a half-moon around the stable. He was dimly aware of the matched shadows that galloped away beneath him, even more acutely aware of the bullets that searched for him, darting forcefully into the bales of hay surrounding him.

He elbowed his way onto the hayloft, feeling the boards shiver as the automatic fire slammed into it. Little puffs of straw blew into the air as the bullets lanced through.

Where the hell was the sheriff when you wanted him? Jackson wondered angrily. Then, just as quickly, he dismissed the complaint. Even if the man had heard the sound of shooting and came running, he would have been outgunned and would have perished quickly.

Jackson rolled over and pushed himself to his feet,

keeping his head snugged down into his shoulders to keep from hitting it on the low rafters. He resisted the impulse to look down to see where his attackers were and whether or not Slye was alive.

"Do you see him?" Kanter asked.

"No," the other man answered.

"Where did he go?" "Up into the loft. You go up and see if you can flush him out."

Quietly, Jackson halted near the edge of the loft where he judged Kanter to be. He peered through a crack, seeing the slender man huddling close to one of the nearby stalls. Without waiting, not wanting to give his nerve a chance to fade away, Jackson gripped the edge of the loft and swung himself out, over, and down, aiming his booted feet at Kanter's head.

Agony screamed through his injured palm and he could feel it tear open again. His fingers slipped from the rough wood before he could complete the move, greased by the fresh blood. He felt himself falling, seeing Kanter look up at him.

Kanter dodged away, trying to bring the Matthews up. "Over here, Juis! The qwerk doubled back!"

Twisting in the air, using the last of the momentum derived from his descent, Jackson managed to catch the slender Future Rebel with a glancing blow. Left off-balance, Jackson felt himself hit the ground wrong, felt the air explode from his lungs. He pushed himself over, scanning for Kanter. He saw the Future Reb clawing for the lost Matthews, knowing the man would have a fist around the butt of the pistol before he had the chance to react.

Footsteps pounded dully overhead and Jackson knew the other man would reach them in seconds.

As Jackson forced himself to his feet, he knew he would never have time to reach Kanter before the man unleashed the destructive power of the pistol. Bright light caught at his attention, drawing a brief and frightened glance at the kerosene lantern hanging from the support strut by his head. He wrapped a hand around the thick pole and pulled himself toward it, curling the fingers of his right hand around the lantern's wire handle. The flame wavered and the fuel sloshed wetly inside the reservoir as he ripped it from the nail holding it.

He threw it with all of his strength, feeling it slip in his grasp, willing it to hit Kanter with enough force to at least allow him to close the distance between them.

Kanter dodged, sinking to one knee as he took a double-handed grip on the Matthews.

The lantern hit the railing just behind the Future Reb and smashed with a metallic thump. Kerosene left dark, wet trails over the wooden rails of the horse stall.

Inside his chest, Jackson's heart almost came to a stop as he saw the triangular barrel of the Matthews drift toward him.

There was a faint whoosh of displaced air, then flames seemed to eagerly wash over Kanter's body, tracing the spattered remains of the kerosene. Fingers of it whispered along the slats of the wall and the horse stall. Within seconds the fire had formed a blazing cocoon around the Future Reb.

Kanter dropped the pistol as he tried to brush tears of fire from his eyes. He tried to run. A scream ripped from the man's throat that made the hair on the back of Jackson's neck stand up.

Jackson watched the man run, unable to do anything else, staring at the fiery footprints Kanter left in the straw covered floor. Buddha, he had never intended this.

In the center of the double doors, the Future Reb stumbled and fell, still beating at the flames smothering him with blazing arms.

"Kanter!"

The hoarse shout drew Jackson's attention from the burning man, reminding him he wasn't alone. He glanced upward, surprised at how quickly the fire had spread through the stall. Gray-blue smoke formed a shroud that drifted up to the hayloft, making it hard for Jackson to see the remaining man standing there.

The smoke touched Jackson's eyes with baby thorns, burying itself under his eyelids. He forced himself to move. The man in the hayloft raised his gun in response.

Jackson threw himself forward, reaching for Kanter's dropped Matthews. Bullets kicked into the dirt behind him. He slid across the rough ground, coming to a sudden stop against the stall railing. Flames licked at his face and he dodged away, nostrils filling with the cloying scent of scorched hair. But the Matthews was in his right hand.

He fisted the weapon, estimating where the last man had been when he dived for cover. His finger curled around the trigger. The Matthews tried to twist and turn in his hands like a python as he channeled its fire into the loft overhead. He saw splinters of wood kick free as he emptied the 50-round clip, trying not to think of what the projectiles would do to the flesh on the other side of the barrier.

When the roar of the pistol died away, he listened, wondering if the man had moved to safety. Nothing. Only the shrill whinnying of the horses and the heavy clomp-clomp-clomp of their feet as they moved within their individual stalls.

He grabbed a rail and pulled himself up, unwilling to drop the empty weapon.

Silently, a heavy shadow dropped from the loft, thudding brokenly onto the hard ground.

Jackson raised the Matthews instinctively, as if it would ward off any attack by merely being there. The dulled and glazed eyes of the man stared emptily at the stable roof.

A burning sensation traced his left arm. When he saw the fire feeding on his shirt sleeve, he dropped the Matthews and beat the flames out before they could do more than singe the skin.

He stumbled from the stall, wondering why no one

from the town had come. Surely someone had heard the shots or could see the fire. He made his way to Slye's side on shaking legs. Smoke burned down into his lungs, became a churning and painful miasma of smells as he breathed through his nose. Straw, dung, urine, all of it hot and burning.

Dropping to his knees over Slye, he checked for a pulse at the big man's throat. Hadn't he succeeded? Buddha, how could he have failed to save the Time Policeman's life if he was still here? He felt the jugular beat under his fingertips, thready and too quick.

Unreality pressed in on Jackson's senses as he gripped the big man under his arms. Slye was dead, the time travel madness whispered into Jackson's mind. Dead, dead, dead. How can you save the dead, Jackson? And why save them? Are you saving him now so you can kill him later?

Jackson tried to will the voice into silence as he dragged Slye toward the double doors. Buddha, he didn't know how to feel about his attempt to rescue the Time Policeman. Triumphant? Victorious? How could he feel that way when . . . when . . . He looked at the bodies around him, giving the still burning corpse of Kanter a wide berth as he continued to drag Slye.

He remembered Joy's words, of how Jackson Elgin Dubchek was one of their time-line's greatest enemies. Was this the reason? Because he had killed these men tonight? Or was there some other way he was going to betray them and their mission? But how would they have known? No one knew his name.

Buddha, if only he knew if his efforts were right or wrong. If only he could be sure of himself. But there was no way. Not according to the theory Czenlyn had of the alternate time-lines and the orphan time-lines. Every move he made was both beneficial and detrimental. Good and evil. Saintly and satanic. There had to be an answer somewhere. Buddha, there had to be. He couldn't continue to live his life in this sick confusion.

Cool air washed over him as he pulled Slye into the middle of the street. He fell to his knees, exhausted from his efforts, sucking in the fresh air greedily. Even this, he thought, even saving Captain Laszlo Slye, soon-to-be late of the Time Police, good and evil tailed this decision. How many people had died through acts for which Slye was directly responsible?

Shaking the thought from his mind, Jackson made himself stand again. He had no choice, he told himself.

You give yourself no choice, the time madness whispered evilly in his mind. Slye could die here, now. Things would change. They do all the time. Nothing is/was/will be as it shall/should/could be.

A paper fluttered from one of Slye's shirt pockets and Jackson caught it. He bent to replace it in the Time Policeman's shirt pocket, then noticed his name at the top of the paper.

With shaking hands, he held it out, letting it catch the almost electric glare of the full moon. Jackson Elgin Dubchek. Lester Wu. Rosita Alvarez. There were other names but they were unknown to him.

A bass drum boomed hollowly inside his head.

This was the list.

The list Rosita Alvarez had told him and Suzanne of in 1968 only moments before Slye killed her. It was the list that had been recovered in the past detailing the people who would interfere with Temporal Projects in the past. Slye had recovered it.

Numbness filled him and he felt tears seep into his eyes when he realized what he had to do.

He could almost feel them through the paper. LIVES. Rosita Alvarez's. Lester's. The others he did not know, could not put faces to. Sweet Buddha, he held them all. In the palm of his hand. So many lives.

Even his.

He had the power.

He had the power to save them all.

To save himself.

But.

But doing so would warp Time as he knew it. Maybe even destroy this self he had grown to be. Or would he be trapped? A phantom orphaned in Time?

If he had never been displaced in 2183, Suzanne and he would never have learned of Temporal Projects' attempts to alter history. Irene would never have found out events had been changed for certain. There would have been no one to rescue Ana.

Jackson wept.

For himself. For all of them.

Why did he have to sit in judgment on the lives he held in his hand? What right did he have to weigh them against the little he had accomplished? Why did he cling so tenaciously to the nightmare that his life had become?

Quickly, before he lost his resolve, he tucked the paper back in Slye's shirt pocket. Then pushed himself to his feet, staring down at the unconscious Time Policeman.

Buddha. All those deaths. All the deaths he had at one time accused Suzanne of being a party to, had blamed entirely on her father. Yet it had been his hand that had finally damned everyone on that list to the full punishment meted out by the Time Police.

Guiltless, Jackson? he asked himself. How often did you complain of your innocence? Well, you can't. Not ever again.

He wondered how long he would live to regret his decision.

Hoarse shouts started in the distance, sporadic at first, then gaining frequency.

Jackson looked up, seeing a half dozen men spill from the saloon and start running toward him. A glance back at the stable showed flames starting to lick from the roof. Smoke was a lighter blackness against the star-filled night.

He ran back into the burning building and was almost blinded by the light and heat. Spiderwebs of leaping flame dangled all over the interior of the stable. His fingers clawed a bridle from a wall hook and he dashed down the line of horse stalls, wondering if he had time to free all the animals before the first of the men reached the stable. Several of the horses were all ready loose and galloped away from him through the open doors.

Only three stalls remained occupied and he scared the horses out of them easily. Selecting a roan-colored horse from the last stall, he talked softly to the animal, watching the rolling white of the animal's eyes, trying to match the tone Rachel Czenlyn had used when she saddled their mounts. He tried to put the thought of the men running toward the stable out of his mind.

He touched the horse gently, rubbing its neck, then he slipped the bridle over its bobbing head. Using the reins, he lead the horse into the center of the stable and mounted bareback. The horse needed no encouragement and trotted eagerly toward the doors.

Before they could reach it, a burning support gave way and came crashing down only inches in front of the horse. The animal came up, rearing, smashing its head into Jackson's face. Dull throbbing started inside his head as he fought to stay mounted, grabbing fistfuls of the horse's mane.

Then it was on all four legs again and leaping over the burning beam.

Terrified, the horse almost ran over the first man coming into the stable. Jackson tucked himself down, almost lying on the animal's thick neck as he pulled the reins, changing directions and resuming a semblance of control over the maddened flight.

A chorus of shouts rang out behind him but no one appeared interested in giving chase. By the time they got organized and sorted out the dead bodies, Jackson was certain he would be far enough ahead to reach the time machine without further incident. He hoped.

CHAPTER EIGHTEEN

In the middle of nowhen, the time machine stalled.

Jackson could think of nothing else that quite described the sensation. Multi-colored stars hung frozen in the blackness of nowhere on the other side of the crystal windows. Even the control board ceased its flashings. The lights usually blinked through a continuous sequence during the jump but stood dormant instead.

Inertia tried to push Jackson back into the padded seat as he reached for the initiation switch. Suddenly there was so much pressure on his body he didn't think his lungs would work. He remembered how he had felt when Czenlyn advanced his thinking that he had been gone for so long from his native time-line that he could no longer go back. Remembered how the big man had said he and the LONE STAR book were incongruous with the time-line they inhabited now.

A chill thrilled through Jackson as he watched his thumb narrow the distance to the initiation switch. He struggled to breathe, reaching up with his other hand to strip the face-mask away. Irene's words of warning hung heavily in his mind.

He hit the initiation switch.

The time machine chugged forward. And bounced gently off of something that had found a way to exist in nothing.

The lights in the time machine dimmed, muting out to the point Jackson almost couldn't see himself, only a dulled and pieced together reflection in the crystal windows. Terror slashed a cold path through his intestines with a razor-skinned squirm.

He hit the initiation switch again.

The time machine spun. A few of the lights flashed. The time machine spiraled into another spin but still didn't make any forward progress.

Was this what Czenlyn meant by the barrier he had bounced from in his attempts to reach 2248? Buddha, it was getting so hard to breathe.

He scanned the arrival date again, thinking that maybe he had entered something wrong in his hurry to flee 1836 and the pursuers he felt certain would be after him. His body still ached from the fight in the stable and the bareback ride on the horse. He had limped painfully to the time machine. But the ache he had endured then and now were nothing compared to the burning thirstiness of his lungs searching for oxygen. He was starting to feel light-headed.

Was he draining the life-support system by continued use of the initiation switch?

He didn't know. The coordinates were right, though. Set for him to arrive back in 2074 only fifteen minutes after he had left. Surely nothing could have happened in that time. Czenlyn had died in the past, Irene had told him.

Jackson ignored the remembered words, consigning them to a back part of his mind, letting the struggle to survive wash them away.

He hit the initiation switch again.

Without warning, the time machine skidded sideways, possessing no forward movement at all.

Had that ever happened? He didn't think so. He tried to relax back in the padded chair, tried to cope with the carbon dioxide desert erupting in his chest.

The time machine continued its orbiting motion for a moment, then fell forward, as if tumbling over an abyss into an ocean of nothingness. The pressure dropped away from Jackson's lungs and they filled with deep quivers.

Shivering and shaking, the time machine was suctioned into a tunnel that had been carved from the black ocean of nowhere, shooting faster and faster toward whatever destination the wandering coordinate board had locked onto. It spun, slipped. The sides of the machine kissed the walls of the tunnel that could not possibly exist, sending showers of golden sparks tailing in its wake. If someone could see it, Jackson felt sure they would think they were witnessing the fall of a comet. Panic gripped him in steel-taloned fingers when he recalled that most comets burned themselves up before they ever fell to earth.

Nausea ripped through him. He wanted to grab for the face-mask but was hypnotized by the warming cherry-red glow starting to spread over the exterior of the time machine.

A flash pulled his attention forward again.

Something? Ahead of him? But what?

Another flash popped in the no-space ahead of him, for a brief instant defining the walls of the tunnel through time as yellow and gold sparks circled within a whirlpool just big enough to accept the time machine.

He fought back the dry heaves that signalled arrival, trying to catch a glimpse of whatever it was he was following. Then the time machine shuddered through a final barrier, flinging itself into a wild topsy-turvy convolution that seemed would surely burst the seams and spill him into the middle of whatever existed on the other side of the crystal windows.

Then he landed with a jarring thump that loosened his teeth.

Something screamed a warning in his mind as existence settled around him with the immediacy of a dropped piano. NOW splintered into him with a force he had never felt before. The darkness around him was still complete but he had a feeling of BEING. No longer lost. Arrived. But where? When?

He glanced at the coordinates on the control board as he ripped the helmet off. Thirty-three hours and some few minutes had passed since he had left this time line. Not the fifteen minutes he had programmed in.

Remembered images of the trailing gold fire in front of him flashed into his mind.

He had no doubts that it was another time machine. But how had it altered his destination? Or had it? Maybe the time-line was being peeled off just as Czenlyn had predicted it might. But what would happen to those people living in this NOW? Would they be locked forever in a 2074 that no longer existed?

Or had Temporal Projects found a way to wall off certain time periods, solidify them so that no more tampering could be made in the threads of this particular Time?

Too many questions, Jackson told himself, and too damn many possibilities. He unhooked the seat harness and slid free of the restraints.

The door hissed open at his touch. Muggy and hot air swirled around him, combating the controlled climate of the time machine. The heated oppressiveness won out, peeling away Jackson's comfort.

Fingering his way across the control board, Jackson

found the switch for the exterior lights. Blue lighting flared to life and washed the surrounding walls colorless.

It took him a moment to strip away the stark unreality around him and recognize the room as Czenlyn's second basement. Thank Buddha, he breathed silently as he crossed the room to the wall switch and thumbed it on. Florescent lighting stormed into the small room, chasing away the shadows, turning the blue cones from the lamps on the time machine to a grayish mist.

Then Jackson noticed the second time machine, sitting in the center of the room just behind the one he had arrived in.

Someone had methodically beaten it to death. Shattered crystal glistened on the concrete floor.

Jackson crossed the floor unbelievingly.

The interior of the time machine looked like some type of incendiary had been set off inside it. Burnt padding hung from the four seats like huge black scales.

Tentatively, Jackson reached out a hand and touched one of the seats. Warm. Still warm. It hadn't happened long ago.

A feminine scream echoed into the room, letting him know the secur-seal on the hidden door hadn't been properly set.

Rachel!

The identification of the voice rattled through him, pushing him back to his machine. The replication of the burned husk sitting before him. He pulled the fletchette pistol Czenlyn had given him from between the seats and armed it.

Rachel Czenlyn screamed again. Only this time it was quickly cut off.

Realizing he had to leave himself a back door, he took the rat-tailed cord from the back of his time machine and plugged it into the wall outlet. The power supply showed the batteries had been drained down to one-quarter charge. The outlet was a special one, designed by Czenlyn to bring the time machine up to full power within an hour.

Jackson tried not to estimate how much time he had to let the batteries charge.

Heart hammering inside his chest, he moved up the narrow steps leading to the secur-seal and palmed it open. He stepped through the rectangular opening, coming into the upper basement near the wall, moving up into darkness. Odors of canned fruits mixed in with the muggy air, punctuated by the smell of burned rubber and plastic from the time machine below. He tripped over a sack of potatoes before he knew it was there, sprawling, managing to catch himself on his wounded hand. Dirt clung to his palm, matting to the drying blood.

He gritted his teeth against the blinding pain, forcing his breath in and out at a normal rate.

Rachel was up there somewhere, he made himself think. In trouble. Maybe Tyrell Czenlyn and his wife as well.

He wiped his bloody hand on his jeans again and took a firmer grip on the fletchette pistol. Buddha, how he wished he could go for help instead of this. How could he trust himself to carry out any kind of rescue attempt? Only moments ago, 238 years ago, he had condemned a list of people to death and displacement because he had been unable to sacrifice the meager existence he had been left with. And he had justified it by stacking up all the positive things he had accomplished at the expense of those lives. Now, he stood ready to throw all that away.

He closed his eyes as he paused by the door leading to the upper levels of the hacienda. Buddha, he was no holo hero, ready to save world. No Buck Rogers able to dodge between laser beams to halt the countdown of some megaton nuclear bomb only seconds before the device set off a chain reaction that would shear the earth in two. Not even a Dorothy able to save Oz from the Wicked Witch of the West with a bucket of mop water. He was a linguist. Out of his depth. It had taken him two attempts to kick the events of history around enough to save Ana.

A pained scream cut through the darkness and through the uncertainty that held Jackson in thrall.

He pulled himself around the doorway and sprinted up the stairs. A man's rough voice, angered and tinged with excitement, shouted something Jackson couldn't understand. Brimming with fear, for himself and Czenlyn and Rachel and her mother, he tripped the switch that released the false wall of the den. It slid back noiselessly.

Daylight splashed over Jackson, almost blinding in its unexpected intensity. He leveled the fletchette pistol before him, centering on the bigger of the two figures in front of him.

The Time Policeman's hands were occupied with Rachel Czenlyn. The girl was lying on the carpeted floor, struggling to free herself. Her blouse was torn, exposing the deep tan of her belly and the stark whiteness of her undergarment. A dark circle had started around her left eye, above the swelling of the cheekbone on the same side and the trickle of blood that drifted from her bottom lip.

Jackson watched the Time Policeman's head come up, the polychromatic helmet glinting brightness as it shifted, saw the man reach for the Matthews holstered on his hip.

Triggering the fletchette pistol, Jackson zipped an erratic line of multi-colored darts up the Time Policeman's chest. The last of the burst clawed their way into the man's unprotected throat, quivering as they hung there.

Dark anger bloated inside the crystal eyes of the Time Policeman. The arm continued moving, hooking the Matthews from the holster. The barrel started to come up, then appeared to get too heavy for the man. It dropped back to the floor, followed a half-second later by the Time Policeman's heavy body.

"Where's your father?" Jackson asked as he helped the girl to her feet. So much confusion whirled inside his head. Why now? Why had the Time Police found Czenlyn's hide-out now? Sweet Buddha, Czenlyn had to still be alive. He was the only one who could help Jackson make sense of things and wouldn't try to keep things from him.

"Jackson." Rachel stepped into his arms, crying, trying to hold her torn blouse together like a small child.

Jackson held her for a brief instant, then pushed her back gently. Her face. Her face was so torn, so bruised. "Your father," he reminded softly.

She shook her head. "I don't know, Jackson. It's been so confusing. We didn't even know they were here. Then they were. They killed so many of the servants. We were having dinner."

Jackson watched the den doorway, knowing the bull-fiddle moan of the fletchette pistol had to have been heard.

"Father pushed me out of the room, told me to run. I couldn't. One of them caught me." She started crying again, trembling. "I couldn't believe the things they told him they would do to me if he didn't tell them about you. I've never known men like that."

"Neither have I," Jackson replied honestly. "Rachel, listen, we haven't got much time. I need to find your father."

She looked up at him and new tears slipped down her face. Her voice broke. "They left him in the dining room."

"Where did the other men go?"

"Outside. To check the guest houses. They were looking for you, Jackson."

"I know." He held her for a moment, and stroked her hair, wondering how she had managed to hang onto her sanity throughout the attack. "How many of them were there?"

"Four. The other three went outside to look. This one, he pulled me back here to . . . to . . . "

"I know, Rachel. I know." Jackson stooped and recovered the Time Policeman's Matthews. Anger burned deep inside him. Czenlyn had welcomed him into his home, made him feel comfortable. They had never developed a friendship that was seated in shared experiences or shared passions. But there had been a bond. Both of them had been hunted by Temporal Projects. He couldn't leave now, not without trying to find the man. But going up against three Time Policemen was sheer lunacy.

Then again, Jackson told the rational argument ricocheting inside his head, all of it was when you got down to it.

"Wait here," he told Rachel. "If anyone comes through that door besides me, go downstairs to the time machine . . . "

"It's broken. They blew it up."

"The one that brought me here is there," Jackson said. "All you have to do is hit the return button and it will take you away from here." He looked into her dark eyes. "Okay?"

She nodded.

Jackson shoved the fletchette pistol inside his waistband and flipped the safety off the Matthews. He willed his hesitation away, swearing to himself that the first time he saw the crystal eyes of a Time Policeman, he was going to point the trigger and have no regrets whatsoever. Kill or be killed. Buddha, how long had that been the law of Man?

He rounded a corner, listening intently, trying to fathom some early warning of his enemy's arrival.

A choked gasp caught his attention and he whirled around, bringing the Matthews up in both hands.

Tyrell Czenlyn swayed uncertainly on the stairway before Jackson. Behind him, to the right of the stairway, a door was open, leading to the front lawns. Czenlyn opened his mouth to speak and a bloody froth slithered onto his chest. He was using his hands to hold himself up. He released his hold with one hand, trying to point at Jackson, then fell forward.

Jackson rushed forward, putting the Matthews down beside his leg. He cradled Czenlyn's head in his lap as outrage filled him, burning twisted knots through his stomach. The doctor's shirt front was a mass of burned and tattered material covering a bloody flesh sack scarcely able to contain the vital organs inside.

"Dr. Czenlyn," Jackson whispered. He couldn't look away from the battered face. How close had he come to being where Czenlyn was now? Hours? Minutes?

"Jackson?" Czenlyn's voice was a hoarse croak. The pain-filled eyes made an attempt to focus but gave up.

"Yes."

"Jackson." Czenlyn nodded and closed his eyes. "I knew you would . . . would come back." He coughed. Red stained spittle dotted his chin.

Jackson could almost feel the life leaving the man's body. And it was all his fault. If he had stayed away from the man, none of this would have happened. Buddha, Czenlyn had lived a life apart from the influence of Temporal Projects for twenty years without being discovered. It had taken less than twenty days for the Time Police to find him once he had let Jackson into his home. Why did everything he touch have to die? So much death. It wouldn't be long at this rate before he was steeped in it.

"Not your fault," Czenlyn whispered. Then Jackson realized he was saying he was sorry over and over. He felt tears burn through his eyes. When he looked down at his hand to shift the big man's head, he was unable to tell where his blood stopped and Czenlyn's started.

"Where's Rachel?"

"In the den."

.Is she all right?"

"Yes."

"There was a man . . . "

"I shot him."

Czenlyn nodded happily.

"Your wife?"

"Dead. They murdered her for trying to help me."

Jackson tried to find words and couldn't. Buddha, he felt so helpless. He was a linguist. A man who lived in words. How could he come up lacking now, when he wanted them most?

An agonizing cramp shook through Czenlyn, turning his face into a tight, white mask.

Jackson tried to hold the man, tried to ease the pain. "You're going to have to help me get you to your feet."

"It won't do any good, Jackson." The doctor's eyes found Jackson's. "I'm as good as dead now and we both know it. I'd never survive a time jump. Even if you had some place to take me." Czenlyn's hands closed on Jackson's wrist. "Your time machine is still operable?"

"Yes."

"Good. They smashed mine."

"I know."

Czenlyn fixed him with a stare that Jackson could tell was fading with each passing second. "Save Rachel," Czenlyn whispered forcefully in his croaking voice. "I've made my peace with my God, but you've got to save her."

Jackson nodded, struggling for words. So many languages locked up inside of him. So many thoughts, ideas, and expressions. And he was mute.

"Promise me," Czenlyn said.

"I promise."

Life fled from the big man's body, leaving Jackson

with only a corpse.

Rage and pain burned turbo-fast, nova-hot. Buddha, it was so unfair. Together he and Czenlyn might have had a chance against Temporal Projects, might have been able to stem the tide of historical changes Voxner had introduced.

Not now.

Not now.

Gently, he laid the big man's body down on the blood-stained carpet. Through blurred vision, he closed Czenlyn's eyes.

"Jackson!"

Rachel's scream galvanized Jackson into action. He caught up the Matthews and sprinted for the den, feeling torn and aching muscles protest in symphonies of crackling synapses.

A dark shadow clung to the window of the den, casting a gray pall over the interior of the room. Rachel stood behind her father's desk, holding a bundle of small notebooks to her breasts that she had obviously taken from the open wall safe behind her.

As Jackson brought the Matthews up to point at the window, the shadow drew back an arm and smashed it through the glass. Flying splinters of it sprayed inward.

The Time Policeman started to enter, booted feet crunching through the broken glass.

The Matthews jerked in Jackson's hands, squirming in his slippery grasp.

The Time Policeman tried to open fire with his own

weapon but the stream of bullets blew him back outside the window.

Without pausing, Jackson dropped the empty weapon and crossed the room at a dead run. If the remaining Time Policemen hadn't known something was wrong at the main house before, they surely did now. He caught Rachel by the arm and pushed her toward the hidden door. Books tumbled from the girl's arms.

Rachel fought against Jackson, trying to recover the fallen books. Her dark eyes were hurt, angry. "My father spent his life researching these journals. He believed in their importance. I can't leave them here."

Jackson helped her pick them up, unable to take his eyes away from the shattered window. He had no choice. He couldn't visualize himself attempting to knock the girl out and carry her to the time machine. That only happened on James Bond holos. Carrying the books he held now was going to definitely strain his physical resources. Even with the adrenal boost he was getting.

"Where's my father?" Rachel asked once they had picked up all the books.

Jackson pushed her toward the door. "Dead." He didn't know any way to soften the answer.

A loud voice rocketed through the den, coming from the front room. "Boepple! Where the hell are those qwerks? They got Listin. Boepple!"

Jackson wanted to reach for the fletchette gun in his waistband but he was afraid he would drop some of the books and Rachel would want to stop for them again. "Run," he ordered the girl, and followed her into the waiting darkness.

His heart hammering a mad tribal beat, Jackson tried to run and listen at the same time. He heard heavy footsteps enter the den as Rachel slipped over the bag of potatoes. He reached for her, scattering the journals he carried, managing to wrap an arm around her waist. He kept her from falling, straining under her weight as she found her footing. Then he was scrambling down the stairway after her, pulling the secur-seal tight.

"Come on," Jackson bellowed, grabbing her wrist.

"The books." She evaded his grasp, reaching for the spilled journals.

"Leave them."

"I can't. They're all I have left. Damnit, Jackson, I can't."

Cursing her and cursing himself for being a fool, Jackson dropped to his knees and helped her pick them up again.

Someone beat on the heavy metal door over the stairway. Then the pounding quit.

Without pausing, Jackson dumped the journals in the back of the time machine unceremoniously. He returned for more. The mugginess of the basement air intensified. It took him a moment to figure out why. Then a dark spot appeared on the chrome surface of the secur-seal, turning black.

Laser.

The thought dumped new panic into Jackson's all ready overloaded senses.

Rachel grabbed the last book.

He helped her into the time machine just as the lock system holding the secur-seal tight dropped to the concrete floor with a loud metallic clang. The door lifted grudgingly, squeaking on overheated and expanded hinges.

A Time Policeman dropped through the opening like a cat, his crystal eyes tracking Jackson's movements with feline fascination.

Jackson pulled the time machine's winged door closed, not bothering with the seat harness or face-mask. He punched numbers on the coordinate console, not bothering to watch what he was entering. Anything. It didn't matter. As long as it was somewhere in the past. Rachel couldn't go forward.

"Jackson!" Rachel yelled, her voice reverberating painfully in the close quarters.

The laser lifted. The ruby beam shot out, flattening against the crystal window in front of Jackson. It oozed over the protective surface, spreading outward like an oil film on a pond.

Jackson's finger stabbed the initiation switch, wondering if a sufficient charge had built up in the time machine to rip them out of the basement in one piece. If not, they would be at the mercy of the laser. At least until the deadly beam cut through the time machine enough to breach the security systems and trigger the self-destruct function.

For a handful of seconds, Jackson was frozen, not knowing what was going to happen. Then the time machine lifted like a torn kite in a gentle breeze. A breeze that quickly transformed into a nightmare of hurricane force.

Jackson felt the time machine spin, locking into the same grid that had dictated his arrival before. Everything turned black, then flared yellow and gold as the time machine rattled down the tunnel it had sought out before. Only this time the bottom of the invisible tunnel followed them out, pulsing, pushing, driving them before it. The pressure inside the time machine increased dramatically.

It was closing, he realized as he fought the vertigo. He heard Rachel being sick beside him. The tunnel was closing. Or being walled off, he corrected himself. That was what he had bumped into earlier. Orphaned. That was what Czenlyn had called it.

But how?

Was it something he had caused? Or was it happening as Czenlyn had feared it would? The anomalies Czenlyn had noticed in Texas history had cast that particular time-line into conflict with the Time Projects directed events dominoing through the decades. Was this the end result of it?

Jackson didn't know. There had been so much he could have learned from Czenlyn. Now he would never know.

The time machine popped free of the impossible tunnel, corkscrewing into nothingness. The pressure dropped away, letting his lungs work easier.

The time sickness gurgled inside him, pulling at his stomach with greasy fingers. Images holoed through his mind, bringing mixed emotions. He glanced at Rachel, huddled in her seat, fighting against the nausea. Buddha, they had lost so much. Then he lost consciousness, sometime between this moment and the last.

"Jackson?"

Jackson stirred, feeling the familiar nausea wind through his intestines.

"Jackson?"

He looked up into Rachel Czenlyn's bruised face, remembering everything that had happened.

"Are you all right?"

He knew she was talking about the blood that covered him. Some of it his own. Some of it belonging to the others he had fought with. Some of it her father's. He sat up in the seat, painfully dragging himself into position despite the series of dry heaves that clutched at him.

"Where are we?" Rachel asked.

Jackson looked away from her after noticing the swelling on the side of her face had started to go down Evidently they had both been out for awhile. He surveyed the rolling hills of white snow that spread ou before them, the broken ice-covered cliff face hanging over them. "I don't know," he replied.

Judging from their position on the side of the mountain, Jackson assumed the time machine had not made a gentle landing this time. Instead, it had slammed into the snowbank, burrowing into the soft whiteness and into the hard, frozen ground beneath. He glanced at the coordinates computer and found it blank. Without it he couldn't even tell WHEN they were. He kept the worry from his face, deciding not to tell Rachel yet. She had enough to deal with all ready without adding to it.

He shifted in the seat, noticing the EMERGENCY! UNIT ON RESERVE POWER EMERGENCY! sign flashing for attention. Wherever they had jumped, it had taken a hell of a lot of power to get there. Or maybe it had been sucked off breaking free of the closing tunnel. At any rate, as soon as he put the POES in place, the time machine would gradually recharge. Hopefully.

"Can't we go somewhere else?" Rachel asked. She seemed hypnotized by the vastness of the snow.

As long as we didn't break something critical, Jackson thought. But he said, "Not yet," then explained the Portable Ovshinsky Energy System and how it converted solar power for the time machine's use.

"What do we do now?" Rachel asked.

"I don't know that either," Jackson said. "At least not yet."

They fell silent. Jackson knew she was trying to deal

with the enormity of it, with being able to leave one year for another within seconds. No big red apple falling in New York City. No Dick Clark holoed into being for the three-hour party beforehand.

"Jackson?"

"Yes."

"Will you hold me?"

He opened his arms and she moved into them, crying as softly as a small child. Jackson felt agony from her weight against him and used it to fuel the small ball of anger deep inside him. He looked out over Rachel's head, seeing the blinding whiteness of the snow but seeing other things too.

He had been hounded, hunted, abandoned, displaced, and stranded. By the Time Police. By Voxner and Brelmer. All because of a list that he himself had made sure they retained. And still he had no idea of how his name got to be on that list.

Maybe it was time to find out.

The thought warmed him. He trailed his fingers through Rachel's dark hair.

The answer had to lie somewhere in the past, he told himself. In one of the pasts that were open to him. All he had to do was find it. Despite all the death he had seen in the last few hours of his personal existence, despite his loss of Czenlyn's expertise in time travel and the insights the doctor had derived from his own voyages, despite the fact that he had been betrayed and forgotten by a woman he probably loved, Jackson felt triumphant.

He had survived.

And the powers behind Temporal Projects were going to regret it.

THE END

Warren Norwood spent his childhood summers reading *Tarzan* and *Tom Swift* books one right after another, so its little wonder he grew up to write science fiction and fantasy adventures. His first novel, *The Windover Tapes: An Image of Voices* was published in 1982, and was followed by three more books in that series. He has since published *The Seren Cenacles,* on which he collaborated with Ralph Mylius, *The Double Spiral War* series, *Shudderchild,* and *True Jaguar.*

Norwood and Gigi - his wife, fellow writer, and collaborator -- live outside of Weatherford, Texas. In addition to his writing, Warren teaches at Tarrant County Junior College, and is learning to play a growing collection of musical instruments, including a mountain dulcimer.

Mel Odom is a native Oklahoman, though born in California. He spent his formative years listening to his mother read the uncut versions of THE WIZARD OF OZ, SWISS FAMILY ROBINSON, and THE AMAZING SPIDER MAN, as well as other classics. Once he received his first library card, he embraced science fiction whole-heartedly and unleashed his imagination through the works of Robert A. Heinlein and Andre Norton. He has been writing professionally since 1985 when he made his first short story sale. He lives in Moore, Oklahoma with his wife Karen, and their children, Matthew and Montana and one who holds a reservation for March 1989. Besides working on TIME POLICE, Mel is also working on a popular men's adventure series.

Mel and Warren do not discuss college football when they make their plotting decisions.